# NOT A CLUE

# NOT A CLUE

CERTAINEMENT PAS · A NOVEL

## CHLOÉ DELAUME

*Translated and with an introduction by Dawn M. Cornelio*

UNIVERSITY OF NEBRASKA PRESS · LINCOLN AND LONDON

Cet ouvrage a bénéficié du soutien
des Programmes d'aide à la
publication de l'Institut français.

Library of Congress
Cataloging-in-Publication Data
Names: Delaume, Chloé, 1973– author.
| Cornelio, Dawn M. translator.
Title: Not a clue = Certainement
pas: a novel / Chloé Delaume;
translated by Dawn M. Cornelio.
Other titles: Certainement pas.
English | Certainement pas
Description: Lincoln: University
of Nebraska Press, 2018.
Identifiers:
LCCN 2018009204
ISBN 9781496200891 (pbk.: alk. paper)
ISBN 9781496212962 (epub)
ISBN 9781496212979 (mobi)
ISBN 9781496212986 (pdf)
Subjects: | GSAFD: Suspense fiction
Classification:
LCC PQ2704.E346 C4713 2018
DDC 843/.92—dc23 LC record available at
https://lccn.loc.gov/2018009204

Set and designed in Questa by N. Putens.

For Tom.

Thank you for your love, your encouragement, your patience.

Je t'aime, mon cœur.

For Chloé.

#resist, matrimoine et sororisation 4ever

# CONTENTS

# INTRODUCTION

DAWN M. CORNELIO

After first reading *Certainement pas*, I wrote an article that started something like this: "How can you juggle an omniscient narrator, a murder victim boiling over with accusations, at least six possible murderers—each with their own entourages and psychiatrists at Paris's Hôpital Sainte-Anne—a blog that speaks in the first person, and an author whose intervention is limited to refusing to intervene?"[1] Today, as reader and translator, I would rephrase the question and ask, "How do you *translate* a novel with all of these elements and also do justice to a unique literary voice and style that uses language both as a tool and as a weapon and is actually teeming with cultural references that range from the classics of French literature and cinema to pop music from throughout the twentieth century?" The answer to the revised and expanded version of the question is found in a word I learned back when I read the novel for the first time. That word is *clinamen*.

What is a "clinamen"? Just in case it's new to you too, according to Lucretius, expounding on Epicurus's atomistic doctrine, a clinamen—derived from the Latin *clinare*, "to incline"—occurs when there is an unpredictable swerve of atoms. While in current, common usage a clinamen is defined as a bias or inclination, in philosophy and literature the term continues to convey the notion of an unexpected deviation that is responsible for a change in the order of things. Indeed, Samuel Taylor Coleridge, Harold Bloom, Gilles Deleuze, Simone de Beauvoir, Jacques Lacan, Michel Serres, and perhaps James Joyce, among others, have all reflected on, developed, applied, or even refused the viability of the concept. The influence of the clinamen comes to Chloé Delaume through her profound and long-lasting interest in the writings of Alfred Jarry, the College of 'Pataphysics, and the Oulipo writers, such as Georges Perec and Boris Vian.[2] In Delaume's writing in general, and in *Not a Clue* in particular, *clinamen* should be taken as a watchword, for there is no level of the text that is not marked by the phenomena of unexpected swerves. Juxtapositions of "high" and "low" culture are abundant, punctuation often used selectively and idiosyncratically, syntax and grammar are so stretched to the absolute limits of their flexibility that reading becomes a roller coaster ride, as the sudden swerving of the text takes the reader in unforeseen directions, time and time again. Bringing *Certainement pas* into English here means embedding within it a certain number of new clinamens as unexpected cultural and linguistic twists become part of the novel and extend its spiraling out into unanticipated territory.

*Certainement pas*, published in France in 2004, is Chloé Delaume's seventh novel, one of over twenty titles she has written since 2000. All of these have the stated purpose of expanding the reader's idea of what literature is, of making reading a participatory activity, of refusing to be cultural entertainment, of disrupting literature, and of trying to overthrow the "Banana Republic of Letters" the author feels most contemporary, commercialized literature contributes to, with its pleasant and easily consumable and digestible stories. Moreover, the majority of Delaume's writing falls into the sometimes controversial category of *autofiction*, a wide-ranging style of writing in contemporary France, among other places. The neologism was first coined by the writer and critic Serge Doubrovsky, who described his 1977 novel *Fils* as having "confié le langage d'une aventure à l'aventure d'un langage en liberté" (confided the language of an adventure to the adventure of a language in liberty),[3] thereby emphasizing the importance of language and means of expression in this new combination of lived experience and fiction. Underpinning Delaume's own extensive auto-fiction is the death by murder-suicide of her parents: in 1983, in the family apartment and in the presence of the then nine-year-old girl, her father, Sylvain Dalain, shot and killed her mother, Soazick, before killing himself. Nonetheless, it would be an inaccurate reading of her literature to consider it as any kind of therapy, a plea for sympathy, navel-gazing, or anything other than a Doubrovskian adventure in literature, living, and self-creation. In fact, Delaume's efforts to be her own creation, rather than being the result of her parents' death, go beyond her writing to her life, her name itself an example of this. Born in 1973, Delaume's birth name was Nathalie Abdallah, but after moving to France, the family decided to try to minimize its Lebanese origins and legally changed its surname to Dalain. However, the writer refuses the first and last names given by her parents and has lived and worked under the name Chloé Delaume almost exclusively. Except for a small number of early career articles and short texts published under the name Nathalie Dalain, all of the writer's work is signed with her self-chosen name: Chloé, from the lead female protagonist of Boris Vian's *Froth on the Daydream* (*L'Écume des jours*, 1947); and Delaume, from Antonin Artaud's *L'Arve et l'aume* (1947), his "translation" of a chapter of Lewis Carroll's *Alice in Wonderland*. For many years the author described Chloé Delaume as a fictional character who was the writer, narrator, and main protagonist of her texts; more recently, however, the statements "Je m'appelle Chloé Delaume. Je suis un personnage de fiction" (My name is Chloé Delaume. I am a fictional character) have diminished in appearance, and Chloé Delaume is not present within the pages of in the author's most recent novel, the feminist and political *Les Sorcières de la République* (2016).

Beyond her names taken from literary works, intertextuality—references to other writers' works and other texts of her own—plays an important role in Delaume's work. In the chapter entitled "Sixth Officer," the writer makes reference to two of her other novels. The chapter itself is written as a letter from Chloé Delaume the author to the narratrix of *Not a Clue*, is dated Simsial 34, 2004, and includes the names of two fictitious towns, SimCity and Somnambulie. SimCity and Simsial are not only references to the Sims series of video games;

they are also a reference to a project focusing on the life of her Sim and her life as a Sim. It was composed of a blog written by Delaume as a resident of the video game SimCity and a series of public performances centered on readings and demonstrations of the Delaume-Sims in action and culminated in the 2003 work *Corpus Simsi*. Additionally, the town of Somnambulie is a reference to another work published in the same year, *La Vanité des Somnambules*, one of whose key points is Chloé Delaume's failed struggle to take control of the body of Nathalie Dalain. Elsewhere the mention of the novel *Le Vagissement du minuteur* (*The Wailing of the Timer*) by Clotilde Mélisse is a double reference to Delaume's own work: Mélisse is the fictional double of Delaume who, according to the author, can say things she herself cannot; and the title is nothing but synonyms for Delaume's most well-known novel, *Le Cri du sablier* (The Cry of the Hourglass).

The references Delaume makes to other authors and works outside her own are much more extensive than those to her own work and often much more understated. One of the main characters in *Not a Clue* is a young writer by the name of Mathias Rouault—many people will recognize in that rather uncommon name a wink at Flaubert's *Madame Bovary*, since Rouault was Emma's maiden name. Beyond this reference, namely in the chapters concentrating on the amnesiac character Aline, several lines from *Madame Bovary*, specifically a song sung by a blind man as Emma dies, appear a number of times. Likewise, the subtitle "Conversation sans Loir ni chair" in the chapter "Professor Plum in the Ballroom" refers to a work published in 1935 by the dramatist, poet, essayist, and statesman Paul Claudel, although the chapter follows up with quotes from Balzac's more celebrated *Illusions perdues*, relating to the publishing industry. Here the example of Claudel brings us back to the notion of clinamen because in *Not a Clue* I chose to retain the reference to Balzac, but for reasons both of recognizability and the retention of a bucolic contemplative meaning, I replaced the Claudel text with a reference to Thoreau's *Walden*, thereby incorporating, I imagine, an unexpected swerve out of French into American culture. Therefore, the subtitle "Conversation sans loir ni chair," a reworking of *Conversations dans le Loir-et-Cher* (a département in central France), becomes "I went to the Castle because I wished to live deliberately," an adaptation of "I went to the woods because I wished to live deliberately." Among other writers quoted or alluded to through intertextuality are Simone de Beauvoir, Marguerite Duras, Lewis Carroll, Valérie Solanas, Samuel Beckett, Joris-Karl Huysmans, Vercors (the pen name of Jean Bruller), Margaret Atwood (in particular her scarlet cloak–wearing handmaid), Dante, and Victor Hugo, whose famous line "un ver de terre amoureux d'une étoile" (an earthworm in love with a star) occupies a particularly interesting space in the novel.

However, these examples from the classics of French and world literature do not exclude the possibility of sometimes playful but also meaningful allusions to popular culture, ranging from the TV cartoon series *Minus et Cortex* (*Pinky and the Brain*) to Disney's version of Jiminy Cricket to *Harry Potter* and from the white slippers in Charlie Chaplin's *Limelight* to a 2001 French romantic comedy, *Se souvenir de belles choses*. While it goes without saying Jiminy needed no modification to be brought (back) into English and that it was easy enough to revert to Pinky and the Brain's English names, such was not the case for the two films mentioned here, whose adaptations in this translation can be read as examples of clinamens that result in the translation taking just a few more unexpected turns than the source text. Although *Limelight* is obviously an American film, it is also well-known internationally, and Delaume includes in her novel a mention of "deux chaussons blancs" (two white satin slippers), the theme associated with the ballerina character Terry and whose lyrics summarize the plot of the film. However, in the English version of the film, the same song is simply called "Eternally" and is a rather unimpressive, unoriginal love song. In this case, in order to keep the narrative related by the lyrics, I substituted the "red shoes" for the "white slippers," thereby bringing in not only Andersen's fairy tale but also the cinematographic adaptation by the same name, which was released just four years before Chaplin's *Limelight*, thus making a temporal connection between the two movies. In the case of *Se souvenir de belles choses*, although the film was released under the title *Beautiful Memories* in the United States, I was afraid the film wouldn't be known widely enough to create any resonance. I have replaced the French movie with the Goldie Hawn–Kurt Russell romantic comedy *Overboard* since the tone is similar and the basic premise of memory loss is shared by both movies.

Beyond the white slippers, Delaume includes a number of song titles and lyrics throughout the novel, most of which I opted to change to English-language songs. For example, the snippet from "Harper Valley PTA," "Mrs. Johnson you're wearing your dresses way too high," offers the same kind of innuendo as that found in "Sidonie," originally sung by Brigitte Bardot: "Sidonie a plus d'un amant" (Sidonie has more than one lover). A more difficult decision was what to do with the Charles Trenet song "(Le Menuet c'est) la polka du roi" that Delaume intertwined with the narrative throughout chapter 9, since the story told by the song advances the unfolding of the character's delirious dance with his psychiatrist. In translating, it certainly would have been possible to translate the song literally or even leave the lyrics in French, as I did with the titles of the books the character Mathias wrote. Although there would be advantages and disadvantages to either of these options, I chose a completely different set of pros and cons, by deciding to change the Trenet song to a Leonard Cohen song, "Take This Waltz." The pros of the decision are the shared focus on dance and the tragic tone of both songs, but the cons can be seen in the looser link between the song and the novel and the replacement of the source culture with the target culture.

As with all translations, nearly every word in *Not a Clue* is the result of a decision: to be direct or indirect, to create something that feels surprising or familiar, to displace the reader or the text. I will admit to being proud of some decisions and the discoveries that led to them, although for some I will always wish I'd thought of something better. Without a doubt there are instances in which I had a decision to make and wasn't even aware of it. However, a translation is in many ways as personal a creation as a novel. As William H. Gass wrote, "In a translation, one language, and one particular user of that language reads another"; and "What we get when we're done [translating] is a reading, a reading enriched by the process of arriving at it, and therefore, really only the farewells to a long conversation."[4] Since Chloé Delaume's *Certainement pas* is as much—if not more—about literature itself than it is about the characters found in its pages, I will also admit that I hope that *Not a Clue* is not only about the characters and about literature but also, at least a little bit, about translation and that it includes a few clinamens of my very own invention.

NOTES

1. Dawn M. Cornelio, "Les Limites de la narration minée," *Contemporary French and Francophone Studies* 13, no. 4 (September 2009): 423–30 (my trans.).

2. Indeed, their influence is evident in Delaume's use of the board game Clue, with its characters, rooms, and weapons, to structure her novel, which is something of a Oulipian constraint in itself.

3. Serge Doubrovsky, *Fils* (Paris: Éditions Galilée, 1977), back cover (my trans.).

4. William H. Gass, *Reflections on the Problems of Translation* (New York: Knopf, 2000), 47, 53.

# NOT A CLUE

# Studio

There are six of you in the room. A dark room, with a single window clouded by bars. You've gotten used to these anemic shadows, so used to them that your eyes don't even bleed anymore when your gaze crashes into the menacing rust. There are six of you, you're tired, slouching opposite each other toy soldiers lined up three by three, solitary residue after a scavenger feast. Through your fabric you should feel the steel frame splitting the imitation leather. Of course you don't. Of course, obviously. Your eye sockets uncoil, your pupils happily dart off toward the big ashtray. Always filled to overflowing, that big ashtray. Cigarette butts, gobs of spit, cookies, papers still spotted with minced-eyelid grease, little barrel plump with the detritus of the daughters of Danaus. It's the only one, the chosen one, the big brown many-dented ashtray. The point of convergence of your three outstretched fingers, second knuckle pointer middle finger like a buttercup, feverish catapult thumb, sharp tremor, revolting nail, it depends. It remains the epicenter of this room, where, on this day, there are six of you.

The linoleum is old green, once celadon bordering on turquoise, formerly reassuring. It's a reasonable supposition at least. Indelible marks, so many scars, carbonic craters: not everyone here has been a follower, not everyone submitted to the harsh reign of the tyrannically big ashtray. Seats and floor match, an insistent hue. The achromatic rings under your eyes protect you, so you think. All this green will slip away, won't splash onto anyone, all this green will refute itself, be neutralized before it kidnaps your hearts as they flutter at your lips, before you're nauseous from the wait. It's because of the place itself. Your quixotic struggles stir up the bad-weather air, nutshell blindness infiltrates your eyes, ivory-tower cozy every day you're a step closer to the sisters of Anne with their canonization-faded pupils. White-hot silence, simply devoted roped-party leader, internal speleology, solitary descent to the very center, bumping into salty petrified tear stalactites, on your secret pains grazing in echo.

The walls aren't green. Not to bring it up again. The floor must be made of hope so your feet can stay anchored though lacking a grasp on reality. So the walls are yellow, a slightly dirty ochre yellow, a little dull, more discreet. To the left of the door with an unwelcome opaque window inset, a rather ugly painting has made itself right at home. A crude, pastel trompe l'oeil. Awkward invitation to bucolic reveries, bower crossroads leading to a Provençal scene oozing with rich laughing vales and dense thickets.

You couldn't care less about all this. You're all even more sealed off from your environment than from yourselves, have been for a long time. How many hours spent in this room with no attempt to tame it, how many orange trees in your hearts and old willows in the garden, how many. How many. I know, you have no idea. Sometimes one of you or another, another even more damaged than you if that's even possible, sticks their mouth against the plexiglass, closes their intrepid eyelids, and blows smoke toward this tender horizon. The smoke rings come back lavender-sticky and reeking of laundry detergent. In this South the sun is always bronze, it's the nicotine halo that ensures the sparkle.

There are six of you, and you killed me. One of you or maybe each of you. Yes, that's right. Each of you. The ones who love me must have missed the train, dirty Orient Express seat. I'm not a vengeful ghost, a familiar phantom, a homeless cricket, a spirit rattling yours tapping on a table ringed with people. I'm not an angel either. Really, not in the least. I will not redeem your sins. I won't punish you. I won't announce anything to you. I can see you're very disappointed, but that's not my role. Nonetheless, we all have our own role, even more in this place than anywhere else. So terribly much more in this place than anywhere else, you know that, everyone has their own role. It's all very organized. I'm here and that's all there is to it. For as long as it takes. Time for one simple game, just the time for one simple game. The last one for all of you. The last one for all of us. No one has a choice.

I'm Dr. Black. My very identity, even in government records, my psychological profile, everything, down to the tiniest details of my biography, to this very day is blank and in your hands. I will be your palimpsest. Because I am less the incarnation of a victim than of murder. Murder, drastic change. The unexpected taking of action, the praxis of your drive.

Since 1949 a hundred million people have gathered, between three and six players, seated around the representation of my apartment, moving from hypothesis to supposition, from assumption to presumption, until they narrow it down to a proud *I accuse*. For these past nearly seventy years, accelerated early Sunday morning rhythm, these millions, yet no one, no one, ever lingers over my fictional remains, no one ponders the motive for this ever-solved crime. Never has blood ever transported such indifference.

There are six of you and you killed me. You think you're in the smoking lounge. That freezing little room next to the day room. You think you're safe for a crumb of an hour, meals are served so early. You think you're isolated, crippled with comforting autism, hunched down over your rancid heart. You're wrong. That's not where you are right now. No. Right now you're in the Study. You feel the air suddenly turn heavy and warm. Your lips get dry, the window hastily swallows up its bars. The tar-covered calluses on your fingers let go, what does it matter if your filter-tipped light cigarettes put a lonely end to themselves, what does it matter, there's no more ashtray. I'm Dr. Black, I'm dead. There are six of you, and you killed me.

Your names will be assigned to you simply for the sake of convenience. And coherence too. A rare commodity in your lands. Your age, your appearance, your past, your profession like your appellation will at first seem to have no immediate relation with the identity that will be given you.

There are six of you and you're sick. You have come, some of you have come, of your own volition. For others a loved one, a soon-to-be amputated family member, dropped you off, or a nondescript worried third party. No matter the case in so doing they used the term *entrust*. To try and numb the objectification. You entered this place, Unit 13 Piera Aulagnier Wing, for one sole reason: your internal logic is just too sacrilegious for you to be left on your own.

Only intermittently are you in the real world now, your lips hardly able to communicate. Your internal murmurs, your repeating fables, every night they inhabit the building that protects the outside from your sneaky witticisms and your intensity. During the day you don't speak. The hallways soak up songs of despair and reddened laments. You are a chorus of misfits. A disability concert strumming its incompleteness in putrid cinnabar major.

You're useless now, the dregs of the carnage, grotesque gagged druids skirting the feast where you should preside as good citizens an overripe apple in your glottis, a bouquet of parsley earplugging your ducts. You are no longer fit for consumption but you are still cowardly tousled shriveled up bluish fear in your gut, unable to face the why that saves, the why of contamination, the why of error. As you scan the question you relentlessly fear that you remain daughters of Lot, turned to statues and salt when the internal clock chimes the hour of reckoning.

We're going to play. Together, of course, separately. I won't be alone, I'll have assistants. Tonight your brains are little clods of humus whose decomposition you don't quite grasp. Your mind is compost, your mood hoarse shavings. You're lost within yourselves. That's the worst thing. Your bodies are too vast, your brain ricochets your stony thoughts. That's exactly why I'm here, to make you resonate. To make the death knell rattle rusty pores and synapses. There are six of you, three men and three women, the game will be balanced.

We can start. The layout respects the original. In other words nine rooms can be read going clockwise. Hall at twelve o'clock. Lounge.

Dining Room. Kitchen. Ballroom at six o'clock. Conservatory. Billiard Room. Library. Study. The Conservatory and Lounge are equipped with a secret passage connecting them. As are the Kitchen and Study. Note 1: in some versions, the Billiard Room is called the Game Room. It's more practical but not as pretty. Note 2: the apartment has no bathrooms or bedrooms. Many players are surprised by this austere option. There are no spaces to move across, since your formatting failed. There's no board to unfold, no pieces to set up. I said you're going to play. But definitely not *enjoy yourselves*. No rushing from room to room, no shoving in the hallways. Either. I made it clear special rules, added *unnatural* game. I didn't say naturally. There's a handful of dice, but it doesn't matter how they fall, nothing is random. Make no mistake, each and every one of you. Randomness has never ever played a role in your destiny.

I'm Dr. Black, there are six of you and you killed me. They say you're insane. It's an accepted fact. They say you're insane simply because someone who's maladjusted to reality can't be in sync with it. Your sticky organs overflow with agony, your suffering swells into plump Furies, it's too late to recycle you, use you for transplants, you're nothing but refuse whose social matrix can no longer be reloaded, it's impossible for it to move inside you, its roots contract into a wounded anemone on the verge of penetration.

Find the right cards, the right combination. You have eight rooms left, the Study doesn't count, you've been told. You have eight rooms left, and the choice of weapons. Have a good look at the list: six, in other words, one for each of you. Candlestick, revolver, rope, lead pipe, dagger, monkey wrench.

And above all, yes above all, remember why. Why you killed me. Remember the instant my breath escaped before your eyes dull with lust, haste, greed; remember the instant, because the instant was specific and it did exist. There was a before. There was an after. In between there was. A drive, a desire, and then the willingness.

Don't say, it all caught up with me. You gave in, and that's different. No one gets caught by the unspeakable, no one. The old proverb says so. *What's bred in the flesh will naturally come out in the bone.* Nothing is less natural than compromising your principles. You were born sons of the Word. Language doesn't bend. It remains irreducible, and that's why it will outlive mankind. Don't look for an excuse among the generations. Yours, whatever it may be, in its different layers carries angels, aborted demons, warriors, creators, and bell ringers. The proof is in your contrasts, here pink cheeks and there pepperiness invading the hairline flower. Stop waving your softer pathologies at me like a bunch of screaming spotless flags. For you insanity is simply a consequence. I insist on the term. Simply a consequence. I insist on the term and on its adverb. The instant when awareness leapt out at you, exhausting your lucidity-gashed flesh, you remember. So don't pretend. You're hiding in a minor disorder, it lets you flee the sordid acidity of what could be called responsibility. In your charming rooms, every day you avoid the questioning that should be unique, invasive, methodically analyzed. Why, why you killed me. All day long I see specialists kneeling at your bedsides, their scalpel champing at the bit with impatience: why, why didn't he didn't she keep going. At night they take your screams for spreading symptoms that must be alleviated to relieve your shrill-shredded throats, while with each second your whole being yearns even more to simply dissolve into the obscure clamor verging on oblivion.

On the grounds, in the refectory, the hallways, the smoking lounge, the cafeterias, and studies, you see your doubles, you think. The people in the gowns that tie in the back. Who mutter in distress, all their energy in howling and sharing. You're wrong to see them as a safe haven to migrate into. The people in the gowns that tie in the back have never been part of the world, they remain incorruptible, you are foreign to them. They know that feverish you seek rest, salvation, and something to quench your thirst for ignorance. They let you remain generous bow down straitjacket verbena pediment, they let you take part in single-file rites bottom-of-the-cup three tablets twenty-five canary yellow drops, you drink the potion, but you still don't know how disjointed the rite is for shamans. There are six of you, you are alone, a stuffed mynah bird stands in for your memory, your tartar-clot tears scratch your corneas plow your cheekbones into furrows more sterile than horror could ever be.

I offer you the riddle a sphinx suggested to me. In the morning immaculate naive I stream. At noon muddled inner ear I stumble. At vespers I turn over, wondering, who am I. To survive figure it out. I repeat. Figure it out. And take off that modesty it doesn't match your complexion. I'm going to tell you a secret. Your head is not what's sick. Your head is fine. It invents nine lives for you, an escape cat flap, Cheshire smile. No, your head isn't sick. It's your ventricle. A shell hole in your atrium, emptiness pumped, staggering emptiness at your aorta, emptiness embalming your tracheas. And tonight, in this room, the Unit 13 smoking lounge, otherwise known as the Study in this Interior Game of Clue, you are not Dr. Lagarigue's patients. You are my killers, your own murderers. Tonight, you are six characters in search of a heart.

# First Officer

They don't let me say I. I'm not allowed. This is my first invitation ever. I'm afraid of being clumsy, muddled, a little awkward. Of failing in my task, though that's all I really am. See, words fail me, though I know them all, though I wield them all, juggling from word one, triple-axeling paragraphs, arabesquing chapters finishing period double toe loop. Words forsake my alms purse, I'm touched, can't you see. It's more than simple satisfaction, than dazzling happiness, than a barely grazed fantasy now palpitating so suddenly real it makes your eyes water.

Please know, I am ageless and yet I have never ever been. Never really been. Deprived of organs, I am a voice, barely a voice. A disgorged trickle, a red braided strand, a knitted vein. I am everywhere without existing. Can't you see. I speak for everyone, but I am not. I take care of everyone, linger over every detail, yet no one, ever, worries about me. Every day keeper of the keys I go on, no one shows me respect, interest, or even deference. Anyway, I wouldn't ask for so much. Just for someone to think of me a little, of me a little once in a while. Maybe not like a person, someone, an individual. But like an entity, that would be nice, I think. Because I do think, you see. Yes, like an ever so slightly tangible autonomous entity.

Gazes slip right over me, even the fall rain seems less transparent. It's unusual for anyone to linger over the fine minutia of my little reports. Sometimes I'm avoided: I'm thought to be boring, burdensome, and useless. I am condescendingly examined for purposes of dissection only. A living autopsy: there are probably prophecies lying in my entrails, I know every destiny, from the moment of the embryo my delivery is sought.

You can hear me, right. You can hear me, I'm talking about me. I'm not complaining, you know. I'm confiding, it's different. Also I'm explaining things to you a little. Explaining is something I know how to do. Explaining, exposing, quantifying, and analyzing. It's just that I have a scientific mind, that's what's always needed, even in the other hemisphere. But I don't have any, hemispheres I mean. I would have really liked to, though. Have a brain and blood, blood coursing at full speed and then fleeing after a cut. Getting a cut, I would've liked that too. I know all the words that can be used to describe a wound, no matter its origin or even its depth. I know all the words to describe the turmoil flowing from the gash please keep comma and how to combine them so the syntax is best clotted, sticky, or hemophiliac. I know pleasure's properties, pain, and paradoxes. I know them right down to their structure, their sounds, and their morphology. I know them, they are my flesh, Christ's flesh, right, take and eat all of you, it sounds familiar, it's my routine. Because if I am a nobody, at least I have a function.

I am a living pillar, without me the greatest edifices, the greatest artifices, would heart murmur in the end. I am a stylistic mode, in my bosom I carry knowledge that no Rabelaisian abbey and no mortal could ever imagine. I'm genderless but have dissolved into each one since the very first line that ever was. I have neither past nor future. I am for all currently, a thousand and one simultaneous nights. I am more listened to than heard. People implore me, I spread. I am the guide, informer, holder of all formal and future vices. With a simple line I point out a destiny's clumsiness, employ a pair of quotation marks to inform the reader of contextual savor, whip up armies from genealogies of Dantean Waterloos, foresee nouns the conspiracies being plotted.

I am the omniscient narrator.
This is my only known name.

The masculine status was imposed upon me without consultation, otherwise I wouldn't have let myself get pushed around. Omniscient narrator after all what does it even mean. A data base, to be sure. Flicking in indentation, hanging off tables, flying off thirtieth step, wintery landscape, pink garland and pine treed first lines aroma of predestination. Keyhole description, perpetual violator of fictional intimacy, relentless plowman of languishing secrets. The omniscient narrator is the Banana Republic of Literature's intermediary citizen. I am Master Crow upon my pages I sit, distilling passives and shameful thoughts. I am the handful of reeds *King Midas* peddling to the west wind *has donkey's ears*. It's been so long since I've had a closer look. The masculine certainly cannot be my own. I stay in my dressing room from the beginnings to the absolute ends, parroting, I open the curtain a sliver, I meddle, I intervene, scheming, I jest. I am the chief caretaker of the fictional world, I demand feminization and a raise.

I'm delighted to have been given the chance to speak. I will always be grateful to Dr. Black for choosing me to help him out. Doctor, thank you (head nods and applause). With the reader denying my existence, don't imagine I can feel anything at all during my unending third person singular third person plural. Yet I'm bored to death till I cough up the final period. I grieve too, and often, sorrow like an anvil and lava when I have to bear witness, relating my dying heroines' final spasms. Fake omniscient narrators, in other words characters themselves retracing a story whose every recess they know for having lived it sometime before, don't have a monopoly on fictional pain. No matter what they say, obviously. Sometimes I cry right from the watermark and the ink dribbles from certain words. Conscientious editors give the printer a good going over, handkerchief remaindered copies. But there's no solution, in the reprint my tears again sully the embossing, the bible, or the vellum. Because I do feel, don't you see.

It's a little different for you. I won't cry for you six. I am the omniscient narratrix, the legend to your roadmap. You will come in my wake. I will clear the way for each of you, preside over your abusive groping all throughout your larval investigation. I'm the one who gives out the roles, holds the information, oversees the order you go in. I'm first violin smuggler. Coronation leader.

You're wondering, each and every one of you, when and how you killed. Why remains your own business. I'll plant pious adverbs, see how useful I am to you.

I am the omniscient narratrix. I have a fondness for italics, they smooth any curves on the hips, but I won't give in to vanity. You can relight your cigarette. I hereby proclaim the official and definitive opening of the first round. I'm your crutch. Arise from your astonishment.

# Miss Scarlet

Initially, she was supposed to die. Initially, from the initial. Last name first name, first-letter acrostic, Aline Maupin, an ordinary yet certainly incurable illness crouching in the hollow of the A, an ordinary disease, why not an ornamentation-encrusted orphan. An A inlaid with acute pain, its horizontal bar set with glitzy asthma, an unsteady A from the moment it was typed on the birth certificate. A staggering A even before anyone brushed against it, its outline bearing cerebral aneurism or anything else for that matter, anything deadly, pernicious, irreversible. Last name first name, let's get things in the right order, Maupin Aline, yes, the right order, getting things in the right order because order is important. A toxic capital-letter last name, M hiding in its crotch an irreversible accident, an accident a fall, a skid. M moment, breaking point, deviant upstroke path, violence of a frontal or stony impact in the back of the skull, it doesn't matter. Globule evasion recorded, intimately, originally marked wrought iron soul intestinal tubing.

Aline Maupin was supposed to die, one way or another. A swift demise, surprise mourning, leaving all who outlived her to survive the five liters of blood with a grueling butterfly stroke. Or else. An agony extending nonchalantly across leap years condemning close friends and white coat–wearing personnel to let slip an incomprehensible sigh when the encephalogram finally showed how flat she really was.

On the brink of twenty-seven springs in other words nine thousand eight hundred twenty-eight unbirthdays, Aline Maupin was meant to rot. Rot with the determination of little bodies swollen with mischievous abandon, deliciously rot. In a satin-lined coffin, guaranteed 100 percent solid oak, with four handles, waterproof decorations, one thousand three hundred four euros. She was supposed to decay very slowly following a moving ceremony in which family, friends, relations, would have competed with tears and warmth.

Aline Maupin was supposed to die. Die and that's all period. How wasn't wouldn't won't be the problem, the question. The only thing that matters is that in the end no. Aline Maupin was supposed to die but she woke up one day in a perfectly maintained, polished room since the facility was in Neuilly-sur-Seine.

The first thing Aline saw was the whiteness. A trumpeting, opalescent whiteness, superimposed bleach dizziness. Then it was a sharp, thin, unknown hand, a set of tiny bones gloved in flesh so pale that the sheet seemed dirty by comparison. Imperceptible tendon shiver, the pallid spider moved one leg, then a second. At the third Aline coughed. Originally she'd wanted to shout, but you can't always do what you want to. Her breath was rising up from too far away, her lungs had forgotten the virulent autonomy that can harpify vocal cords. Her throat had seized up in the six months that had passed, clogged with aphasic phlegm, mononucleosis silence. Ripping the veil, the hanging, tearing, raising the starched velour curtain, gutting the folds, the masterful contralto furrows, the whistling blade-sharpened la, the Valkyrie spinning propeller.

The complex machinery she was connected to informed the medical staff that the girl in 43 must have let someone kiss her. Deep brambles, slain dragon, life surged back in puffs, wild rose flash fires setting the whole floor ablaze. Over her door the light turned red, rhythmic insistent blinking, silent hypnotic siren. It was dawn at a few dead minutes past 5:00 p.m. They were busy at her bedside, they smiled at her, probed gauged vital signs, observed that everything was fine, administered a few remedies and fluffed the pillows. The patient seemed dazed. The chief physician leaned in, murmured the usual words. The usual words, the used-up threadbare words, too worn to make a rope, a tightrope, so tight, acrobat's lament to go back to the circus, a Barnum brouhaha of white coats in the room, *the red shoes* repeated Aline's brain *the red shoes* hammered Aline's brain, flaming cortex and synapses all along the launch ramp, the ringmaster announces, Aline the human cannonball sudden immediate takeoff, *the red shoes* whined Aline's neuronal peat bog, I'll contact your family concluded the white rabbit in a satiny hiccup.

The first impression. The first impression, the very first one that Aline had of her wait-tenderized cockpit upon awaking, was excruciatingly painful. I hurt Aline said to herself. I'm suffering, and I'm saying I, yes but in fact what am I? The words trotted tiny in the little pink skull, knocking as they passed into the scalp's oozing fat. The words bounced back, bumping into each other all the more in the chaotic lard, creamy, rancid margarine, the brain a churn with so many shards that each sentence became a thorn of incoherence.

Something happened to me, Aline expressed to herself, petrified at the idea that the real stranger was residing more in the *m* and the *e* than in the radiating ideas in her database. Beyond its iv bandage mitten, Aline's hand went out, quaking cartilage, on tepid reconnaissance. The skin on her face whispered its sharp, paltry secrets in braille. The circles under her eyes were painful, saturated with ancient salts and syrupy toxins. On the bridge of her nose blackhead granules. Her nostrils quivered with fear, to the touch of her phalanges her muzzle, appropriately, seemed proportionate. Perhaps even charming. She found this reassuring. She continued to investigate toward her chin pressing lightly. Her index finger lingered on her dry lips, rubbing, carrying away dead skin relics. My mouth must have stayed shut for a long time, Aline thought. Her mouth, a cloister with doors covered by prolific ivy-like chapping, hoisting up a tongue tip arduous opening. A rubbery little tongue, said Aline to herself, pinching it. A thirsty little sponge, hardened with silence, much more like carton than elastic. I pronounced words with this bitter canker-covered slab of meat, said she to herself feeling it. Although. Maybe not. It's possible, completely possible, that her sentence was quite different.

I certify that Aline did examine herself in this way, and, and in doing so, she remarked on a number of things to herself. I record the content. But leave the form to me. It would be harmful to the narrative to reproduce her words. Aline's tongue is damp, soft-boiled egg slimy. Because you see Aline is a real woman. Not a fictional character. Aline always expresses herself in the cowardly vernacular, smooth phrasing, sometimes a little rough, punctuated with healthy slang and trendy terms. As the omniscient narratrix, I'm duty bound to raise the level. I do my job: I recount the external and internal facts. Please, however, do allow trustworthy me to attend to the keys and picks scattered across the sheet music. I'll let you hear Aline's voice soon enough. You will, Miss Maupin, be allowed to speak to your heart's content. Time will be provided, no one needs to worry. But I'm holding off until our dear patient makes even the tiniest bit of progress in the acidic art of upstrokes as well as in her quest. Because to my mind there's nothing more vulgar, you see, than a strict inscription of orality. Except for the use of exclamation marks, but that goes without saying.

I pronounced words with this bitter canker-covered slab of meat, Aline therefore said to herself. It's just that I don't know which ones, or which eardrums they managed to slip into. Aline's blood pressure increased. Something between a waltz and a fearful minuet crippled with riddles. *Often the warmth of a summer day* intoned Aline inside *will make a young girl dream her heart away* chanted Aline's whole interior. Something like a fragile fluttering followed by mothball hammering pulses took hold of her being, leaving her panting, so many questions unknotting in ribbons, one two three one two three the bluish silk of the years one two three one two three lace reminiscences with the twirl of the hoop. I don't know if I like to dance, thought Aline, her eyes dry with resignation.

The word butter started marathon mixing again in Aline's cerebellum. A greasier, more opaque butter in which Aline's reason drew craters, little amber craters with wide fork stabs of mental oxidation. Slabs of word butter in which she dug a little hole a little repository in the peaks, feverishly waiting for the memories to curl up inside, eventually overflowing, melting the butter with the intense heat of the finally familiar. She would have liked, Aline would have liked, it if the word butter volcano heated up at least a bit inside her brain, making way for a sudden sound, smell, image. Her tallow Pompeii existed somewhere, there will be digging to be done, Aline reassured herself, sensing that the lava wouldn't have preserved anything. Because her own personal lava was a word coulis, a syntactical ossuary, in which the whole dictionary was piled up head to tail. Not remembering her own words, her own uttered words, was being at a loss for words after the fact.

Nothing was left of her past. Neither the memory of far-from-beautiful things, nor the smallest fragment of her identity. She guessed her sex by shyly approaching her dark crotch, felt her grainy skin above the bony mass. Certainly female feminine, I'm sure yes, Aline said to herself. I'm sure, I'm confident. I observe I deduce I understand. I'm not a knowledge virgin. I'm too old to be a virgin anyway, thought Aline as her hand lingered over the bushy pubis.

In her head, Aline was talking loud. In your head it's always very easy to talk so loud you bother yourself. I'm a girl in the hospital, increased Aline's internal volume. Alone all alone in a white hospital room, I'm a girl who doesn't know which someone it is Aline's internal decibels threatened to explode. A body without any title deed, that's what had been given to Aline, a body without the blueprints, without the keys, how could she, right there and then, hand and wrist veins iv exhausted, avoid the sensation of having broken into herself illegally. She eagerly rummaged around each room, but nothing, always nothing, not a clue, not a trace, not even the tiniest bit of debris seemed familiar. Wearing out her pupils, she scrutinized the floors, corners, chipped baseboards, always nothing. Her brain remained clean, scrubbed to excess. Fresh-plastered paint-smelling insides. I used to live here, though, Aline heard echo through her vast emptiness. I lived in this body and thought in this head, but it's like yesterday never existed.

She took a long walk through herself, striding across her emptiness with big steps, roaming through her limbs and globules vainly searching for a fragment of the past. The body's memory, Aline said to herself, they talk so much about the body's memory. Looking for a scar I'm so tired but with no physical assessment just memory pain or pleasure. Aline imagined a number of lives for herself, possible combinations. She made herself the heroine of temporarily abandoned manuscripts, had some fun inventing a thousand and one nocturnal reconnecting futures. The blank page, the precarious space impregnating her for a few hours with soon-to-be discarded plots and profiles was comforting to her.

I still don't know if I'm pretty, Aline suddenly worried. The seconds went by as slowly as mercury dripping onto a wood floor. I must be, or I will be. What name would I like. It's important to have a name for yourself, a name that can keep you warm. My parents chose it while they were watching a movie, or by poking a pin into a list of baby names. Maybe it was the name my mother gave her favorite doll when she was five years old. Maybe my father thought it was rather unbecoming and imposed his own choice, a family name, an adored grandmother who'd passed away too early amid crustacean tears.

The word butter was followed by a sparkling syllable-and-capital-letter garland on which every name blossomed in Aline's brain with renewed dew-entangled joy. I know a lot of names, Aline gushed forgetting the wait as well as the truth. She worked at holding on, arranging the leaves and petals as if when she completed her classification she'd be able to choose her favorite corolla. Julie, Charlotte, Emma, Lydie. Véra, Laura, Angélique, Aurélia, Béatrice, Sylvie. Albertine, Odile, Amélie. Or maybe even Marie. In the end Marie's not so bad. A name for nuns and wayward hookers. Ten feet from the bed, in the wooden closet, a black mink coat patiently waited for its owner to slip it on again. And as the hanger sagged beneath the fur, Aline sighed with satisfaction, in a carriage her Marie was hurtling down the sterile hills of the great internal emptiness, leaving a few blue flowers to blossom in her wake.

Aline wouldn't be anyone as long as she was alone. She wasn't anybody the whole next night. In her sleep, Aline dreamed she was blonde because of the long light strands she'd noticed lying motionless on her shoulders. She came back empty-handed for the rest: her subconscious had walled itself in, in vain she ground her nails against the cemented memories, her Pandora remained locked rough with hostility. Aline dreamed she was blonde, but she was too far away to get a glimpse. The forest was deep, the roses needed urgent painting, the dormouse stuck in the teapot and the hare furious. Thus she shortened her periods of REM sleep as quickly as possible.

The door opened and closed three times, but she didn't hear a thing all night long. At seven o'clock they had her drink some water. She hated the name they gave her then so much that her esophagus refused to cooperate. Aline Maupin the liquid transformed into angular rocky ground your name is Aline Maupin each swallow thistles scratching Aline Maupin mucous membrane oxygen stones hydrogen agates my name is Aline Maupin vomiting little marbles bouncing off the chin.

At seven thirty, two aides ran a wet soapy towel along the ninety-five haggard kilos. I want to see myself it's not time my ribs stick out so much my skin too fine a peel a linen film stretched to breaking. I want to see myself it's not time I insist my legs solid knots branches I hear their dry wood splitting. I want to see myself I said I want I see my arms olive branches slowness decomposed movements jerking at the elbows chopping joints and my stomach how it. Mirror. The face owes it to itself to be a Polaroid, the past in sepia running off fashioning even the tiniest little wrinkles Aline whistled quietly, some tribes fear the capture of their souls in glossy photos the negatives little soul cages little freak show cages little country fair cages the bearded lady the soul cage come in come in whistled Aline way down inside, how old am I and yet I don't see anything. An amnesiac in front of a mirror has the same reflection as a vampire. My body isn't teaching me anything, raged Aline in D minor, I'm nothing but absence a ball of veining viscera knit together behind all this tissue. My features are regular, my deep-blue eyes would brazenly slice milky skin if they weren't as inexpressive as a cow's. Freckle constellation, natural without sun, easy, not a single dimple but a path, comatose stuffy-smelling under-eye circles, if tears carve out canyons my heart was a flat land. Immaculate, intact, lack of hydration on its upper layers, my skin has nothing to say nothing to confide in me. I slept for such a long time my eyelashes grew. Unless. I saw the death of the swan and my eyelids wear its agony as a decoration. Nothing's escaping from me, airtight is the soul cage, my soul was returned to me washed, spun, pilled. Does a young child howl in pain when he sees what he is. I am worried, worse, terrified. And yet my two eyeballs remain mollusk stares, I'm looking at myself in clammy silence, my iris precious, my pupil shooting daggers. I am absence walled canine a gambling den without mystery behind all this tissue. Aline stuck in a fingernail to see. To see herself stick in a fingernail, in the fringed heart of her upper lip. A reflex or a tic or maybe the first time. The first time I've done it the first time I've watched myself do it the first time what does it mean mean to me the first time. A minuscule trench a micro swelling a pinch of redness. I'm in pain, Aline says to herself. Not a lot but a little. A little bit anyway. I'm in a bit of pain, Aline says to herself, but maybe not enough to. For ducts blocked to tears, the stimulus insufficient. My eyes never shine, there's no way to cheat, they say the window of what is in my case a child of nothingness. I am emptiness, concludes Aline. I can precisely deduce what I inspire in anyone who meets me. And in anyone who has met me, too. There's no way to cheat, I'm not in mourning, my eyelids would be black. I am nothingness, Aline knew. Alone you open the soul cage before you push the latch. Sitting cross-legged on the bed, Aline let her face liven up to check its finery. Resting, expressive, resting. I have the whole range, squeezed out Aline's little inner voice, you'd have to be a chalice overflowing with such vacuity to master the solfège of the positions. The day it is the name I have the body is silent but betrays itself, I learn. I am emptiness in a thin body that will soon manage to reestablish the balance of its curves. Breasts, hips: the weight of weapons. I can make out that my lower back will be plump as it sags, emptiness always chooses its foot soldiers from behind. I also know that being woman—she hates me, being an intelligent woman—she ignores me, being a superior woman—she holds me in contempt. Men must really like me a lot, Aline exiled herself within. Her little voice couldn't sing.

At seven forty-five a nurse took her blood pressure, changed her IVs, and talked to her a very little bit. Her voice was trying to be gentle, but Aline could sense it was heavy with worry, mired in hierarchical recommendations, and didn't ask a single question so as not to bother her. I'm not an orphan, the distant little voice in Aline's very depths hesitated to rejoice, my genitors will come soon. A mother a father old keys for my damn locks lead keys a mother a crowbar a father a hatchet break apart the door that hide-and-seeks the emptiness, break down holy battering ram the door the closet Blue Beard but a headless body multiplied by seven or by the Trinity still remains shut down even after resuscitation. Does a head rolling away from the guillotine lose its blood or rather its memory first. The last memory the convict keeps, how does he keep it. I'm thinking in gulps of air, opened up Aline to swallow the pill.

At eight o'clock they brought her two crispbreads that she dunked in some weak tea. In the morning I swallow how many sugars in single hot beverage tea coffee milk chocolate how many nothings or sweeteners in mixed hot beverage tea with milk tea with lemon coffee with milk kind and type of preparation to be determined recurring or fluctuating presence of an occasional or daily ritual with or only cold beverage fresh or concentrated juice preferred temperature single or combined citrus orange grapefruit lemon fruit and vegetable cocktail soy or nothing. Nothing at all. In the morning nothing at all or bread and butter or crispbread or pastry or cereal yogurt or Greek yogurt or bacon and eggs or everything. In the morning is that seven o'clock or eight forty-five or ten thirty or whenever I want. In the morning don't even bother talking to me. In the morning I'm in such a delicious mood they nicknamed me the lark my pretty little lark my dear little lark it's so nice to see you to hear you to touch you as soon as I open my eyes. Aline was chewing very slowly, letting each minuscule bite be cuddled incisors palate molars taste buds. She chewed till everything turned to liquid, vainly waiting for her madeleine moment. If seers once read the future in entrails, where is the past if it's not in these saliva-bundled crumbs, pondered hoarse Aline. Dissecting my ex-self in bland tongue rolling, what do my memories taste like, I hope they're compact, a little less flavorless and not so heavy. While the tea was lukewarm, she thought it was more polar than an arctic squadron, cementing her conduits just where she was expecting lubrication. An iceberg in my throat, titanicked Aline and her mistreated nerves, a crumb of memory for how many below the surface. Resuscitated, did Lazarus always have the taste of ash in his mouth, every day did he rediscover the taste of apple, or had his icicle nap anesthetized his jaw's jubilation. Aline swallowed diligently. She swallowed each dose molasses as if her body were being fed for the first time. Do I have children. Emptiness often has children. It's natural, it's emptiness's destiny do I have a husband to have children for. Emptiness reproduces in order to have something to feed on. No spontaneous generation. I'm a newborn in a vast adult body, shivered Aline, lacking assurance, a newborn with a dead memory and potentially blown circuits. Aline distinctly visualized a toaster, but was entirely unable to determine if it had belonged in her own kitchen or to an acquaintance, an advertisement or the family shelf. Maybe it was just a mental image, concluded Aline in a whisper. The head doctor had just come in.

The strange thing about amnesia is that it can affect its subject in a very partial way. This means Aline Maupin now knew nothing about herself, but she hadn't forgotten anything at all about the rest of the world. She remembered wars, what time the train would arrive, the rule of threes, and Coco Chanel. She knew the five continents, the name of the president, and the habits and customs of Western illusions. She remembered that at 6 rue du Vieux Colombier there was an agnès b. shop, but she couldn't give her own address, the name of her parents, or her date of birth.

Dr. Benzecri knew from her family that Aline was partial to Parisian parties, counting a number of celebrities among her acquaintances. Parisian celebrities, obviously. Young people with sharp fins, smug fat cats under threat from the taxman and their cholesterol level, the gangster set from the gossip columns who were happy to raise a toast as long as the bottle cost more than three hundred euros. Magazines were brought in, the TV turned on: Aline faithfully reproduced CVS and rumors, having no difficulty recognizing sitcom actors, reality TV puppets, face-lifted emcees, and even more serious individuals, going so far as to notice their capillary modifications. She remarked on the covers, leafed through the articles and nodded, never ceasing to point out the faces touched by the grace of the cathode tube. The nurses themselves whispered to each other about the extent of this knowledge, all the while picking up one or two juicy bits of gossip. Only the heart of the matter. The doctor suspected what was coming next. A kind of intuition. From earliest childhood Dr. Benzecri had felt slight buzzing in his left ear, a muffled swarm announcing a future worry. So, ever since he'd been at Room 43's bedside, his eardrum had been playing Cassandra with absolutely unpleasant insistence. He asked his patient to think farther back, but nothing helped. Photos from a party he was certain she had attended, simple because she was in them, left her utterly speechless. She only had to have crossed paths with someone for her not to know who they were, unaware, unable to give their profession and their name.

Too fast with her we're going too much too fast quiet concern a rest time will heal her time restore the scattered little pieces ugly little pieces like the echo of her soul little pieces chalk because she always fades back protecting from the storm torrent reality Aline inside waterlogged Aline inside bogged down how to armor her against the dripping self already splashing her at the edge of breathlessness how to protect her from permeability, Dr. Benzecri indecisively tortured himself as he picked up the phone.

In order to distract the patient and study her progress while waiting for her condition to allow her to receive visits, she was given blank pages. A lot of them. The first day she didn't do anything with them, crucified bed and IVs. The second day she touched them as she wrinkled her forehead so deeply that the nurse was afraid her veins would implode around her mossy temples. On the third day at about six o'clock Aline asked for a pen. The fourth, fifth, and sixth days the little white pack of paper thought it had been abandoned for good. The seventh day

Aline meticulously folded each sheet in half and slipped them into the groove and made herself some ugly little makeshift notebooks. On the cover of the first, Aline drew many indeterminate shapes, immediately interpreted as simply decorative by the medical staff.

The truth was something else again. Aline was afraid of everything that came out of her. She didn't like her voice, a nasal trickle powdered with openings that were too cavernous on the vowels, clearing the way for the kinds of drafts particular to heavy carriage doors that protect certain classes with door codes and bronze door handles. With a sharp spasm she'd aborted her first laugh, her throat paralyzed by its cackling fruit. Oozing the great nothingness, how can I be able to expel so much everything, she disgusted herself as she cleared her glottis hard enough to tear her uvula. So she was often quiet, preferring the rhythm of her internal echoes, the monotonous chant of doubt, the litany of fear, more directly in agreement with what she seemed to be, to really be for good. I'm Aline Maupin, her body resonating with temptation and her voice like a maraca, hammered Aline deep down inside, I'm Aline Maupin but after all maybe. I'm not who you think I am. Her own sweat bothered her, as if her glands were actually too incompetent to secrete droplet scent balance. My words cluck my movements a peacock's tail I think in fan shape how could I survive handwriting analysis, spasmophiled finger-and-thumb-tensed Aline.

The loops and rosettes that Aline was drawing were accomplished in single lines, without lifting the pencil. The ballpoint pen tip adhered to the paper without ever piercing it, hypnotic nonchalant movement. Some space remained blank, framed by the dark lush doodles. The orgy of curves invading the cover was by no means made up of timid attempts at illustration, contrary to the deductions of Dr. Benzecri, whose tinnitus by the way was still on the rise. If Aline was blackening the sheets' original whiteness with upstrokes, it was simply for the sake of procrastination. Pushing back the foreignness docking always more deeply and intimately, amnesia is a bottomless well, dizzied Aline, people think that when they have no memories men lose their balance, and nothing is more gaping than passivity. I saw face and body first dive.

I explored corners enduring swan dive. I heard my voice and sniffed my skin, my auditory canals along with my scratched sinuses relapse. I thought the floor would stop falling away. Yes. When will the floor stop falling away, all I do is fall, panicked Aline, does my inside have a false bottom. When Aline's fingers decided right hand to grab the old Bic, her whole body shivered with the organic mechanism engaged. She was a simple witness to the first line, then to those that followed. Aline held her breath and threw herself into the heart of the spared rectangle, center right of the page. Do I decorate my *i*'s with childish balloons, are my capitals constructed with energy or laziness, do my *f*'s flare out cancan like Nini Flat-on-Her-Back, or are they a stern frozen font. Shaking and awkward, words appeared in little bunches. Writing like a schoolgirl's, wide and loose, impregnating the loops with helium and nonsense. I could feel it so much, waivered Aline's tiny exhausted, entrenched voice, I write like emptiness, not even developing not even a crabgrass sprout, just perfect emptiness. At twenty-seven, having a child's quirks in drawing a consonant, such breathlessness with the aspirates, decrepit punctuation, nasty senility, I write like a corpse or a stillborn earthworm. And for the first time since she'd been reborn, steam came to Aline.

When the day finally deigned to decline, Aline had filled every space on each double folded page, cover back front. Thanks to some Tranxene 50 mg, Dr. Benzecri discreetly entered Room 43 and recorded the following:

Notebook 1: Overboard Maybe
Notebook 2: My Life: A User's Manual
Notebook 3: Why Anne Is a Dog's Name
Notebooks 4 & 5: Illegible

Meanwhile, Aline was dreaming abrupt. She was hurtling down a hole with sibylline walls, a vertical tunnel, a narrow steaming gut. She didn't feel carried away, but rather abandoned like an old piece of greasy paper ending up in the gutter just because that's its place. You're number 6, the Hatter informed her. Don't try to pass me, I'm way ahead of you and your holier-than-thou attitude. But I didn't do anything, Aline answered him, her voice echoing more than a little unreasonably. I don't talk to girls who tilt their consonants, especially when they're third to last, winced the Hatter, completing a double somersault demonstrating years of practice. Sit back down, we're going to have tea. Please understand, Miss Maupin, I'm number 2 and we want information. Aline got ready to tell him something, but the Hatter almost disappeared, a little point farther down in the distance, much farther down, infinitely farther down. In six months I'll have touched the center of the Earth, whispered Aline to herself. It must be too hot there, and that's what woke me up. She smoothed out her dress, which ballooned out as she free-fell. It's possible that I've gone all the way through, the shortest distance from point A to point B is always a straight line, but does that rule apply to speleology. Her elbow banged into a cup, a saucer, another cup. The Hatter liked taunting the latecomers. I'll spend the fall in Beijing well, if it stops in time Aline calculated mentally as a teapot hit her full force. You hate blue, don't you, uttered in the dark a toothy, thick-lipped croissant floating on its own at her level. Don't be surprised if it's cloudy, it's just that you've gone out the other side.

When she woke up, Aline had some bruises, and a few cat hairs were scattered across her gown.

# Miss Scarlet in the Kitchen

**Round 1**

**(5 + 3, Total on the Dice = 8)**

You gave us such a scare. There's no doubt about it, you really gave us such a scare. And on top of that your mother waited more than a week before she told me, I don't know if you understand, more than a week, you could have been dead, besides she thought you were dead, we all thought you were dead, there's no point in lying, artificial respiration the doctors had told us nothing proves she'll come out of it, we were even thinking of unplugging you because of the cost but Charles insisted on taking care of everything, he's the one who had you brought to Neuilly, your mother good-for-nothing as always do you think she could make any decisions, I was too far away I took the job in Lisbon you know, it's a pretty city I'm happy there and Marie-France likes it a lot, I don't speak Portuguese very well but I get by okay and besides at work everything happens in French or English anyway and English is my strong suit, you take after me as far as English is concerned, taking after your mother you wouldn't have gotten the good grades you did in English, do you remember what your mother looked like when you failed your *bac* with such high grades in English of course you do. There's no way you forgot something like that. There's no doubt about it you really gave us a scare. You'll have to be nice to Charles okay, because I don't know if you have any idea how much the guy has spent, if it wasn't for him we wouldn't be here shooting the breeze right now, you can take it from me. He's the one who let your mother know when you woke up, you know your mother off who knows where again spending her alimony with Josiane, lucky he got in touch with her, but I warned him, I warned Charles I told him the lay of the land, you know, because your mother doesn't show strangers her real self, I told him what she's really like that way he'll see what she's up to no problem and she won't be tricking anyone. That's just like you. You sleep for six months, then say you're tired. You should be in tip-top shape, you know. We'd all like to sleep for six months, between work and Nancy cutting her teeth we don't get five minutes, we never sleep through the night, I can't tell you how tired we are. Exhausted is what we are. It's going to be hard, Aline. You understand, things are complicated right now, I have too many responsibilities at work, and hospitals give me the creeps in the first place, so with a hospital for nutcases, you can imagine. That's one of your mother's ideas anyway. Since you live in the 14th arrondissement, we'll just transfer you to the loony bin. Well, I'm saying that, but you couldn't stay in Neuilly anyway, they didn't know what to do with you. But that doesn't mean your mother couldn't do something, take you home to her place or something, I don't know. Special care my eye. Just more to bill the insurance for nothing. They don't know what pushed you over the edge, they're not going to be able to figure out what will make you normal again either. Well, when I say normal, it's just a word you use. You are normal, you're just a little shaken up, but it'll pass. Maybe tomorrow morning your brain will straighten itself out and everything will get right back on track. This thing isn't going to last five thousand years anyway. You're going to have to be strong my girl, okay, no giving up, I didn't raise you like that, we're tough in this family. Well, especially on my side. You think it feels good to have your kid in a psych hospital, honestly it doesn't. You're not crazy, you have no reason to be here, period, new paragraph. There are no crazies in the Maupin family. It's a good thing your grandparents aren't with us anymore, I swear. It's just that it's not an easy situation, you know. One minute you're on death's doorstep, the next you're a vegetable, they get us all confused with euthanasia and everything, and then finally Her Highness wakes up one fine day but doesn't remember anything.

No, I'm telling you, you have to be tough. Luckily, our hearts are strong. Anyway, what's important is that you're better now, right. Like they say, as long as there's.

## Notebook 1
### (Overboard Maybe)

The dance at Vaubyessard following the dinner at 7:00 p.m., what an idiot I put my gloves in the bottom of my glass. I haven't forgotten the smell of truffles, you can't forget it, the supple note taunting the warm air climbed like ivy along the numb aroma of flowers and the upper crust, the smell of truffles certainly challenged the aroma of meat. Essence of fennel, I haven't forgotten that either. Pure water doesn't exist, the river is a peaceful sewer, Cidrolin refused the chlorinated tap, and Lamélie enjoyed it in the pontoon sun. In the hall a woman was singing, it wasn't the same day, the same month, or even the same year, but she was singing, I'm sure *Mrs. Johnson you're wearing your dresses way too high.* I can hear her slender voice easy as anything. I can also make out the rusty despair of a senile throat, dulled by wounds and tears, accompanied by ghosts grimacing as one, that still finds the strength to shout *Maréchal* never will I come to you never have I come from you. I can also describe, with absolute exactness, the main door of the Snoutfigs cathedral, the Land of Lace, and the Squitty Sea. I remember all that and so much more, who knows, even more.

## Round 2
### (4 + 1, Total on the Dice = 5)

She started with us three and a half years ago, it was in December, no, January, we'd just expanded, and there were boxes everywhere. Charles had recruited her as an intern, through a friend of a friend, without even asking for a cv. As long as they're blonde and under thirty, Charles doesn't care about anything else. After all, it's our job to take care of everything, to find them things to do, to check up on them, it always ends up on our plates, we're used to it. Except for her, we saw her coming a mile away. Lolita is what we used to call her. She didn't know how to do anything except flutter her eyelashes and follow Charles around like a puppy dog. We've seen scatterbrains before, there's been a parade of super-short skirts, spaghetti straps, and thongs, which is apparently what it takes to replace Viagra. Every season there's a new supply— paper, forms, office supplies, and bimbos, but it's the same in every company. But like her, no way. I've been here for ten years, and a girl that types with two fingers and spends fifteen minutes looking for every letter was honestly something new. She didn't know how to answer the phone either. We always had to explain everything, she never remembered anything, the coffee machine was always a mystery, and we didn't even ask her to go anywhere near the fax machine and the photocopier, every time it was the same thing, it was always a catastrophe in the end, she'd get all red and cry, god, did she ever cry, she'd stand there with her mouth open and her nose running, acting like her dog just died until Charles would hear her and come yell at us, she was top-notch, a real office tragic actress, she was. I've seen other gold diggers after contract work, younger, prettier, and craftier, but never one like her. She would practice her poses, biting on her pen and glancing at herself in the window, adjusting the way a lock of hair fell or a neckline that wasn't sexy enough. A real prototype for an upwardly mobile little slut. She would always stay late, so Charles would believe in her dedication and limitless motivation, though mostly to get a good sniff of her new territory. Marion and I used to see her going up and down the hallways, after a certain time, her face would relax, her barely hidden secret desires couldn't be contained anymore, every movement betrayed her cheap ambition, her eyes oozed her lust when they fell on the assistant's desk, like a fingernail scratching the associate director's leather blotter, the trembling of lips when nearing a bouquet of roses the bookkeeper got for her birthday. We knew she wanted it all. All of it. Usually the girls shoot their wad because they don't have anything to lose. They settle for very little, a contract just over minimum wage, a piece of jewelry, a helping hand, a pro forma promise, and three notes on a violin. Generally, they're realistic. That's why they're not too dangerous. They know they're a pain for us, but they're only temporary, we're not there for the same reasons. You know, Doctor, these girls are very conscious of their weaknesses. Some are almost apologetic about using their bust, resorting to almost unfair competition, and wringing the neck of the sisterhood. Because they're realistic, I'll say it again. They know it's all they have going for them, and that inside everything rattles around when they go down stairs. When they start sharing, they're a little ashamed when they admit they can't close a file. That's why we tolerate them too. There are thirty-four employees in the company. We're an equal-gender team, just by chance, but we want to keep it that way, we want to show Charles, and the others too, because it goes without saying that he put men in the key positions, that we know how to get the job done, and even better than they do. It's not easy with their lewd jokes and dubious double entendres as soon as we show a little initiative. I understand. Of course not, it's natural, that's what I'm here for after all. With Aline it didn't take us long to figure out it was doomed. Because she wasn't like the others, the ones we usually have, I mean. Aline wasn't realistic. And that's what worked for her. She had no idea, so she got it all. Behind airheaded Barbie mask, she's a real war machine. But a war machine that's actually nuts, that was her strength, that much is clear, not lucid but so nuts she couldn't actually fail. We could see her eyeing Charles like he was her chance, you know what I mean, like it was him and now, that she had to force the lock by any means necessary, and quick too. Where other people gave up, settled for a little bit, she put in twice the effort, patience, and dirty tricks. She observed the terrain, listened at doors, verified information, but always acted like a bit of a dimwitted filly. The others always dove in head first, Aline blew hot and cold, one day charming with her hair down, attentive, submissive, the next day armed with a Kim Novak bun and eyes pointed in the exact opposite direction. One morning she'd scold Charles about some unimportant matter, repeating word for word the criticism she'd heard through the executive assistants' office door, thereby appearing extremely competent and just a little courageous for being so insolent but for everyone's well-being, the company's, and her embarrassed boss's, predicting the future anger of a client who'd already complained farther down the food chain. Another she'd break down crying if a single harsh word was uttered, shivering like a baby bird mired down in a file that was so thin it looked like nothing but a brochure. Charles thought she was smart. The bizarre kind of smart that's not immediately visible, mixed up in muddled neuroses, strange, mysterious neuroses, deserving of some attention. She hadn't even been here for two months, and she was all he talked about, he would say she was sweet. You know, I'm forty-two years old, I wasn't born yesterday. When a man, no matter how old he is, tells you a girl is sweet, you know it's game over for him. She was doing it all at the same time, she wanted everything, like I told you. She didn't have to put out till after her first promotion. I admit she amazed us all. Charles is married, he's a serious businessman, it wasn't as easy as it seems. She never tried to push aside his wife. She understood she never could. She did better. She made herself part of their couple. A ménage à trois, if you like. Actually not three but four, Charles's wife has a lover, but that's a different story. She wanted it all, the position, the power, the lifestyle, the days when she could perch on her Pradas looking down on the new interns, the nights when she could drink Cristal Rosé wrapped up in a dead animal. She was capable of anything, absolutely anything to get there. Charles isn't that easy to get along with, he works too hard, you understand. She swallowed some tall stories, went through some bad public scenes, anyone else with the least bit of self-esteem would have thrown in the towel. When he bought her an apartment, we thought we'd have some peace. That in the worst case she'd sit home waiting for him, as is customary. But no. She wanted it all. She got it all. He created a department for her. Just for her. He hired three people who do her work for her. She came to every meeting, every single one, especially the ones that didn't concern her. Charles himself would always bring her along. She'd repeat the ends of his sentences, systematically nodding her head like those stuffed dogs you see in the backs of cars. Daddy's Yorkie, that's what we called her behind her back, except Christelle from communications, she didn't pull any punches. As a matter of fact, that's why she got fired. You know we're not completely stupid, we figured she'd give us a hell of a hard time, but still. Once she had her social status, her business cards with her tantalizing title, her brand-new BMW, her 1,200 square feet, and her shopping that would make the girls from the Emirates turn pale, we thought things would calm down. There were even some people who said that after all maybe she did love Charles, that thirty years difference isn't important nowadays, and then other people like me who aren't so easily fooled who said she'd been playing it close to the vest but now that she'd won there wasn't anything left for her to take. That was without thinking about the rest. The rest, well, is that she's a bitch. A real bitch. Who plans in advance and ruins everything. And not just to save her own skin, notice I didn't say a whore, I said a bitch, it's not the same thing. Do you have a dictionary? No, no, I mean it, it's important. We may as well be precise while we're at it. Thanks. I'm not very fast, sorry, it's stupid, but I always have to recite the alphabet in my head to find the right letter, I can never get the right order right away. So, here we go. Whore. (1) Prostitute. (2) A woman of loose morals. (3) Willing to compromise oneself for monetary gain. I'd say that Aline did indeed act like a whore, among other things. But not that she was a whore. Let's see the rest, no, no, I'm telling you. Here we go. Bitch. (1) A female dog. That's the original meaning, they say so themselves. (2) A lewd woman. (3) A malicious, unpleasant, or selfish person, especially a woman. So, you see. That's Aline exactly. Because not only is she contemptible down to the bone, but with everybody who's gotten the ax at the office, I can assure you that people who complain about her are the only ones left. Once she was settled in, Aline managed to isolate herself. It's not for nothing that our bottom line is in free fall. She only cared about her kingdom and about exercising her power. That's where the problem lies in fact: even if it's usurped, it's still power. And for lack of using it for work, since she didn't know what the hell to do, she used it on other people. Or rather against them. Other people are concrete. Individuals with bodies and affects, relationships and emotions, ideas, goals, and actions. She started cleaning house around Charles. Hell of a spring cleaning. She sent everything flying. She set him against everyone, especially his closest collaborators. Classic, right. Except in the end it really hurt. I'm not even talking about the depressions, packages of Valium next to the paper clips, sales reps who could only sleep when they took Rohypnol, before they ended up in the unemployment line, vacant positions immediately filled contrary to common sense and the harmful atmosphere it created in the company, no. I'm talking about Charles himself. He brought it on himself, according to some people. But we felt sorry for him, even now he still makes me feel sorry for him. He's made a fool of himself, she's turned him into a complete moron. You should have seen him at trade shows or in business meetings with her. He was proud of his Yorkie, lost all credibility before he even opened his mouth. Every time, he introduced her saying, This is Aline, my girlfriend. Discreet bourgeois charm Aline, my girlfriend. What happened to the word mistress, they think if they make it disappear, if they avoid trotting it out, then the situation isn't so ugly, so grotesque, more acceptable, that the people opposite them don't end up visualizing the grayness of his flabby tummy rubbing up against her taut skin. Really. That should help you understand why Aline's not getting flowers from us. I'll tell you a secret—I took up a collection this winter when Charles was talking about a coma. For two months we've all been sorry she didn't get flowers for her funeral.

## Notebook 2
### (My Life: A User's Manual)

It's impossible to love my mother, if you, and I, don't mind my saying so. Love is worse than remembering: it feeds on memories, but you can't cheat with it. I couldn't touch my mother. When she'd come near me, the nausea was sharp, sudden, and uncontrollable. I hesitated a moment, a shard of a second, before hiding my disgust. Out of cowardice, I'm pretty sure. My cheek would bristle, the fine hairs like armor, I didn't want to have to explain, and I certainly didn't want to apologize for how irrational the feeling was. So I refused, once and for all. Every drama has its compensation. I suffer from being a vacancy, but what can compensate for my right to refuse the vile profusion.

I never said *mom*. I couldn't bring myself to. There are some words like that that are too foreign, words I lost when I was sick. Lost along the way. Unless they're the ones that deserted me, aware of the fact that their very substance would always be impenetrable, without life experience so many words lack meaning. Hollowed out when they're still on the shelf, so many words like dead fish and I can't even feel their roughness or single guiding thread obstruct my nostrils, carcasses of words by the dozen, and I can't grasp their curing salt, I'm the one who's still unaware of the tears immobilizing them. Mom isn't the only one no longer in me. So I know why *father you abandoned me*. My mother is a piece of information, an additional turn of the screw. That's all mothers really are in the end. Items to add to the file to prove you exist. My mother, the source and origin, me her heifer make a note that's right genetic traceability has to be recorded.

I won't write about the head-on collision, my eyebrow should have stitches the way I ran full force into the mirror. My mother sees herself in me, and I can read my mother. Rather than amnesia, I would have preferred alexia. I said as much to Dr. Lagarigue that same day: rather than temporary incompatibility, it's actual conflict. Gabrielle Maupin goes by Gaby and really loves going to the gym, with me, it seems. We were so close it was scary, and I'm not trying in the least to deny that her whole being can be ripped apart by the indifference I'm offering her, by the gaping trench that I'm easily forcing myself to dig out by the shovelful. But who cares about tears and the sincerity of her chirping. Because everything has been said: this woman, in addition to her highly visible tan, yes, this woman, my mother, has an ankle bracelet.

## Round 3
### (6 + 3, Total on the Dice = 9)

She doesn't want to go home, not even to stop by, what do you want me to do? I wasn't waiting for you before I gave her a day pass, she didn't want one, she's still refusing now. She's fragile enough as it is, I don't want to upset her. I'm not sure shocking her is useful, you really have to be careful. Yes, of course I contacted Marenstein and Pierroli and the behaviorist with the mustache that the neurological institute suggested. They don't understand it a bit, what can I tell you. Yes, retrograde amnesia. The psychogenic kind. Hang on, please. Mr. Fouillot, you can see I'm on the phone, no, I'm not talking to your mother, no, of course I'm not talking about you behind your back, now please be nice and leave my office, then as soon as I'm done, I'll come see you, that's right, exactly. Sorry about that. It's much more complicated than that, Antoine, a lot more complicated. It's not even really a false memory. You must be kidding, we'd love that, if it were Korsakoff's syndrome, at least we'd know what to do. How can I explain it. She doesn't remember her mother, but she does remember Emma Bovary. No, not the book, the girl. You're mixing me up, Antoine. The only memories she has come from literary objects, except that she perceives them to be real. No, no way, I can assure you she is not psychotic in the least. That's the problem. She has a fictional memory. You said it, Antoine, you said it. This is the proof it does exist. No, she's always very lucid about it, and I know it hurts her. The strangest thing is that according to her loved ones, she isn't an intellectual, she quotes characters and situations from novels that she remembers very clearly, yet her family and her friends, too, are sure she couldn't have read the sources. In here she's always reading, yes. She's quite pleasant, well, we think she's pleasant, according to them she's changed. Radically changed. Certainly passive, rather classic all in all, divorced parents, an absent father, a mother who reads *Psychology Today* I'm kidding Antoine, I'm kidding, I really liked your interview on fetal anxiety in an urban setting, it was very relevant. Yes, yes, there's no problem there, she's highly capable of adapting, her cognitive functions are intact, nothing to mention concerning her short-term memory either, but as far as long-term goes, nothing helps, there's not even the smallest crumb, fictional recollections the subject has incorporated as real, and she quickly realizes the problem as well. Of course I'll keep you up-to-date. Don't hesitate to call me about Mrs. Cassianis's transfer, of course. And tell her I'll keep seeing her every Wednesday at the CMP. Are you going to keep her in for long? Lithium stabilizes her nicely, but you know how they are, they always have to stop their treatment, this is the third time for her, one of these days she'll understand. Okay. You too, Antoine, bye.

Circular NAC001

[*Not a Clue* page 36, line 5]

My Dear Readers,
In my role as the omniscient narratrix, I'm taking the liberty of stepping in. Would you please grant me the extreme indulgence of excusing the suddenness of this intrusion, cavalier as it is if nothing else, I hope you will, retrospectively, see its merit. I hesitated for a long time, I can tell you, about appending myself, shyly, yes, but firmly, into this chapter, where I have no objective reason to be. Nonetheless, I thought it was necessary to very briefly explain some of the notions at play here. I could have certainly restricted my educational drive to the narrow office occupied by footnotes. Alas, as you are aware an omniscient narrator's work consists of walking through the vast land of novels under his responsibility as well as rappelling along the many intimate crevices streaking across them, before committing himself to their highly enlightening inscription. Thus it will be easy for you to agree that, ontologically, I must suffer from claustrophobia. Consequently, I'm taking the liberty of submitting to you below a few definitions culled from a specialist publication. Without really making any of the events understandable or coherent, this short insert will at least have the merit of compensating the handful of lost souls who opened this book in the hopes of being caught up in the dizzying whirlwind that worshippers of cultural entertainment call "a story." Once, according to the current terminology, they've at least learned something, I invite these individuals to immediately turn on their TVs. Because in a time when, more than ever, the media allows fiction to permeate reality and situationists to roll on the floor, it would be out of place to chip

away anymore at the profitability of their days off. If you hold a BA in biology, psychology, or any other appropriate terminology or if you are rightfully on the verge of losing patience, I warmly recommend that you find something else. Otherwise, everyone's going to take off, and I have no desire to be left alone with my characters: you have no idea how annoying they are.

Sincerely,
The Omniscient Narratrix

**Memory:** Cognitive process allowing the preservation and retrieval of past states of consciousness and associated elements, including previously acquired information and impressions recorded in the brain and that continue to influence in the form of habits. It also allows reviviscence of former affective states, working on representations, without our being aware of it.

**Short-term memory:** Buffer state in the memory system in which information is stored for treatment by the articulatory loop and the visuospatial sketchpad.

**Articulatory loop:** Memory mechanism that stores and treats phonological and verbal information.

**Visuospatial sketchpad:** Memory mechanism that stores and treats information in terms of visuospatial imagery.

**Long-term memory:** Capacity for storing information beyond the short period of time afforded by short-term memory. Transmission of information to long-term memory occurs through the process of consolidation that begins as soon as the information reaches the short-term memory. Long-term memory is subdivided into declarative and procedural memory.

**Declarative memory:** The kind of information, such as facts, events, images, proposals, that is stored and accessible in the form of explicit knowledge recorded in the long-term memory. It is subdivided into episodic memory (stocking and recovery of events or episodes personally experienced; the information is stored in long-term memory in a specific temporo-spatial context) and semantic memory (stocking of generally acquired knowledge; reference memory is generally spared in cases of total amnesia).

**Procedural memory:** Acquisition of perceptual, motor, and intellectual skills or facilitation techniques for the execution of a variety of mental operations.

**Amnesia** defines a total or partial loss of memory, either recent or distant, along with the ability to complete new learning.

**Psychogenic amnesia** consists of sudden onset retrograde amnesia, often due to an emotional shock, and that may be reversible within a few days, as in fugue states or cases of memory loss due to specific situations (crimes, e.g.). Nonetheless, it can remain ongoing, as in cases of pseudodementia. The characteristics distinguishing it from organic amnesia are the speed and circumstances of its onset, the loss of personal identity (rare in cases of organic amnesia, except when advanced dementia is involved), the normally preserved ability to complete new learning, and, often, psychiatric antecedents.

**Retrograde amnesia** consists of a memory disorder involving the events preceding a trauma or the beginning of an illness. It generally concerns the minutes or hours preceding the accident. Normally, islands of memory are discernible during this period, which can last several years, although more recent events in relation to the onset of cerebral damage are more susceptible to being forgotten than facts in more distant memory.

**Islands of memory:** Isolated portions of memory preserved during the episode or the period of retrograde amnesia.

**Fabulation:** Fabrication demonstrated by statements that are completely foreign to the circumstances, associated with consciousness, memory, or intelligence disorders that free imagination from any filters. Answers immediately given without regard for the truth. This is sometimes apparent in cases of Korsakoff's syndrome (spontaneous fabrication) and also as a coping mechanism for memory gaps for a variety of cortical disruptions (provoked fabrication). Fabrication is not constant and is not a defining element of an amnesic syndrome. If present, it will be more present in the acute period of the illness. Fronto-cingulate dysfunction seems to be related.

**Korsakoff's syndrome:** Toxic (chronic alcoholism), infectious (tuberculosis, cerebral tumors), traumatic in origin, or due to nutritional deficiency, this is composed, on the psychological level, of continuous or retrograde memory-fixing amnesia, compensated by a mix of fabrication and false memories. This type of amnesia is caused by cortical lesions, in the area of the hypothalamus and the mammillary bodies, in particular. The patient suffers from a state of confusion; he presents attention deficit and disorientation in space and time. On the physical level this disorder is associated with polyneuritis generally affecting the lower limbs. The evolution of the ailment is generally chronic in older subjects and includes more or less severe intellectual decline. The disorders can often be serious in nature, with rapid and fatal evolution. In younger subjects the ailment is curable if treatment is early and intensive.

## Notebook 5
## (What the World Whispers)

I watch TV for hours at a time. My principal sources of contact with the outside are TV, newspapers, radio, and what our visitors have to say. And this last group is not to be trusted, they're revisionists with our best interests at heart, voluntarily erasing any speck liable to upset us. We often prefer our own personal fictions to the ones that are offered to us. Sometimes we take a TV movie for a documentary, or vice versa. When we realize our mistake, it doesn't bother us in the least. Sometimes we even take these lighthearted mix-ups for a very healthy reading of reality. I have a few questions to ask Dr. Lagarigue about (1) how September 11 was dealt with in her practice, (2) how Arnold Schwarzenegger's election as governor of California, specifically for the patients who saw him calmly announce to the crowd, "I say hasta la vista, baby, to unemployment," while a nurse made sure they ingested their daily dose of neuroleptics.

Sometimes it's hard to be the only amnesiac. Being the only amnesiac: feeling like an amputee but not really a patient, patient as a noun, suffering less than the others. I'll never tell the hospital personnel that I have this hideous feeling all day long. Telling them would be my downfall. They'll say it's probably quite true and send me on my way. I don't want to leave. Not because I'm afraid of the outside, because I'm afraid of me on the outside. I'm trying to soften the angles on the problem with a couple of hypotheses. (1) I'm narcissistic. (2) I'm in denial. (3) My pathology is no less severe than anyone else around me but it is less visible to the naked eye. (4) I'm a narcissist in denial, and amnesia is not as noisy as schizophrenia, especially at mealtimes.

## Round 4
## (6 + 2, Total on the Dice = 8)

It's good, it's not as peaceful here, but it's still more pleasant. No I mean it, I'm lousy at Ping-Pong, really, I promise. It's annoying not being able to leave. I don't know Lagarigue said next week, I hope so, 'cause I'm sick of this. And so are the kids I think. Almost three weeks, what about you? That must be starting to seem really long, poor you. Yeah, I understand though. My husband is adorable, really, he doesn't put any pressure on me, he takes care of everything, but it's hard, I know I'm lucky. I miss my little ones, it's awful. Same as you, that Mommy was going to get some rest, but after a while they start to wonder, which is normal. Four and eight. Not on me, but in my room I do, I'll show you them tonight, for now I'd rather leave Aline alone. Hubert and Ludivine. My kids are really great. It kills me that I'm not good enough, I'm always afraid of not being a good mother, anyway, I'm not a good mother, as you can see. That's nice of you but it's because I'm doing better too. Lagarigue says the same thing, but really, look, it's a mess, it's Easter vacation, and instead of taking them to the park or, who knows, going away to Deauville, I'm stuck in here. No, I don't play, thanks. No, I don't know how to play. David, I'm telling you I don't feel like playing. What a pain he is, he's overexcited today, it's exhausting. No way, if we move to the bench in the back, you can be sure that Jacques will start in again, and personally, he exhausts me. Are you kidding, he's not nice at all, I don't know how anyone can think he's nice, that guy is totally creepy, all you have to do is talk to him for five minutes and you want to throw yourself under a bus. See, he depresses them too. He's bitter down to his bone marrow too, as soon as he shows up he starts giving off these negative waves, I've never seen anything like it. No worse than Albert, of course, we all agree on that even Marika although she's a serious one, that Marika, yes you do Marika's the black girl who's always asking if anybody has a phone card, yesterday afternoon Aline and I counted and she repeated her question thirty-two times, it doesn't matter if you answer she doesn't remember, the nurses couldn't take it anymore, we ended up laughing hysterically in the end, that's right with those braid things, exactly, I didn't know the word you know, well anyway, even she can't stand Jacques. Yesterday afternoon I ended up next to him at the table, Aline and I were talking together, she'd just found out she was a manager, but she didn't know what of so we were talking about it, and Jacques butts in, so she asks him politely if he has a job, he says he was an IT engineer but that it was sordid, that's the word he used, sordid, a sordid IT engineer, but honestly with that guy you really wonder what's going on upstairs with so much unemployment, anyway she asks him what he'd like to do for a job and he answers with that voice he has, man does his voice annoy me, the guy's too soft, soft people depress me, so he answers her: the only thing in life I'd like to do is drink from morning to night. Can you picture the scene? Seriously, sometimes I feel sorry for Lagarigue. Oh he doesn't have Lagarigue, he has Brochet? It might be better that he's got a man taking care of him, you know. What Jacques really needs is a good kick in the ass. Yeah, I know, you're right. But still for us it's really not the same. Do you have a light? A little like Geraldine, 'cause I stopped the lithium. It had been over a year, I was feeling really great, I was doing all kinds of stuff, diving, amateur theater, catechism classes, we even spent a month in Senegal, but it was so hot in Senegal it probably wasn't the best idea, I was a great mom, my husband was really happy, so I figured it was okay. Yeah the same. It's such a pain in the ass, you feel like you're sick. And at the same time if you get sick as soon as you stop the treatment, then maybe you really are sick, you're not wrong. This disease is a real bitch. And I don't know about you, but for me people don't really understand. When you say you're depressed they think you're just sad. Yeah right. Or go organic, they love that too. Or having warm milk before bed. No, getting exercise, you have to get some exercise. That's exactly what my old boss said, they're all the same, it's incredible. You pay too much attention to yourself, too, we forgot about that one. No I don't dare, anyway they wouldn't understand, they'd think I was crazy, my mother-in-law doesn't even know I'm here, we told her I needed some rest, she must think I'm in Vichy. Lagarigue told me the word bipolar is very popular, but I don't know where. I'd like it if it were, hey if you have to be nuts you may as well be, what's the word you use, Sophie, trendy, yeah, that's it. You feel liking shooting yourself as soon as you stop taking the pills, but we're totally trendy, so we've got that going for us. Maybe Kate Moss is bipolar. You can certainly be bipolar and anorexic, there's no reason why not. Geraldine, will you give me a cigarette, no I have some but my pack is in my room. I'd rather not, Aline's father's there, or maybe it's her boyfriend and she has strange taste. Or at least she did. You said it. Thanks, no I'd rather have a light one. I'm already so anxious, if I had amnesia on top of it, I don't know what I'd do. Were you there, Carole when she realized she didn't like milk? It's weird, I'm telling you. She fills up her bowl like everyone, she heats it up in the microwave, she sips it calmly, she starts to drink it and suddenly she stops and goes to us ew, milk is disgusting. The things you see in here, I'm telling you. I told my husband about it, for once I could tell him something without it making him sad that I'm here, really you too, our men are the same, it's because they really love us, but they don't understand, it doesn't help, you agree. Or maybe it is us. Exactly, we think it's normal. Right now, for example, David's been screaming for ten minutes that his name is Chaka Zoulou and no one's even noticed. No, Sophie has the lighter.

## Notebook 1
## (Overboard Maybe)

Charles was my grandfather's name. I don't know if that's any excuse. When my grandfather would kiss me, I would rub my cheek and say stop, you're prickly. I'm certain about this memory. Not because it's buried someplace deep in my brain, a movie, or a book. Just because humans respond to the stinging ordinariness that lets averageness bloom. When Charles would kiss me, I'd rub my lips and say something, but I don't know what. What I'm sure of is that I said it quietly, very, very quietly so he wouldn't hear, but down deep inside of me I yelled it very, very loudly. Or not. There are several options to choose from. Hypothesis 1 is that the screaming was like a landslide in my head, a landslide of tombstones, with every kiss I could see death, bad breath from an old mouth, my tongue exploring this old mouth, my tongue afraid of coming back from that old mouth with a piece of old tooth sucked up by mistake, an old tooth is nothing but an old bone, kissing Charles, French kissing his corpse, or rather his skeleton, right exactly, they'll say I'm exaggerating, that Charles is barely sixty years old, who's going to say I'm exaggerating, who's going to say that Charles, at not quite sixty years old, doesn't have an old mouth yet, at what age then do men have an old mouth, at what age if not at sixty can you say a mouth is old, so old that it's why their breath is heavy, bent to bursting with all the liquids drunk, all the food ingested, all the cyprine emissions licked up, all the sex-generated froth deposited even deeper than Charles's old throat, than his old throat with its greasy tonsils, sixty-two years old do you think if it's gotten better. Hypothesis 2 is that the screaming was loud enough to make my head explode, when the kissing went on so long I could feel that my scalp go from smooth to gritty, too much screaming from the needles, a pincushion in my skull, a threatening piercing, that's all it could be, no, no Hypothesis 3 or at least not that one, not the one that implies it was pleasant never mind tolerable, I know what sacrifice smells like, the smell of a ram or a virgin, the stench near the altar when the daggers are sharpened before the phlebotomy, I stink like a great bloodletting, I reek of sacrifice, I say so myself and know that even if it wasn't me, not me yet, not that me, despite being purified and more than amply washed, despite being purged of mud-drenched memories I know it will cost my body and the rest dearly, the tiny remainders of a tattered moral, for me political is linked to correctness, it's impossible, no, I am looking because you have to look. Hypothesis 3 I went deaf inside myself particularly.

## Round 5
### (Double 5s, Total on the Dice = 10)

I increased the Maupin girl's Tercian to fifty drops. And it's not a bad idea to keep the bottle of Hextril in the medicine cabinet, I prefer if she has to ask for it, all that gargling is getting to be an obsession.

## Notebook 2
### (My Life: A User's Manual)

I don't know if picking up information is that helpful or good for me. Lagarigue says we're making progress. I smile at her and don't say anything. Obviously, we're making progress. I only ever cry after I get back. We talk about my being transferred to a specialized facility, neurology, memory, they say that Sainte-Anne is not where they can help me at this point. By helping me they mean *triggering* things. I'm not really into triggers. Lagarigue is happy because an hour ago those are the words that brought back the first real memory, and if we tap the vein she can justify my staying here to my family. Officially I can stay if I want to. Officially they can't do anything to me. Officially I'm responsible and alert. The government doesn't give a shit about retrograde amnesia, better yet, the government must think it's pretty practical. I've been rebooted. Malleable and ready for work. It's often practice that makes perfect critical judgment, what's more scrumptious for this good old market than my meat, empirically tenderized and marbled. I won't tap the vein. I'll close the quarry. I'm afraid of something she doesn't want to understand or, worse, that she can't grasp. I don't give a shit about my clinical state. I want to stay on the first chapter, there's no way I'm going to rush off into volume 4.

So, a little while ago in her office, Lagarigue said trigger like she says lots of things. Just to be specific. And something happened, something new, abrupt, and horrendous. I wasn't paying attention to the sleepy meandering of the analogy. I naively thought that my memory had given its soul to the devil and left me to cultivate my own garden, a big uncultivated garden that I'd just fill up with my own crabgrass. When

I heard the word trigger, I thought of the word activate, which led to push. And when push was stirred up, everything came to a screeching halt. I saw Mrs. Courcelles talking to us. Mrs. Courcelles was a teacher in my old high school. She was the head French teacher. All of a sudden everything was a mess in my head, all five of my senses going off, my class, the commotion the old-autumn smell the cramp against my ballpoint pen the taste of gum dusted off the faces in a familiar nightmare. If I'd only seen it, maybe the dizziness could have been controlled but everything rushed vortex past all at once, canals unblocked, it was surging back so fast, when you lose your memory you lose its rites and its rudeness, its super-tight curves and everything that makes it so annoying and primitive. And at the same time, it was all the names too, a disemboweled column spitting out self-confident last names with the matching first names cut off but sometimes the reverse, an overabundance of stories and sterile replies elevated survivors without any affective hierarchy. And to top it all off this terrible catastrophe let little bits of future swirl around, insignificant facts and information capable of restoring this data reboot deep down inside me, relics of course yes, we have a memory for only one reason: to wallow in nostalgia.

I saw them and felt them, coding within my skin traveling through my circuits till my guts were ready to burst, Marc Baudin Lise Carlier Emmanuel Douet Maxime Guélin Dominique Matignolles Angélique who always came in late Stéphane Porcher whose nickname was Sperman deflowerer of Karine Fillaud Béatrice Stevenson Cécile Richard Nathalie Riquet Ghislaine Abécassis and her stupid friend who listened to Bob Marley because he was too cool you know Anita Remano who is now a product specialist at Royal Canin. Marc What's-His-Name married that stuck-up Sylvie has three kids and lives in the Jura Édouard Salincourt who took over his father's heating oil company Julie who threw up on me on New Year's Eve at Marie-Jeanne's who works at Carrefour now Zoe who must work in Lille Yvan who pretends to be a DJ Patricia who took acting classes and an ad for bleach Tristan who simply messed up his life a ten-year reunion the idea of group suicide when we saw our grades and that's not even everybody. I liked my

emptiness better, my gapingness was hardier than this sticky ossuary of sickly little embryos aborted by cervical information, waving
their atrophied arms and legs everywhere what for who for, I wonder.

That's all memory is, a row of awful cesspools, sluggish places of
death, a picture tacked up behind every door, a door for every period,
one picture per calendar, and memories in the middle, memories are
dead moments, and among the smiling dead, ready in a jiffy, you force
yourself into the pose thinking it would be nice to be able to wander
through your own funeral parlor age by irreparable age. Jack Torrance
also knew that memory only exists collectively, memories as little bottomless, residual basins, nests of parasites, may as well infect the whole
thing, but how can I be sure that the names that I'm writing, the bodies
splintering me on this day the guts really did forget my face, features,
and voice long ago. I know that few of them remember me at all I wish
no one remembered me anymore. If they force me to remember, it's not
for my own good, no, it's not for that. That's why I stoop to fair trade. I
want to take without giving, it's no one's business but my own. I want
my doors rough, double-locked haughty. I don't want to end up at the
Overlook, there are enough people there without me. It's funny, she
says, that *trigger* is what triggered things. It's funny, she says, without
even thinking: she says, it's funny. Develop, she's thinking, undoubtedly.
My sea is walled, Doctor. No, I didn't answer that. I would have liked
to, I really would have, but I wasn't brave enough. I settled for answering: you think I'm healing, but I know I've caught the malady of death.

Trigger, activate, push, and Mrs. Courcelles all transported me
somewhere. I didn't really like where, but somewhere. The lesson
was on the Enlightenment, I can still feel the palpable boredom, I'd
forgotten that, not the boredom itself, definitely not, I've felt boredom
a lot since I woke up. But the memory of boredom. It's warm and a
little sweet. It's enticing and comfortable, too, but it weighs on your
digestion. Maybe because I'm taking note of all this my memory is
feeding me new data, family meals with hard-to-swallow menus and
eternal cups of coffee drunk in the living room. It's certainly possible.
Everything's ruined now. The valves are open, I'm going to die under

the weight of the supreme lie. That's the end of the new me. Stains will pour out. I know there's nothing to get out of it. I feel full, heavy with a brood of bedridden fetuses. I'll never discover anything new again, except some feats and opinions that no Dr. Faust and no troll will be able to spare me.

It was a story, with a moral, a crude parable as it was popular to use. On one side of the Earth there was a button. On the other side, a Mandarin. For some obscure reason, the two were linked. Whoever pushed it would have power, a lion's share of riches, the whole kit and caboodle. Whoever pushed the button would kill the Mandarin. Just as Mrs. Courcelles had cleverly pointed out, it went without saying that the identity of the Mandarin was and would remain completely unknown to the button pusher. Nothing but a body on his or her conscience, a distant body. No one would ever know, she'd added. Only the button pusher would have any idea that someone else had lost their head for him or her. I can really still feel the slight tingle going up and down my spine until it terminated in my unwilling body. I can feel like I did then in Lagarigue's office, I can feel it just like that very moment in high school in Sartrouville. Memories are tapes you watch over and over again, as long as you know how to get your hands on them. A slightly raucous silence almost inadvertently washes up at the edge of the teacher's desk. Mrs. Courcelles lets enough seconds tick by to make her point, then, looking at us with disdain, she states: well, I'm not sure—silence—that there isn't someone—who would still push that awful button—silence. With full force I experience that brief moment again, yesterday just as right now even less than tomorrow. Shame sprouting before it blooms, the insolent pleasure of a dirty little secret. I told Dr. Lagarigue not to mix everything together. The more we move forward, the more I'd like to run away without ever stopping, without even looking back. The more I investigate, the more I can't stand myself, the more I'd like to flee far from this body of mine, the more I want to throw myself up, empty my insides out, anorexise my memory, blank-slate the slightest foundation. You'd have to be incredibly stupid not to push that button.

## Round 6
### (6 + 1, Total on the Dice = 7)

You shouldn't linger in the cafeteria like this, it's not sensible and you can see you're keeping the workers on duty from doing their job. We have to close up, come on, you know we can't leave it open in between meals, you have to go back to your room Miss Maupin, or next door to the TV room, or to the smoking lounge, you usually like to go to the smoking lounge. Margot, go get Boris for me. Aline, be nice, what's going on. Yes he is, I saw him five minutes ago, he's doing treatments in the hallway. Calm down, breathe, there, there you go, breathe. Boris is coming with the meds, you'll feel a lot better, you'll see. But what do you mean, *you haven't finished sitting down to your meal yet?*

## Notebook 1
### (Overboard Maybe)

Charles comes every Thursday. He brings me daffodils because he says I like them and it's daffodil season. Charles constantly wants me to like what I used to like. As if it would make any difference to him. Charles is a little naive and very fleshy. I've made a secret vow to never remember Charles's body naked. I've made a secret vow to never remember what they call a man's desire when the man in question is Charles. That makes two vows. If they come true, I'll have to go to mass twice as often.

## Round 7
### (4 + 3, Total on the Dice = 7)

I like coming here. It's too bad it's not open very much. In the morning it's only from eleven o'clock till noon because we eat at twelve thirty. They don't have enough staff to come get us on the floors. And sometimes it stays closed 'cause there aren't enough nurses. Yeah, I think she's a nurse. She works at the reception desk too. Well, maybe she's not a nurse strictly speaking, she doesn't give out any medication. She's part of the care team anyway. Like the man behind the bar. He wears a uniform too, but I think he just serves drinks. They must have some special training, here you'd have to. There are some special cases, you know, it's normal. My roommate's okay. She's just manic-depressive, we can talk, I like her. Nothing, she was a sales assistant but now she just looks after her kids. In other words there aren't a lot of single rooms, they keep them for the most disturbed ones, like the old lady with the green bag. They're not hospital slippers, they're washcloths. Yes they are, look, they're made out of terry cloth and they're not the same color. You're blowing it out of proportion, it doesn't matter she's got socks on anyway, and besides it's not that dirty. If they let her do it, they must have their reasons, at the very least it's a bit of local color. I don't know anything about that. You don't always have to figure it out, you know. You imagine it's connected, that everything always means something, that each and every thing is kind of internal code and once you find the right key you can decipher anything. Lagarigue even told me that sometimes she doesn't understand anything about it. I think that's kind of reassuring. Shit, you're slow. It doesn't matter what the illness is, there's room for chaos, that's what it means. Or free will, why not. Yes we do. No one is completely predetermined, not even a textbook case. Take the guy in the jogging suit back there, for example. No not him those are pajamas, the one on the left, there, next to the girl talking to her Twix. Yes. Well you can see he's psychotic. Mm-hmm. There are tons of them here what do you think. What gets under his skin is that the system is out to get him, everything is based on that. Mitterand had the Grande Arche built on purpose just to show him how powerful he was after he'd graffitied Anarchy all along the RER tracks. Yes he did I'm telling you. And they've injected him with cameras too. He's really into nanotechnology, and he knows Foucault by heart too. I already knew Foucault before, you're full of crap. I've been hanging around the guy for quite a while. I've actually gotten used to him. At first it's scary, then it makes you laugh, next you communicate with it, and you end up deciding there's no smoke without fire. I'm kidding. Although. I talked to some former patients who only come during the day now. Some of them have been running into him for ten years. When I look at him, it's like I'm seeing all his circuits laid bare, the connections, the switches, sometimes I can guess when they're going to have to give him a shot. You could almost think that a psychotic is a cool, very precise clock. It starts, and tick tock it's off on another spin around the dial. And then all of a sudden it gets stuck and goes offtrack. As if sometimes the mechanism was off. Not like it was out of order, no it's not that. More like the subject was tired of its own gentrification. Not that psychosis is comfortable. But once you've settled into it, it must really purr, even if it's really violent. So sometimes things rebel inside. He hasn't mentioned geopolitics in a week. He just wants to marry a cheerleader and is trying to find out how to meet one. Don't you think it'd be nice not to be under a yoke like that or to constantly rebel against your own subconscious? Yeah I suppose. A coffee. It looks like I'm boring you. No nothing. They have a real espresso machine have you seen it. When you say how awful do you mean in general or just when it's not espressos in particular, because that's really all I drink. Of course they do. Otherwise there'd just be a vending machine. The cafeteria's not just for acting relaxed and friendly, like come on guys make yourself some friends being sociable is great to fight emotional problems. You're not too sharp are you, Charlotte? In here they can watch our progress and keep us from going too far. Pretty sneaky eh. If something happens in here you can be sure it gets recorded. We're all under control twenty-four hours a day, no need for cameras. My laugh freaks me out too. But I can't compare, maybe I'd think the one I used to have is worse. After six coffees they won't serve me anymore. Then they say it's decaf. But the decaf is disgusting, so they give me some crappy soda or fruit juice that's so heavy I feel like I've just eaten a full meal. See, it's not expensive. With two sugars please. The day before yesterday or maybe Tuesday, I forget, I blew a gasket, see, because there's a girl they let drink up the whole stock of Diet Coke, and they let her, they give her six cans at a time with a smile on top of it, and with all the caffeine it has in it I'm telling you she's taking advantage. I don't really feel like getting any air, but we can turn down the music if you want. Can't stand

Lara Fabian. No way. I have all her records? No there's no need, I'll see when I get there, at some point I'm going to have to go home and have a look at everything. Will you get me another coffee? What was I just saying. You're kidding. That's why the cafeteria on the third floor and the Relais H on the grounds are so important. Without the cafeteria and the Relais H we'd all go crazy, I'm telling you the truth. And on top of that we're lucky, our wing is just opposite, for the buildings on the other side it must be a real pain in the ass. Not everyone no. You have to get signed authorization from your psychiatrist, even if you don't do anything with your two hours or your four hours, if all you do is the round-trip. A lot of times we organize it among ourselves. Since they leave me alone I can get my sheet almost immediately, and then I let them know, sometimes I forget but since Lagarigue remembers I get my pass every day. I let them know before I go, that way I come back with cigarettes and magazines. The number of magazines you can read in here is ridiculous. My bedside table is worse than the hair salon. Yesterday or the day before I bought *Cat Fancy*. Frankly neither do I. Not exactly. It's either that or women's magazines. Not trendy no, don't go overboard, but still there's a shopping page and a column with personal stories, this time it was about Kristo, an overweight Burmese on a diet. The picture'd give you the creeps, I swear, it looks like a bag filled with who-knows-what, it's not even that it was spilling over, its ass was in the shape of a rectangle. I don't like your laugh either to tell the truth. I don't know what got into me, I'd already read the rest and there was a Siamese on the cover, Siamese are really cute. When I get out I'd like to get one, a Siamese I mean. Really? Two? God, how you can be best friends with some girl who named her two Siamese Dolce and Gabbana is beyond me.

## Notebook 1
### (Overboard Maybe)

I didn't just have my first cigarette two months ago. I started when I was about fifteen, on vacation in Brittany. It had to have been at night, I felt the smoke warming my lungs, which were retracted from the cold, salty sea spray. Or maybe it was around noon, and I'd chosen a menthol to be like my mother. She laughed when she saw me cough, told me to brush my teeth and that it was time for school. Not necessarily finding witnesses. The first cigarette must not have been as good as the first one I had myself. Charlotte brought me a carton of Philip Morris Blues. I thought they had less taste than the Luckies I bought myself. Too light, they burned too quickly, too hard to inhale enough, one frustration after another and then an awful migraine.

I liked that my body already knew how to smoke. In here it's easy to feel the serenity. Pleasure is a different story. I get up a lot at night to go to the smoking lounge. I sit in one of the armchairs, the noise of the lighter always echoes a little, so do the movements of my lungs. I can feel the word solitude. I know it's not the first time, but it's the most complete, the fullest, I'm full to the top with this word: solitude. It's nice. The building is empty like I am inside, a little desert set at the edge of a much larger, three-story one. I don't know the exact number of square feet. I feel reassured although I'm never really afraid. I haven't been afraid for a long time now. I blocked up the damn process as much as I could. I dammed it up out of love, just out of love and nothing else, almost, out of love for the word solitude. I love the word solitude, I want to be this word, to be one with it. To do this only emptiness, real inside emptiness, devoid of memories and the already rancid past might be able to help me. Memories are the reason the insides of skulls smell so musty. Solitude smells like plains, apples strewn across the fall and the splashing of mountain streams unleashed across rocks that are still warm in a dying August. Dr. Lagarigue always finds a way to mention progress to me, but I know there's no progress. My memory is dead. Sometimes I wonder if I'm the one who killed it. This question is normally underlined by a snarky little laugh.

I lit my first cigarette in the middle of the night, in this slightly cold room known as the smoking lounge. But in my head I was leaning on a railing facing the wind and I blew the smoke in the face of a Provençal sun. I tell Dr. Lagarigue that I'm building myself memories. They're so perfect that the old ones don't feel at home anymore. I know it and

I don't care. Anyway, a memory is nothing but a little bit of a lie that we hang onto in order to laugh or to cry a little harder. Might as well make them up. It's working pretty well, at least for the time being. Maybe I'm losing something. It's possible but I don't care. In fact, no, I do care because I can tell I haven't lost anything. I think I got rid of it.

I don't dare mention it to Dr. Lagarigue, first of all because she's a smart cookie and second because she wants what's good for me. There's nothing worse than smart people who want what's good for you. I don't know why I'm saying that. It sounds like something my father would say. I trust myself. Maybe I shouldn't: the more I learn about myself the more I am. Disgusted isn't the word. I feel contempt for myself, that's more like it. That's why I trust myself. I'm showing that I'm lucid. I'm showing a sense of distance too, distance and critical sense. Given the data it's a sign of something. Something different. I'm different and that's the only reason I'm lucid. It's hard for me to be one with myself, it's easier with the word solitude. If I wasn't lucid, I could do it.

I would have preferred waking up somewhere else. Sometimes I hide my Tranxene tablet under my tongue and make my glottis bob under the noses of the nurses who are possibly completely aware of what I'm up to. The nurses are very clever because they want what's good for me too. I do always take my sleeping pill in the end, it's just that I spit it out for later. I like to have at least a little control over the time I spend asleep or awake, I don't have control over much so I want to keep that at least. When I pull my Tranxene trick, I go think in the smoking lounge. I'm not the first one to think of it and sometime it bugs me, you have to talk for a while, play board games, or get rid of everybody else. For some that's easy enough but for others it's more complicated. I don't really like to have to do that because it annoys the nurses and I really do like them. And plus it makes a lot of noise, and the alcoholics come to see what's going on, the smoking lounge fills up, and everything goes to hell.

I really have a hard time with the alcoholics in here. First of all they pretend they're here for some other reason, sprained neurons, cracked cerebellum, a nasty case of the blues, a seismic depression. Their speech patterns are consistent, so we trust them. We're the B&L's, the Bipolars and the Like. It's just chance that we're together, little clusters of overripe pain, all of our hearts were twisted with juicy, purulent secrets. Our stories twine together with every confidence and each stifled sigh, it seems we cry less if we use the buddy system. The alcoholics are really sly, they try to link up with the vine without understanding that even impaired, the sap owes it to itself to be loyal if it doesn't want to end up covered in scabs. I understand the weight of shame, but after all, the nymphomaniac accepts the truth, the same goes for the addicts and the ones with eating disorders, and for the manic-depressives and the suicidal ones too. Some of the psychotics say they're doing fine, and that's how you can tell who they are every time. What good does it do to pretend, to talk about your every move and crisis, to compare your symptoms to anyone who will listen if it's just to hide the cause, no really, it's really annoying for us. And on top of that they depress me. I'm not saying I'm having fun all the time, but still. When I do my disappearing tablet trick, it's so I can have some peace at night, at least for an hour or two. To think about all the bodies I could've woken up in instead of my own, bodies with lives that are so much worse or with former choices that are so much better. Maybe I could've been a man or a child, after all, why not, a man or a child why not, why not say so to Dr. Lagarigue, that honestly I really don't accept this particular body, this particular life, because maybe it's not mine, no not mine at all maybe it's a punishment a damn idiotic metaphysical punishment, I screwed up bad in a former life and bang they sent me back to a fucking grown-up body to a damn whore's body, because that's what it really is, a middle-class whore's body, twenty-seven years old and the ass of a whore, the tits of a whore, a stomach that's already had liposuction. When I think about all that I need to be alone at the railing so that I can look down and admit that that's exactly what happened to me.

I need to be alone, bundled up in silence so my eyes can let go, free-fall from their sockets into the distance, and the more I look at myself the more my irises drop away, and the more I look at myself the more I know: I can only get away from myself if it's full speed ahead. The B&L's have a tacit agreement. We all know how precious solitude is, our survival instinct may have been laid to ruin we shelter the others as much as we can. We can't do much but we try hard. Sometimes it's hard to give up the room, to hold back the torrent of distress, to hold back the lock as the tidal wave of words bashes into the back of our teeth. We force ourselves to do just that despite it all by, I don't know. Maybe just to be polite. The B&L's have good manners. At three in the morning when the wind sweeps into my dull blonde highlights, I hear a creak crumbs I feel a damp gaze then a sugary bang. Sometimes we play duck-duck-goose, the goose a strange pedigree. I'm alone leaning on my elbows overlooking my peel pock-marked by this self, a distinct little spot in the field of lavender. A door cracked open a soggy handkerchief *this old man he played one* pulled-back snout the gong apologizes in the oil *this old man he played two*. A lot of times I'm the one who comes in just as the Kleenex package is started and on my heels the opening closes handing me over to the hallway and its twin sisters. It's much more than a need, more than a necessity, it's communion with solitude. Only the alcoholics like to talk. Well I say the alcoholics, I should be specific, the alcoholics in the post-withdrawal phase who live in the 14th arrondissement of Paris and who've been in my presence in the smoking lounge of the Piera Aulagnier Wing at Sainte-Anne's for the last eight and a half months. In other words Jacques, Viviane, Jean-Claude, and occasionally Cyril. But even if it's not a very large sample group, please note that I can't look after them. Maybe it's because they're worn-out. Or maybe because they're ugly. Or maybe just because they're unbearably unhappy. I think that's what it is. They ooze suffering, but it's a diffuse suffering, throbbing old jazz music, I hate jazz, I'm sure that even before I hated jazz, that's what the alcoholics in here are, jazz music, swaying pain, a rusty old tune sputtered out by the glottis of an antique saxophone that turns the atmosphere to lead on you with the first two notes. The post-withdrawal alcoholics living in the 14th arrondissement of Paris who've been in my presence in the smoking lounge of the Piera Aulagnier Wing at Sainte-Anne's for the last eight and a half months spin fiberglass as soon as they open their mouths, their breath is so rough, the room becomes the hostage of their asbestos-laden comments, they make the air so thick it condemns our bronchia, the idea of contagion spreads terrifying in a clawed crescendo, everyone curls up tight oh so tight as tight as can be, a compact ball of self, crouching inside to try to avoid the oxidizing assaults of this deceitful lethargy. They have the bitterness of cider, their blood has turned bad, their souls are lead poisoned.

Every place has its pariahs, often the ones it deserves. I don't know why, in here, they're the ones in need of a miracle. Some say that it's kind of their own fault after all. Others whisper that alcohol is a common shortcoming, a shortcoming, a propensity, a Pisa of filthy weakness. For many insanity is a burden scraping down to their shoulder blades since sudden childhood, perhaps they refuse to apply compassion to those who are well-off in the head. Perhaps we're jealous, those of us who didn't choose our pathology, who have to live with it every day, our chatty illnesses impose their diktats upon us, no temporary comfort, no familiar dizziness, is it then possible to envy the apathy, the debris of existence spreading at the feet of our granite pride. We suffer with spirit, we syndrome with grandiloquence, we see no sparkle in their resignation. We are beautiful and mortal in our stone dreams, hardened by the constantly tolling bell, to the west no Eden, nothing will be found not even eternity. Jacques, Viviane, Jean-Claude, Cyril, like their brethren could can and will be able to carry out intermittent pauses, digressions, know the temptation of each side exhibited before the mirror. Too mercury-sticky, it's impossible for us to know temptation. Amnesiacs, schizophrenics, psychotics, neurotics, manic-depressives, and so many more: it's clear that we'll never know straps that can tighten or be removed at leisure, chains of events and expectation are unknown to us, tomorrow night the next hour, no, we'll never manage to imagine it. Who cares about the nasty violent aftershock, they approach pleasure, at least that's what we think. Overboard maybe: my vagina is a crevasse frostbite greed, never in the past did delight ever stumble into this slutty trench. They used to say witches had a mark in the hollow of the vulva, there is no scraping that can scour clean what's inherent.

My memory remains phlegmy imposing arachnid infiltrated alveoli at the slightest curves. My memory is nothing else, black widow mucous, it's naive enough to be belched out by loose coughs but chanting will always give my throat a pounding. A bad head cold must be what turned me into an amnesiac.

# Miss Scarlet in the Kitchen
# with the Monkey Wrench

I wonder where memories go. In fact a memory really can't be lost. All it can do is wilt, gently wither, go bad fade in tender agony, but never be lost. There is no land of lost memories. There is no cemetery of banished memories, not a single one, not even for the most porous, the most debilitated. There is no ossuary, no funeral home where their remains can be laid. Maybe because deep down a memory can never die. Not really.

So I wonder, I wonder a lot, where my memories are, what has become of my plethora of rejects, my pointy-toothed horde of dirty little secrets. Have they been grounded, has their case been dismissed, are they trapped in some vague place where everyone is condemned to some wretched orgy, a catacomb free-for-all their tiny blister death rattles vapor stream abortion. Could my memories be simple components requiring collective memory fermentation. I wonder a lot, but I don't have much of an idea. Dr. Lagarigue doesn't really like this question. She says it does a lot of harm to many things, many things inside me that keep on eroding, like she says for example your principle Aline your reality principle.

That makes three weeks four days and seven hours followed by sixteen minutes since I stopped being careful about what she might say and especially about what she might answer. Because I certainly do know where my memories go. Where they go and how and what I do with them too. I know the song that goes along with this rite, a very personal and rather disgusting rite.

I eat my memories. If my brain is empty it's because one night I stuck in a spoon, a big old soup spoon, not even made out of silver or anything. I dug carefully so as not to mix the edible morsels with just any old thing lying around in there. My head is full of offal. Smooth little, soft, shapeless blobs of dark, angry blood greedily pulsating, intertwined with cables of veins and aquamarine quivering to the rhythm of each transmission. My head is offal. A rough little, harsh, shapeless blob of completely clotted blood cyclically vibrating, strangled by the throbbing dance of the blue flies. Sometimes a bubble pops at the edge of my cortex and out comes a voice calling me by a name as it's liberated, a name that isn't mine, a name that doesn't belong to me, a strange, masculine name, and it whispers words that I don't understand and it whispers words I don't want to understand and it says that the flies are because of me and it says the flies have come just for me, they're the guardians of memory that it's their job that I deserved it that they won't leave that they'll invade everything that they're a little like the voice itself compulsively bursting my head, familiar pressure followed by a rock slide eight words fourteen syllables: *They are the Furies, Orestes, the goddesses of remorse.*

The first time I stirred the spoon around I was a little scared and very cautious. I didn't feel anything, just a kind of pinching around the hippocampus at the initial penetration. Rummaging around in your head makes a weird noise, especially since your ears aren't used to it. Rubbed the wrong way, my eardrums took a few minutes to adjust to the direction the broadcast was going. I'm having a hard time describing the musical score composed by a spoon stirring in a head in order to load up with memories, the most accurate onomatopoeias, the exact adjectives. It's pretty close, I think, to what you can hear if you eat yogurt mixed with cornflakes, with the difference that it's not in your mouth but one floor up.

As I was taking the spoon out of my head, I discovered that memories can be very heavy. It's like almost topaz-colored jelly with glittery confetti in it, I don't know if it's the glitter or its viscous prison that's responsible for the astounding density (9.8 μ). Nonetheless I'm sure about it and can confirm: memories are allotropic.

I brought the spoonful of memories to my lips, a previously unseen texture, between crunchy and infinitely muddy. In the beginning I just wanted to reduce my contents a little, but there's a fine line between bulimia in its initial drive and the irrevocable lair of hyperphagia. Memories taste like carbonic snow and exposed ashes. Apparently, when I was little Daddy used to say: Let's leave the burning embers in the fireplace, tonight Santa Claus will come back to us roasted. Some of my thicker memory mouthfuls tasted gamy, I have to admit. I made no effort to chew the rotting taste beneath the condiments. You're not supposed to play with your food, and I've cheated enough already.

I chewed slowly. My molars mashed up the summer of '93, the day I was born, Saint John's Day folk songs, piano lessons with the *Méthode rose*, my first baby tooth, the fall of '78, my tears when I saw *Donnie Darko*, all my birthdays, my cousins' laughter, the dress I loved too much, Maurice Carème's *Le Hérisson*, the smell of the dunes in the south, double flavor Malabars, champagne on ice, the megaliths in Brocéliande, I devoured my memories, auburn henna that turns carroty, the little boy's smile, the winter of '86, daisy petals, my mother's lovers, Chinese New Year, I conscientiously ground them to bits, some were very stringy, others tougher than cheap meat, my incisors were tearing and tearing rodents are white rabbits, my enamel got dangerously hot, my dentin was on the verge of crumbling but my jaw held out.

It's the leftovers, the memories from the back, the very back of my skull are what was an issue. The spoon scratched sharply, with tenacity. I didn't want to leave anything behind, especially not the sauce base, the buttery base of words bleeding me dry. Moving the edge of the spoon passionately, flirting methodically, scouring clinically, working eruditely to pull out its tongue, a slightly ulcerated pink snail's head standing left mouth corner, a blind snail, we won't go over the river and through the woods anymore the antennae have been cut. No matter how hard I scrubbed this thick film harder than lava clung to the walls, ravaged walls snails house open to the sky renovation work, on its back the snail in a smashed shack, Scotch Brite rubbing rubbing its ruined walls the shadow of memories indelible Hiroshima shaped charcoal, with a wood plane break the tartar off the floor baseboards nooks incrusted interstice memories, making the effort to break my back and my tools, memory tartar is nothing but granite, even worse than what some hearts are made of. My fingers fissure the spoon handle, only jackhammers work, I said to myself, against dry lava, how can I conquer the fermented memories sons-of-rock memory and cousins-of-mica memories, bringing down memories is a complicated task, complicated, difficult, much more arduous than that silencing the insolence and vulgarity of the sun in July, yes much more laborious than strangling the sun to save Icarus arterial consumption, I said to myself I said to myself in the wing chair. My head is Pompeii, especially can't leave mummified cadavers there in the stone, random-access bloodsuckers' stone, lapis lazuli slug stone can make you sadder than the adage, absolutely can't leave stony memories deep down inside, they are an anthology of loose caustic stones that grate and scratch from the brain to the heart.

I put hot water in my head. Boiling water, half a cup. When a pot won't come clean everyone knows you have to run it under hot water, fill it with steaming water and let it soak and add a couple of drops of bleach. I hesitated a little but didn't pour in cups and cups of detergent. It's so easy to be poisoned. I just let it soak, an hour, barely an hour, less than sixty minutes, the vapor-encrusted water in the hollow of my skull. I stirred spoon adapted broth. The defiant memories floated to the surface, nothing simpler for me than to fish them out. I hated the taste of soup in my head. Such a rancid consommé, hard to swallow. Shame and remorse apparently resemble a stock teeming with red herrings. My throat swelled up, my esophagus rebelled as the mustiness of my venality quivered upon my already solstice-minced tongue.

Hubert Gérard Mathieu Stéphane Jean Aaron Patrick Christophe Albert Maurice Alain Bernard Olivier Patrice Jocelyn Thibaut Michel Thierry Pascal Piotr Claude Léon Richard Jean-Luc so many tapeworms paragraphs and paragraphs filled with rough strident sluggish pipeline trash paragraphs filled with nomenclature ulcers ingest assume consonants syphilis vowels peppery spirals list where how many sailors not only captains to chew growling ruddy guttural faces to swallow up Saint-Tropez Courchevel Saint-Lauren Gucci avenue Montaigne gulp down heavy tongues every mouth half-open sewer on breath so white every case half-open on a chain a perfume a watch approval Aline approval, I was saying to myself as I nursed a lobe of their ears. My tonsils burned this grimace soup this soup is too tough but less so than the heady vacant passageway that made up my pre-autophagy data.

A little ball of bark, hard and shiny, and very full like a still fresh though slightly green hazelnut rolling carelessly, surviving in my skull despite the minutely executed drainings. I needed some time and to get my fingers right in to catch it. It was resistant, and sitting on the table quivered like a jumping bean in order to escape me. Inside, I knew it, was Charles, his square clammy hands, his perverse tomcat simpering, his dark gray fur, his eyes, eternally damp with cognac, desire, and breathless stupidity. I couldn't eat anymore. My stomach was tainted by the evening menu, by the small-fry menu and was already begging for mercy, no way to force in so many fats, Charles-margarine would be an excess of fat, the tipping summit, the fuse that would transform my lair into a seesaw. Eating the memories wasn't particularly easy, throwing them up wouldn't have made any sense, I'm not a fan of pointless all-this-for-thats, and the molar-ground memories the enzyme- and digestive juice–harassed memories must really be ugly, not very pretty to see, and it must hurt too, hurt even more to cough up memories than to swallow them.

I didn't stuff myself with memories of Charles. I strangled them with the monkey wrench. Not having a nutcracker, I used what I could. I must admit I did enjoy going overboard with the vice, tightening up the metal, cracking the beige shell till it bled. The hazelnut holding memories of Charles was full of a kind of very dark hemoglobin, with pulsating little jet-black organs. I counted five of them, five symbol-izes man and maybe middle-class female vampires. For a long time I sniffed at the five sinewy marbles, I touched them with my tongue caught by the particular sponginess of madeleines cooked at the wrong temperature. For a long time I rolled the tiny taws inside cheeks and lips. My mucus membranes were distressed by their acidity. I arranged them like internal jewels, grafted between gums and lippy circumflex. The mirror gave me a scornful look, saying Snow White is the fairest you know the fairest in the land, adding, oh you poor dear you think you're Orlan get those out right now. I spit out all the marbles into a blue Sèvres porcelain saucer. They didn't look like little hearts, more like brown beans. One after the other I made them blossom with that monkey wrench. With the first turn of the screw a voice *Often the heat of a beautiful day* could be heard *makes a young girl dream of love*. Hoarse *to gather diligently* unhealthy *the grain the scythe cuts* awful *my Nanette bends towards*. With the second it became haughty *the furrow yielding it* rising in high wavering threatening notes in sniggering arcana. With the third and fourth *it blew* she died *very hard* the atmosphere *that day*. With the last it skinned my ventricles and eardrums to the bone *and the short skirt blew away* blood turned spurted so thick *and the short skirt blew away* the rancid little marble its drops echoing *and the short skirt blew away* thin stains on my fingers. Five little balls of memories emptied and scattered, their envelope consumed, a small shift, honored puddle of mercury, salty, troubled liquid. I lapped at the metal warmed by their seed, right up to the flecked handle. I don't remember his hands on the small of my back or the first sigh I had to fake and especially not the retching that shredded my throat with every kiss.

I'd like to disappear, devour myself like I did my head, snap my bones, reduce my vertebrae to powder under the reign of that monkey wrench. I secretly hoped that some random bite would lead to the nerve, the rind, the very first piece that turned my heart to meat, but it's the whole system, yes my whole system, it's cartilage kneaded with corruption. I'm intrinsically tainted. Not an ounce of libertinism, not a hint of hedonism, no Juliette on her cushions. I wanted I wanted reconfiguration data cleaning garbage dumping the life out of Aline, well the one from before. I didn't give up, I'm on the wrong side. Huddled in my bosom are the blessed beds and wall hangings of holy whorishness.

From the time I was born, or rather a preteen, smashing constantly smashing in back of Dr. Black's head. Every spinal movement, every wink of a shoulder displayed bare appetizing curve, all supply and demand, my body is more a market than an ecosystem I'm a cowardly market stall paid for with biopower, every corner-of-the-mouth twist a cervical hit, I kept putting his fragile little neck between the polar teeth of the rusty wrench described as a monkey, I kept strangling yes constantly strangled Dr. Black between the iceberg teeth, I kept crushing his porous marrow, I specialize in handsome old men and in a good rabbit punch and a good rabbit punch and I'm not white and a good rabbit punch I'm late terribly late eternally late a soul must be punctual if the bleach of redemption is to fall upon it.

Some of my sisters, because my race is fertile, grow and multiply is common encouragement, so many plans across the generations, some of my sisters often invoke war sexuality combat, choice of rancid arms shoot me first. Some professions are teeming with my kind, I won't list them, but not out of goodwill. Simply out of decency. And because everybody, even the Petit Robert dictionary, knows the truth even if the dictionary holds its tongue. Maybe the Petit Robert isn't always candid because it's a man. One or two examples are scorching my tongue, so, unfortunately, I can't completely refrain from such ridiculous denunciations, from knocking down gaping wide double doors. Everyone knows about interns, known as *little hands*. Originally used in the fashion world, can we deny the reasons the term is still in use, knowing its popularity outside this sphere? *Assistants* are a serious problem, too, if you look carefully. Of course in many cases, it's understandable for a woman to reject the dreadful, dated secretary, especially looking at the accumulation of associated tasks. Still, *assistants* gets me excited, I admit it, especially since they were often previously hired as *little hands*. I'm a prime example, but since using my hands wasn't enough, I managed to go far beyond, a whole department. And as for press secretaries, even though, except for a couple of crude puns, the term doesn't have any intrinsic connotations, one noteworthy anecdote sheds light on the reason: the EFAP, their communications school, is located in Paris at 61 rue Pierre-Charron, opposite a proud establishment known as Le Milliardaire, a famous hooker bar where it's not uncommon to run into employers, reporters, and others in the company of women who are still in training. The joke about the horse is not only crude, it's also dangerous because it's cryptic. Sleeping your way to the top is more about laying down. I don't have the strength to stay on my feet, but even as I say that I know my bitter nose is growing a bit. I didn't try, maybe though, honestly, I didn't even think of it. If today's thirty-year-olds position themselves as Pharmakos, it's as much procession inhabited as scapenannygoats.

I'd like it if all this sneezed unheeded, I'd like forgetfulness to pompously nibble all the compensation neurosis larva implanted inside. Even emptied down to the muddy tissues adorning my crotch, I'd remain shaven, forsaken in Nevers, I don't deserve anything but this dank hollow, the hollow in my brain where both my nails break and my voice *and the short skirt blew away and the short skirt blew away and the short skirt blew away.*

I wish I could remember fish.

# Study (Reload)

You're alone in the room. You're alone and you killed me. You can stay where you are and curse your remorse or so many other things. The smoking lounge is quite cool on the verge of summer. Don't touch the dice, it's not your turn anymore. Your case was laborious because of your scattered memory. Handicapped from the word go, I gave you an extra turn, around the board and of the screw.

I'm Dr. Black, I'm your uncle from America. That cute little face of yours took quite a few hits when it ran into the doors and lighted signs. Your frizzy whiskers must've been cut or else no one would've gone over the river and through the woods. The enclosure was set with bushy barbed wire, an approach known to be efficient with scapenannygoats. You incorporated the vagi-clean curettage, your insurance will reimburse you for the operation. I won't give you back what was devoured. I won't give anything back to you, not your memory, not any praise, not even an eye for your eye. That's not what I'm here for. Even if it's obvious that I lied to you. I told you when I came in: I'm not here to judge you. I am here to listen to you, maybe to deliver you, to observe, accompany your foul confessions. I'm not here to judge you, I insist on that, and I add: there's a difference. When I said judge I wasn't thinking about a verdict, I was thinking about the pain, under pain penalty of death, there's enough of that, enough so much that the pain seems like sorrow.

So I am accusing you. What does it matter that you've become aware of the motive, what does it matter that the time of the crime for you is integrated into your biological clock, what does it matter that your tears try to clean the black-and-blue marks making such a mess of my neck, what does it matter that the hysterical, rhythmic lungbursts from your sobbing could wake the dead, including my own remains.

I'm Dr. Black, I'm telling you: I'm the Mandarin. There was an M-Moment, there was a trigger, there was an undeniable choice. May 24, 1995, I submit for your approval seventeen minutes past midnight, seventeen minutes fourteen seconds, my archives, I agree, are among the most impressive you'll find. You didn't have too much to drink. You never have too much to drink. You drink just *enough.* His name was Bernard Levinstein. His belly was as swollen as his wallet. You hesitated quite a while, observing him in the bar, in that bar where Dianeless so many others hunted. You accepted when you saw the oh-so-baroque black of his American Express card. You were wavering the whole last hour, his name-dropping was already troubling you, your quivering ovaries did a little dance. You didn't order one last Bellini. Deep inside you didn't sing a children's lullaby as he punched in the third door security code. You didn't send for the automatic pilot at first contact with his parchment-ribbed skin. You tried everything to get the best moans out of him. You even guided him so he could make you come. Besieging phone you hoped he'd finally call. Your tears weren't fake. You crumbled, you were suffocating with anxiety, rage, and bitterness. You sacrificed that old Mandarin, first cold-pressing of the button. You immolated me, in fact you demanded an immediate investment return. Since then you've not checked your momentum, index finger pad cataclysmic thrust without ever worrying about the slightest consequence. Because Bernard Levinstein finally did respond, a little fixed-term contract on TV, a few society dinners, a handful of connections. And an adorable, persistent, impulsive little flea, you jumped from one head to another, one network to another, from a bald head to a blow-dried one, sometimes you choked on the anti–hair loss, anti-dandruff scents, today's shampoos including the benefits of intrusive fragrances. And the more you gorged yourself, your nose in their roots, the more you filled your ducts with their blood, their blood their precious blood globules every cell a promise of possibilities multiplied by ten, fractal Rh images, in up to your flank, you were dear Aline, but yes, remember, because the more vampiric your state, your essence became, dear Aline, stop your whining, the more you turned me into a trepanned martyr of eternal returns.

Inside me there's not a single organ, not a single thought, that you managed to save. With your bare hands you choked stop your screaming my dear, dear Aline, every, well I wouldn't exactly say every moral sense, but I'm not far from it. You are a rock sea, a hardened pond, a swamp so sterile that havoc itself refuses to grow there. Lucidity, dear, dear Aline, lucidity is something you and you alone have eradicated from your cerebellum. Women are all born lucid, did you know that Aline, it's an advantage supplied by nature to arm them at a young age, nature likes to counter objectification. Without lucidity you couldn't be a woman, you'd be a puppet. But with a subconscious if Lacanian psychoanalysis agrees. A puppet, Aline, dear, darling Aline, take this and blow your nose, a puppet is nothing but a perishable object, a race toward repairs, sisterhood death, neuron excision with the compliments, obviously, of the boss.

There's no pain to inflict no sentence to serve because no punishment can be crueler than the wasting away of your soul, my child. But let me reassure you: your survival instinct has been preserved. When one limb is sick, the whole body unites to perform a separation from the gangrenous organ. It's your heart, Aline, your heart and the small of your back exhausted in their fall, it's your skin, Aline, your ridiculed epidermis, your cerulean eyes and their irises bleached from such crudeness, from nonnative, overblown fiat lux ambition, it's your body, Aline, your divided body because pantomimes always end in puzzles, that commanded you, treated you with autophagy, devouring your memories, eradicating the crime, yumyumming the encephalon, but you must be familiar, right my sweet, Aline, with the itching torture known as phantom limb.

I am that limb, Aline, I'm your brain and so much more. I'm your memory, and it will always survive, you need to understand, this is my role, I am the spectral guardian of the incinerated memories at the bottom of your belly, I'm a crucial guardian and a pile of other things. I accuse Miss Scarlet of knocking me off on May 24, 1995, at seventeen minutes past midnight Greenwich mean time in the Kitchen with the monkey wrench and on and on and secondarily with a soupspoon not even made of real silver. I accuse Miss Scarlet of subjecting, on a daily basis, it's one-way, the Mandarin to the death of a thousand cuts. I accuse Kitchen Miss Scarlet with the backing of the monkey wrench.

You're alone in the room. You're alone and you killed me. There are five of them in the Study, you're alone in the smoking lounge. I'm on the board and won't leave until the end of the game. Omniscient Narratrix, bring in the next one.

# Professor Plum

They weren't locks of hair that Esther abandoned once her eyelids closed, they weren't locks of hair that wound up on the bolster, red, flat, silky ribbons, slightly thorny where the waves curled, little crowns with split ends that highlighted the anemia of their sleeping source such wishing-well curved eyelashes, with no red hole on the right side Esther Duval let her hypnotic roots pour out their serpentine tentacles, Esther Duval daughter of no one according to her, Esther in alcohol-anviled sleep some nights with a one-eyed moon only entrusted her mane to the rough pillows in Mathias's bedroom so it could finish off the last frail verses of its dervishing in languishing, rolling knots.

They weren't locks of hair, they were tendrils, plant or bug or maritime Saint Esther, invertebrate actress and martyr Esther, by the stingy light of the bedside lamp Mathias loved to collect up the seeds of her foolishness, get them to sprout, coat them with syrupy-reference fertilizer, put them through the sifter with uncertain rhythm, flip them, flip them nauseatingly high in his loquacious brain, at that time there was room in Mathias's vast brain, so much room he often didn't know what to do with it, so much room that his verbose insomnias always put it to good use.

Mathias really liked to play in his brain, especially when Esther's little body was within reach of his cortex, it was a dry, veiny body, a notebook or a hesitant palimpsest book, Mathias hesitated so much he always always hesitated some and then some more, back then Mathias had a blue, elastic-harnessed notebook, a pad that had been assaulted, gang-banged by one ballpoint pen and thick-leaded pencil after the other, a dog-eared pad he couldn't let go of, just as he couldn't let go of Esther back when Mathias still had some room in him and in Esther, Esther who would be buried on March 12, 2006, in the cemetery in Carrières, Carrières-sur-Seine (near Paris), with its downtown its riverbanks its viaduct its high school *Les Pierres Vives* and still farther afield its cemetery, fetid suburban houses dark lapping water disparate tufts of grass brown steel fences open sesame cement alleyways straight marble slabs, oh so well behaved, kilos of gravel gravel makes the shoes of the living scream out, notice the cowardly measures, the feverish resistance, the survivors' pride, but who are these organs crunching over our heads wonder the dead with their fists over their ears, a few plastic flowers, look at B-24, a few vases with stagnant water, B-24 hit of course hit and sunk as will be the redheaded Esther Duval on March 8, 2006, a few rancid bouquets, turn left to the south no more to the right, a few shriveled stems rotting in the glass heart, the gold cross next to the Lopez family plot, clean little tombstones for high school girls cut to the quick on the inside of their wrists, our scorched Esther will be hit and then sunk in B-24, on March 30, 2006, because there's a delay no matter the work site it's a fact you always know to count plan include the time the workers need, on March 30 B-24 here's Esther's grave *Esther Duval (1973–2006) You'll always be our angel and soon we'll be with you again.*

Esther's grave is ugly, almost as ugly as the Lopez family plot and Martin and Jacqueline Pasquier's tiny tomb. Maybe Esther's grave is ugly because it's abandoned. Plucked bare of any offering. The Lopezes really like all sorts of knickknacks, the Pasquiers have a half-wilted rose taunting its neighbor in its cellulose robe. Esther's grave is as smooth as the skin she presented to the decision-making blade on March 8, 2006. March 8, 2006, will be a Friday and Esther even more tired than usual. Esther will be **tired**, in other words, because it isn't enough to be precise, **1.** Weakened or exhausted by exertion. Because it isn't enough to be precise *a tired muscle, heart, brain* because any light shed on the motives troubling those who commit suicide *a tired person*, one experiencing tiredness is interwoven with nonsense and blinding dregs filling the air with the stench of catechism and what's worse: citizenship. *To feel very tired.* ☞ **aching, broken, drained, exhausted, worn-out,** don't compare suicide and desertion don't compare broken boundaries to marrow A. **weary,** and cowardly withering B. **dead** (FIG.), understand once and for all **ground-down, overworked, shattered, smashed, spent;** accept it once and for all FAM. **all-in, done, finished, out of commission, pooped, spent, wrecked,** it so happens that sometimes along fallow land certain fields prove to be objectively **beat, bushed, sapped, sucked dry, zonked** more sterile than the rock that will replace the heart of all the survivors (see also To be done in\*, to be at the end of the line\*, to be at the end of your rope\*, to be at the end of your tether\*, to drag your feet\*, to drag your heels\*). Some gardens can't be cultivated *Tired and lacking energy.* ☞ **dejected, depressed, overwhelmed,** FAM. Out of sorts. In human skulls lucidity digs deep tunnels where bitter winds gust *Tired out by noise, by chaos:* dazed, stunned, stupefied. Inside the breeze remains a persistent draft salmonella eroding the courage of birds AMUSING. *He's been tired since he was born, he was born tired* it's called the reality ◊ principle. BY EXT. ARCH. That which shows, indicates tiredness. No matter the context never say think that suicide's the easy option *A tired face.* ☞ **haggard** suicide is the easy voice *A tired appearance* suicide is spineless bundles of cowardice. **2.** BY ◊ EXT. Disturbed. Never ring deceitful trinity faltering mailman craziness *To have tired blood, a tired liver.*—Weak, never say think she's lost her mind correlation reason because the chicken or the egg the worm-eaten soul the pierced heart never say think he she a little sick. ☞ **unwell.** Indecency swallows up the body always steeped in splattering mourning as the remains go by *She's a little tired and won't be in class today.* Suicide is a choice **3.** (1878) FIG. Something that's been used a lot, lost its sparkle, its newness. Binary clinical application every problem has a solution ☞ **crumpled, damaged, deformed, faded, old, used, worn.** Suicide is a decision a decision it's unusual how can you classify such a dynamic act as weak when everyone is subjected to horizontal lineage *Tired clothes, shoes. A tired book.* Suicide always distresses family and friends as opposed to their gregariousness suicide is a testosterone-stinking clinamen suicide is an antidemocratic act suicide is the island of rejection autophagy crucible living currency **4. BY EXT.** *Tired of:* weary of. ☞ **bored, disgusted, exasperated, fed-up, jaded.** Esther Marie Angèle Duval, March 8, 2006, at 11:19 p.m. will know that the next minute and every single one thereafter are nothing but leaden misery (see also **To have enough of**) Esther Marie Angèle Duval daughter of Marguerite Jeanne Clémence Pesséans (housewife) and Georges André Duval (sales agent) born on December 7, 1973, at the Clinique Sully (Maison-Lafitte, in the Yvelines) will figure out for herself that her pregnancy reached full-term. *To be tired of one's mistress.* She won't write a letter and will push closed the door to the big bathroom *To be tired of living.* To combat the smell, she'll empty two liters of bleach on the tile *"Tired of writing, bored with myself, disgusted by others"* (Beaumarchais). She'll wear a pale little smile as she does this, a sporadic twist at the left corner of her mouth, thinking that she was altruistic right up to the end. She'll the fill the bottom of the tub with pink strawberry gel, chromatic preparation, cocktail formulation, Esther will wonder will I dissolve like a duck my soul a sugarloaf will I dissolve my blood is grenadine and my heart brown sugar. Stretched out on the enamel her wrists freed Esther will remember: *Of all the words banished in the twenty-first century, it seems that hope is the biggest pariah of all. Poetry flees for fear of being ridiculous; novels turn the other way so as not to seem affected; writers confronting this obscure mafia quickly come to gnaw on their own knuckles: they're taken for politicians.* Esther will remember, and in her emptying brain the title will echo, the title and the author of such awkward lines, *Escale chez Persephone,* Mathias Rouault, one last little ringlet, one last tango in Carrières-sur-Seine, *Escale chez Persephone* that's where I'm going my love and not just for the winter, not just for six months, *Escale chez Persephone* that's where I'm going my love and I won't be back, I'm not wheat, the beautiful dozing seeds, the nourishing grain, and yet the worms will make their own fat from my body.

As Esther's red begins to dilute, Mathias will be in Paris and unaware of the whole thing. Mathias will be in Paris and will never know that Esther's remains will have to wait a long time to be reheated. On June 17, 2020, her mother, January 25, 2024, her father, April 5, 2041, her younger and divorced sister. Esther will know that her body will be cold and that it will be really bored for a number of decades before the cracked wood several decades before the corroded wood bends beneath another rough box, years and years before the molasses can take, years and years before Catherine on top of dad on top of mom on top of Esther can finish the Duval & Co. stew. Mathias won't know any of this. Mathias won't know what became and what will become of the one he whispered *burn burn this witchcraft* to at night, Mathias won't know and couldn't care less.

Mathias Rouault is thirty-two years old. And on this day Mathias doesn't remember Esther anymore. How many pale Loreleis Laures Beatrices has he consumed locked up in ink it doesn't matter in the end or in the beginning. Mathias Rouault has run out of room in his brain to keep flipping words when he can't sleep. Mathias Rouault has run out of room, it happened a long time ago, a long time after Esther's creeping locks and those of other sleepers who followed her square dance on the pillow parquet.

It's almost time to hear from to Mathias's brain. To hear it narrate the bitter strangulation of each of its zones, no Music of the Spheres for this oozing organ. It's almost time to catch a glimpse of the increasingly exponential paraphernalia clogging the circuits and interfering with the flow in this dilapidated place. But it's still too early. It's barely noon. According to tradition, the train where Mathias is sitting is en route from Angoulême, the literary tradition forgets that the suburbs of Paris are bustling with frustrations and desires that are very similar to the ones sheltered by the hideous word "province," the literary tradition doesn't take into consideration the strength of the ivory piercing the gums of the Paris region's young residents. If it was simply out of literary tradition, all these cemented eyelashes would be less disturbing. When it's only tamed topographically, Paris loses its sparkly appeal, no sunrise view–inspired quotes, just muffled, blistering rage, constantly ravaging the hearts of the Cinderellas on the last RER of the night. Mathias is not a victim of social disintegration. He's just a martyr of the cultural ravine.

When he was in high school, it used to take Mathias an hour to get into Paris, and all alone in the heat of his quest, on Saturdays and Sundays he took twice as much time or more so he could strategically and spirally go from one bookstore or record store to the next, without ever being sure of a lucky strike. He would've liked to have seen his blue-covered aborted texts in one of the magazines littering the shops in Saint-Germain-des-Prés. Not so much for the prestige of it, for the silly satisfaction of printed letters, but for the social side, the exchanges, a feeling of community. In Carrières, Mathias never conversed. He broadcasted. Or resisted collective programing. Unilateral movements, repressed fatigue and anger, a yellow ball of blood slipped between his glottis and his esophagus. He started taking courses at Nanterre, convinced that conversations would be a natural part of studying literature, that he'd stop drowning Esther in his torrential references, imagined he'd have unending Norton anthology discussions, and going so far as to dream of having friends he could rip into the latest issue of the geometrically titled review with.

He was studying at Paris-X-Nanterre (Greater Paris), a train every twenty-five minutes during rush hour, he took the long ramp, a concrete tongue vomited up from the guts of the station, welcomed by being short of breath, greeted by an unobstructed view of the employment center sign, the proximity of the buildings being an Aristotelian irony, a roll of the dice, nothing random. After six months nothing, still nothing. But he'd marked out the territory, double-majored in literature and drama, poetry novels and theater, no literary genre could reasonably evade him, no pimply reader's profile could escape his gaping demand, the dead would be studied in overcrowded classrooms, the living discovered in the cafeteria, with this prospect exciting him beyond all reason, Mathias had a hard-on all during orientation week. The first day of classes was like a cold shower.

The undergrad program in drama, since renamed theater studies thanks to Guy Debord, was mostly composed of illiterates who'd discovered within it the unexpected payments that allowed them to obtain parallel parental financing as if they'd registered at an acting school like Juilliard, along with the studio apartment they always described as being *in a good location*. So almost every single student in the program turned out to be someone whose only goal was *to get noticed* as quickly as possible, jumped at every occasion to read out loud, or do a presentation, or answer a question—no matter how briefly—as if they were *potential casting calls*, since all the instructors in the areas studied were actual professionals in the field, usually directors. From the start, Mathias's eardrums were assaulted by gelatinous tremolos and incredibly pertinent remarks like *What I love about Ionesco is the strength of his titles*; *Sartre's Les Séquestrés d'Altona's completely outdated since you can't understand a thing without the costumes*; *Saturday I went to see a play by Novarino with Hélène and Pierre, it was so incredible I almost wet myself*; or perhaps *Shakespeare's kind of overrated*.

The literature students had the advantage of not inviting him to some ridiculous nightclub where he'd endure a free-form jazz adaptation of Claudel's *Tête d'or* [sic] or Beckett's *Endgame* in sign language [re-sic] or a montage of some starving Apollinaire's advertisements recited with accompaniment by a late-middle-aged alcoholic pianist who was *sooo cool* [re-re-sic], but it still hurt Mathias. It's noon Charles-de-Gaulle Métro station, the girl who knocks into his suitcase, too fat not to clutter up the aisle block the folding seats the suitcase, reminds him of some stupid girl he dated for three years how much time way too much time Mathias thinks to himself, her habit of putting on makeup without a mirror *when I was a teenager I was so self-centered that now I know my face by heart it's useful for putting on blush without looking* and the questions always more questions she never left me alone *Does Rimbaud end in t or d I can never remember* so fucking stupid any desire was pulverized but what an ass she had but no way no really or maybe by cutting out her tongue yes by cutting out her tongue but when she kept at it I'd imagine the trickle of blood dripping down her speechless but mutilated completely mutilated chin her mouth a pudgy puddle of blood ready to overflow a projection of fresh blood what was her name already it was two or maybe even three years ago that midterm *can you come over I have your Blanchot I didn't understand everything but I thought it was really great* I wasn't super-interested but it wasn't impossible she was just barely a B cup anyway. It's noon and Mathias is on his way to the Right Bank, it'll take something like another forty minutes because of the two transfers. It's noon Mathias's brain still has room, this is maybe even the moment when it's the most immense and insatiable, a still unpolluted brain, a still unencumbered brain, a brain still free of future garrotes.

Left behind, he counts, he ranks in real time what he's left behind, Carrières-sur-Seine, the studio apartment on boulevard Gambetta, Esther, the university in Nanterre, the part-time window at the Credit Lyonnais in Sartrouville, the RER-A, Marc, Gregory, and Jean, the Café de la Mairie, the banks of the Seine, the bookstore, and that's when he starts to laugh. He laughs a little too hard and especially in a loud, almost booming voice. According to tradition, Angoulême-leaving Mathiases may not laugh in a loud almost booming voice. There really is more than a just Relais H shop in Angoulême. Literary tradition really must admit that urban sprawl is a horrible thing, a lot more horrible than such a sweet thing as "province." Mathias's brain gobbles up the sentence and will mull it over with a bunch of others till he gets to the Strasbourg–Saint-Denis station.

Mathias Rouault works a lot, really a lot. His brain is more than a machine, it's a word centrifuge. It gorges itself and then makes them dance to the whims of the carousel assembly, Mathias's fingers some-times struggle to keep up with the rhythm, a rhythm that is always fluid, despite some jerky bits, a rhythm so frantic he risks a sprain with every move, Mathias's keyboard clicks in a lively way, Mathias's keyboard proves to him that he's alive, a lot more alive right now, here, beating his keyboard as some would the bushes, pruning his sentences raking up his words plowing through his brain digging white patches into the paragraphs here and there, he's alive, living proof, his body is the interface, his brain is connected only his brain is reacting, often Mathias says to himself I'm a brain and a penis, just a brain and a penis, but very clearly both.

Unlike the not-yet-very-distant time when his major organs shared Esther and his little notebook, these days the only thing Mathias strokes is his computer. And not just its keys. He owns a laptop with a slightly soft screen, he likes to touch the words, puts them under his thumb while his pointer lightly presses. I'm touching my words with the tip of my finger, Mathias says. This must be what literary masturbation is, Mathias smiles. Then he goes right back to his smudged chapter. Mathias was happy in his little room under the eaves, using clichés to find the strength he needed to keep at it. At what? A book, obviously. Mathias is happy. Happiness has always made people stupid, which is just and right. What would all the disadvantaged and social outcasts hang onto if the temporary chosen ones also found power sharpness critical reasoning in abundance. Let's not push it.

Mathias is reveling in joy. His furnished room is dangerously dilapidated and filthy, it's an attic room, with Parisian rent and unpredictable heating. One night Mathias watches the birth of frostbite just as Saint Ludwina once watched the bubonic growth on her forehead. Mathias is a boy. It must be noted that as far as superegos and symbolic fathers go male writers are specialists. Mathias is also thinking about famous dead men who, like him on this December night, were freezing to death as they produced a masterpiece. To alleviate his hunger, which by the way could be alleviated with one simple phone call to his mother, his father, his brother, his grandparents, any of the nice people with whom he has an indestructible and completely normal relationship, Mathias is reading Antonin Artaud in a clear, loud voice, swallowing big gulps of fresh air between each line. Mathias says to the friends he's made in Paris: I'm living on Artaud. Mathias is anemic and has recently become susceptible to aerophagia.

Mathias doesn't have TV. Mathias only reads the literary pages in the few magazines and newspapers where these columns are actually a thoughtful critique and not a long synopsis. So Mathias doesn't buy very many of them. He doesn't pay any attention to the reporters' names, the articles are enough on their own. He's surprised though to sometimes read about writers adored by Martine Baudouin, the bank manager he worked for at the Crédit Lyonnais in Sartrouville, but hardly ever about writers recommended by his favorite bookshop in Les Abbesses. From time to time Mathias gets his hands on a work whose subtlety, comedic virtue, and analytic acuity had been highly praised in the press, which had made great use of terms like *a vitriolic portrait of our society, a whole generation cruelly crushed,* or even, *our modern world placed in an uncomfortable position with unrivaled panache.* Next comes a real feeling of despondency and even profound and very sincere astonishment.

Mathias prints his manuscript, his first manuscript, while drinking dark, expensive wine. *Adénomes et margaritas,* Mathias Rouault, 167 pages. As the pages are burped out, he picks them up meticulously, the pile takes shape, another swallow with each page that fattens it, Mathias is dead drunk by the end of the process. Yesterday Mathias confided to Eugène, a new friend, the strategy he plans to use. He's siphoned three excerpts off *Adénomes et margaritas,* which he plans to send shortly to three poetry magazines. Mathias is not a poet. He would've loved to be, the word breathes a divine tingle down his spine, particularly an outcast poet splendid destiny to be butchered and abused during his lifetime but ashes ultimately canonized in a Norton anthology. Backhand tapping Mathias tames the unruly sheets, then slips the manuscript into a brown envelope that he'll bring to the Copy-Shop tomorrow. He sees his conversation with Eugène last night: I'll be the phoenix of these plagued animals, even if no one wants it in a century I know I'll be understood. Mathias is a little ashamed of letting himself go so far. Luckily Eugène boldly concluded we'll screw them all just before he cut his forehead open against the corner of the bar.

In their defense, Mathias and his brain pound words and grind syntax with enough confidence, seriousness, and good faith to be able to present the fruit of their plume to anyone capable of reading it. The three magazines were chosen by default. The last two literary collectives just closed up shop. One due to the founders' simple choice when faced with the immensity of the work to be done, which Mathias regrets now and will continue to regret for quite some time, his brain vainly watching for the definite and enduring return of what will turn out to be more than a simple magazine: a real anthology. The other due to horrible tangles with a published author whose words reminded Mathias and everybody else with any common sense of the exploits and opinions of Robert Michu, the owner of the betting bar Les Bons Amis in Vitrolles near Aix-en-Provence. There remain a few old members of the rearguard that a pen pusher trainee who loves neither Kundera, Edouard Balladur, or Castel could gladly do without. Mathias therefore has his heart set on *La Revue Noire*, *Musette*, and LIADJ. They all combine poetic practice and experimental, philosophical, or literary texts, the excerpts Mathias chose are in the image of the whole manuscript: precise, unbridled language, that uses the story as neither a pretext nor a hostage, pure words but no wordiness, a unique tongue with its cankers showing. Mathias's texts aren't short stories, and they're certainly not poignant, inoffensive little slices of life like the current critics seem to enjoy so much. Even uprooted from their matrix, they're still autonomous little laboratories. Submitting them is the first part of the plan (Phase 1).

Mathias is wearing a T-shirt, which he hates. He hates springtime's last gasps because of his skinny arms, they still disgust him despite the passing of years. His bones are so visible, his two sharp-bowed arms linked cartilage-elbowed bones, revealing your skeleton to everyone verges on indecency, thinks Mathias every summer, it's like I'm showing everyone my corpse, I'm a Vanitas walking the streets of Paris. Mathias has a meeting at place Saint-Sulpice, at the Marché de la Poésie. Little stands covered in paint even greener than a Granny Smith remind you of lady apples, there's something enlightening about the look of it. The Marché de la Poésie, pretty, picturesque, so delightful with its bright walkways around the fountain, its bright posters hung here and there, charming little Smurf village, the Marché de la Poésie, the big brother of corniness and kitsch, but there's nothing like it so a bird in the hand is worth none in the bush, the Marché de la Poésie, the meeting place for poets for those who publish poets for those who read poets for poetry amateurs and amateur poets, a snowball, some Alpine chalets.

Books aren't burned in a democracy. People are not gagged in a tender republic. They're much too polite. The dark force is neutralized by disguising it as a Provençal crèche figurine. There are only two events in Paris that allow publishers of poetry to interact with the public and, in the case of new publishers, with industry professionals: the Salon du Livre, where, given the exorbitant price per square foot, the majority of these publishers wind up at their regional stand—meaning they get to place their titles between *La Cuisine périgordienne pour tous* and *Les Mémoires de Daniel Cusselin: capitaine de gendarmerie*—and the Marché de la Poésie. Mathias stops at the snack bar, because there is indeed a snack bar. On the small stage an ageless woman is reciting Leo Ferré. Mathias doesn't drink his beer at a table. The entire walkway alongside the snack bar is served by the amplifier linked to the mic of the reciter, and with a strong voice she is now reading a poem of her own composition about love, migratory birds, freedom, and Jacques Chirac, with great exaggeration and in rhythmic lines of eight syllables.

Mathias has an important meeting. The magazines he contacted all replied favorably, their directors are here, the initial contact by mail and phone was cordial. Mathias expects a lot from this meeting in order to move to the second part of his plan (Phase 2). He knows his manuscript can't be accepted by any of the big publishers, not narrative enough, not formulaic enough. He's already quit trying to find the crack that'll let him squeeze into a community, he's already quit looking for drinking partners, *Adénomes et margaritas* ten bound copies, *Adénomes et margaritas* return to sender publisher's form letter Gallimard Le Seuil POL Minuit Denoël he won't try Fayard Stock Flammarion Grasset and the others he knows, get information on the small companies the small spaces the micro gaps, Mathias says places likely to Mathias says the publishing priorities Mathias says lots of things like chosen affinities TAZ common enemies similar interests parallel problems complementary practices, but in his brain there's static because in his brain Voice Number 2 repeats monotone the sample *information we're looking for information.*

Mathias doesn't like turkey and one day he'd like to be able to tell his father I'm better than you are but I still respect you. Mathias hates turkey and the way it's cut, inevitably butchered by his father who still can't remove the breasts. When Mathias and Sébastien aren't there, their mother subjects the poultry to a slightly excessive cooling off time to save her husband from such torture and the embroidered tablecloth from grease stains. Her sons stand up against the ploy, imperceptibly delighting in the unchanging paternal failure. Mathias takes the yule log out of the fridge and thinks to himself that it's about time he stands up a bit on his talons. That's nice but I hope you're not giving up on your degree because troubadour is not a real job. He's father has a full mouth and an imposing crest.

Mathias's cerebellum said:

No, your marrow isn't pure and forever from your throat will sons of bitches belch babble: one is born a cadaver, my darling, one doesn't become one. I will enter into love as others do into orders and I'll bash your skull and tear off the rest and you'll think dawn is an assumption. If I drink every night it's to better skin myself against the thorny fissure that will bruise us.

Annabelle Senan (an intern) adds:

Mathias Roualt is twenty-five years old. *Adénomes et margaritas* is his first novel.

Today on the Pont Alexandre III Mathias has a rather strange taste laminating his throat. His book's only been out for two months and it's already disappeared from the bookstore display tables. Letter R shelves, sometimes one copy. The wind pierces his temple, he waivers slightly watching the waters agitate lasciviously, painful gushing. At a discount stall, the barely open pearl gray cover whispers the naive dedication he'd written to some more or less respected popular critic. A determined dagger blade pushes into his heart oozing thick drops of pride. His publisher said you always have to figure about a hundred for the media copies, for us the books go in the loss column but you have to, no choice at all. So Mathias asks, and the clerk tells him to go look on the shelves but for new books it's about four euros. Mathias thinks about the beer drunk by the critic on the occasion in question and about the other unknowns or established writers who are behind in rounds, maybe even meals for everyone, so many payments receipts minuscule fake expenses paid for by their prose sometimes sold by the kilo. The Seine wasn't so dirty on the embankments in Carrières.

The night is more feverish, and Mathias's fingers are tapping out a fox-trot, his agitated brain initiates another rhythm. Along with the primal anger oppressing his innards a trickle of vinegar covers his mucous membranes. His brain has stopped spinning like a centrifuge, it's more like a greedy paddle oxidized by bitterness and constantly threatening to the lurch of the breakdown.

A book and four magazine publications is enough to apply for a Centre National du Livre incentive grant Eugène says to Mathias. The coffee's bad, Mathias has bronchitis and not enough media coverage to move to the next part (Phase 3). Mathias is having a lot of fun with the magazine crowd. He's learning a lot too. He's realized his knowledge of contemporary poetry is a knowledge of modern poetry, for example. Eugène isn't very interested in Mathias's discoveries. Eugène wants to be a journalist, he does regular freelance work for a trendy magazine, he wanted to write articles for the Living section but they had all they needed there, the book pages' publisher liked him though so for six months he's been a literary critic. He prefers interviews to columns, they lead to lunches with pretty girls who are a little ditzy and often pay the bill. Plus interviews take more space so they pay a lot better. Mathias would have liked to introduce Eugène to his work colleagues but something tells him it's a better idea not to.

Mathias is having a lot of fun with the magazine crowd because the poets do a lot of public readings with just a microphone or a soundtrack sometimes accompanied by video. Some of them even accompany themselves with a laptop, an electric guitar, or a tub full of dishwater. These presentations have a vocabulary all their own. A simple reading with a mic is called a *dry voice*, a reading with a soundtrack, a slide show, or video is called a *performance*, a reading with a computer is called a *laptop performance*, a reading with an electric guitar is called a *Christopher Fiat performance*, a reading with a tub full of dishwater is quite simple a catastrophe we could've done without tonight. Mathias is having a lot of fun because the participants have a keen sense of research without settling for reviving dying avant-gardes, they often argue energetically about positions that always seem pointless, cryptic, or bordering on anal behavior for the uninitiated but which turn out to be crucial when you look closer and especially because you wouldn't think so but poets really know how to have fun between two fights over Guyotat and a Deleuzio-Derridian split.

Mathias doesn't get involved in any off-page activities. He's confusedly conscious that it's not really a continuation, an illustration, an extension of the written work, that something else is at play in these so-called performances, even though some nights attendance is sparse. Confusedly conscious because confused consciousness, maybe even atrophied, already atrophied, shriveled in the acid of his battle plan, Mathias is confusedly conscious that something's going on in his mind-body relationship, his mind-body relationship is in danger, in danger from bodies, but Mathias can't see and couldn't see, never ever will see never will understand that he docked Phase 1 in one of those rare centers of resistance, one of these rare centers of struggle, of reflection, of sparring, one of these rare places where people know that language has to be crimped, snared, sharpened, made uncomfortable so they can slice off, slice into, one of the last fertile areas where the unstoppable crabgrass sprouts. Mathias is not conscious of it but his brain is, though it's already too oxygen deprived to tell him, his brain frightened by the tide of static, his brain minute by minute must unfailingly expel brown swells outrageous lapping,

Mathias is not aware that the enemy exists, that the war is real, the opposition here, that if he's the last one standing they will be the ones, that the merchants can do everything except *take* language. They use it they think, subjugate it they believe, but no slogan, no commercial narrative, no calming novel, no formulaic fiction, no marketing plans can ever make it their own.

Mathias's brain says:

And never will sorrow be made from our flowers.

Sylia Aire (a writer) adds:

For example, I've just read the first novel written by Mathias Rouault, a very promising young writer.

Mathias's brain says:

If mud is certain the molasses in my soul cannot drown anything as long as my heart is basalt and my kidneys you know I owe you my spleen Herculaneum.

Étienne Lousteau (freelancer at who-knows-where) adds:

The pretentious outmoded lyricism and the constant metaphors bordering on the ridiculous quickly become tiring. But despite its posing and pathetic title, *Adénomes et margaritas* is nonetheless a dark novel, punctuated with lightning flashes, to which no reader will remain indifferent.

Mathias's hand begins to say:

Lunch on Thursday? Thanks again. Best. MR.

Mathias knows there's a pitfall somewhere. When he talks to Eugène about what he reads and sees his friend always answers but who's that. Who's that. Who's that is the question Eugène uses the most during their very frequent exchanges. When he hears who's that Mathias knows what to do. He has to answer in a precise order while his brain panics Number 2 *we want information*. In the space of a year Mathias has learned that the résumé of any writer cited during a conversation with Eugène has to imperatively include the following information, or else the file will be refused for lack of evidence.

**Form XK003-87**

General Information—Page 1 of 2

**First Name, Last Name**
**(Origin welcome in the case of pseudonyms)**

**Sex**
❑ Male
❑ Female

**Age**
**In the case of women under 40 indicate**
❑ Still sexy
❑ Doable
❑ Nearing expiration date
❑ Past expiration date

**In the case of men under 50 indicate**
❑ Still in good shape
❑ Still in good shape but lecherous
❑ Paunchy
❑ Paunchy and lecherous
❑ Paunchy, lecherous, and alcoholic

**Marital Status**
**In a Relationship or a Legal Civil Union with, Married to, Living with**
❑ A publisher (male or female)
❑ A journalist (male or female)
❑ A writer (male or female)
❑ An actor/actress
❑ A singer (male or female)
❑ An appropriate person from the Left Bank of Paris (specify who)
❑ Single

**Additional biographical information**
❑ Family established in publishing or journalism
❑ Ex-spouse established in publishing or journalism
❑ Friends established in publishing or journalism or connected to the pre—April 2004 minister of culture
❑ Useful occasional sex partners
❑ High-pathos trauma(s) (specify)
❑ Membership in a local out-patient hospital

**Bibliography**
Approximate number of works published:
Name of publisher

**Means by which the first manuscript arrived at the publisher's**
❑ Another of the publisher's authors
❑ A friend of the publisher
❑ A friend of the publisher's family
❑ The author happened to be doing an internship at the publisher's
❑ Lunch at Café de Flor, an evening at Mathias's, a night at 2 + 2, chez Castel, or equivalent (circle all that apply)
❑ Persuasive service of the oral, vaginal, anal, or equivalent varieties (circle all appropriate)
❑ Mail (since this box is checked in less than 1% of cases, please attach written proof to confirm this information)

**Types of works**
❑ Gibberish (experimental, dominated by stylistic affectation, in French in the original)
❑ Gibberish that takes itself too seriously (demanding literature, in French in the original)
❑ Autofiction
❑ Autofictional gibberish
❑ Autofiction that thinks it's experimental
❑ Parisian autofiction
❑ Parisian gibberish that thinks it's autofiction
❑ Traditional novel
❑ Traditional novel with a tendency toward gibberish
❑ Traditional novel with a tendency toward mass appeal
❑ Traditional mass-appeal novel
❑ Mass-appeal novel that takes itself too seriously
❑ Mass-appeal novel that imagines it includes gibberish (proper hairstyle required)
❑ Mass-appeal novel with gibberish (flop)
❑ Slightly sensationalist mass-appeal novel (social and/or generational aspect required)
❑ Openly sensationalist mass-appeal novel (cover with panties required)

**Personal evaluation and additional notes**
_____
_____
_____

Mathias knows he's being torn apart by one obstacle. Though in the village he wishes to rise to the Castle, he's afraid of being nothing because he knows once the XK003-87 Form has been filled out, Eugène won't stop there, Eugène never stops there, Eugène will hand him the XK003-88 Form like he does every time, that's how it goes, Eugène will ask who's that despite the previously provided information, Eugène will ask who's that just like everyone else who isn't Eugène though they are his doubles his colleagues, just like everyone else on the outskirts of the village on their way to the Castle or already there, the others everybody, absolutely everybody except the 25 people or 50 maybe a few more, a few more really, *Adénomas* sold 400 copies, the publisher is happy, it's a critical success, a symbolic breakthrough, Mathias Rouault isn't nobody, 400 copies that's 400 real people, 400 bodies made of bone and guts, Mathias often thinks of the pile of steaming meat that represents, in the eyes of 400 real people Mathias isn't nobody, if you average anorexic girls stocky students and obese middle-agers that's about 150 pounds per reader, or about 60,000 pounds, or even 300 quintals, Mathias thinks a lot about these big quintals of readers, he thinks about it so often that his brain overflows 10 pints times 400 that's exactly 500 gallons of blood, 500 gallons of readers' blood fill his flooded brain Mathias's definitively drowned brain, the readers' blood ebbs from all his orifices it's unbearable, it flows from his ears streams from his nostrils even the pores of his skin are sweating out stigmata downpours, nauseated grabbing the XK003-88 Form Mathias tries to explain to Eugène, Eugène who's not seeing anything, not anything at all, Mathias is soaking an unending menstrual artery a geyser torrent, Mathias whose brain 1,400 grams his brain his cerebellum is even smaller, Mathias whose brain can't resist can't fight the 60,000 pounds of throbbing meat tells Eugène his numbers, the 28,000 kilos crushing his brain, Mathias hopes the weight is enough to stop the. But Eugène doesn't stop, Eugène doesn't stop there, Eugène never stops. Eugène hands him the XK003-88 Form. Mathias tells Eugène *L'Inceste* by Christine Angot was 50,000 copies, do the math. Eugène doesn't bat an eye. Mathias tells Eugène 50,000 copies is even more readers because books move around, readers lend them to each other. Eugène says to him: keep going. Christine Angot's *L'Inceste* is at the very least 7.5 million pounds of living barbecue. Eugène says to him: that makes 3,750 tons but you didn't count the paperbacks and the translations. Mathias Rouault is somebody somewhere, but he is nothing everywhere. It's a siren face of shame. Mathias Rouault knows he's nothing, and his brain rots more every day, more and more, a liquefying obsession to be nothing everywhere and someone somewhere. Mathias hates Eugène when Eugène says who's that, especially when he orders him to fill out the damn supplementary form. Supplementary yet crucial, Mathias at night is woken up by his brain groaning under the scourge of the damn damn XK003-88 Form, head full of caustic soda, not breathing, his brain moans. Mathias is nothing because.

**Last name:** Rouault
**First name:** Mathias
**Title:** *Adénomes et margaritas*
**Publisher:** Extraction
**Category:** Gibberish that takes itself too seriously
**Agency:** September

**Media coverage:**

<u>Print</u>
**(Number of articles)**
**Dailies:** None
**General publications:** 1
**Specialized publications:** 1
**Women's publications:** None

<u>Radio</u>
**(Station and program names)**
**France-Culture:** Du jour au lendemain
**France-Inter:** None
**Europe 1:** None
**RTL:** None

<u>Television</u>
**(Station and program names)**
**TF1:** None
**France 2:** None
**France 3:** None
**ARTE:** None
**Canal +:** None
**Cable stations:** None

Mathias is nothing because he is nothing in the media, because when Eugène asks who's that he can't say the one that was on the program yesterday, on the cover of, the one on TV who said, the one who has, the one who is, Mathias can't answer that, Mathias isn't the one who, not even a month ago or even who knows when. Mathias knows that Form XK004-88 1/1 is the only thing that'll get him to the Castle, he's convinced of that. The more time that goes by the more Mathias clogs up his brain with Eugène's forms and all his principles about living space. Mathias forgets and a squid of amnesia binds his skull. A squid that ably subtracts tentacles number of truths in favor of mirages embalming bandages of mummified Spectacle.

Mathias's brain says:

Be happy oh my sorrow because it us upon your anvil that I spend each instant vigorously forging the arms of my retreat.

François Hibert (trainer of colts in the literary stable) adds:

Once you've gotten rid of that Lautréamont complex, it might be possible for you to do something. Concentrate on the narration, forget the wordy digressions that weigh down the plot and put the reader to sleep. And don't ever forget that above all the public is looking for an entertaining story that's well written.

Mathias's mouth begins to say:

I write to be read.

What's been captivating Mathias since the beginning of the dinner isn't directly related to what's coming out of Clotilde's lippy circumflex accent. What's coming out of Clotilde's lippy circumflex is monotone-made and morality-molded words, which doesn't surprise him in the least, Clotilde is preceded by her reputation as an anal Right Bank–wrapped neurotic. Clotilde says things like *what's important is to find publishing spaces* or *as long as your process is serious and your publisher supports you, you shouldn't have to worry about the rest* or *the only thing that matters is your privileged relationship with words not with journalists* or *media silence is always better than something indulgent.* What fascinates Mathias isn't the undeniable confidence the two lips show as they pronounce what appears to him to be more of a digression with every passing day. Which means that as Mathias stares at the two lips expelling this web of BS, what his brain is trying more and more pointlessly to communicate to him is the way they're moving. Mathias really wants to climb up on the table, firmly grasp his interlocutor's head with both hands, and quickly shove in his penis, the penis that would force open the lippy circumflex till it was stretched into an absolutely perfect O stuffed full up to her glottis.

Clotilde obviously has no idea about this and keeps prattling on and on, she found Mathias particularly cowardly during the roundtable that just finished ("*Who or what do you write against?*" "*Myself*"). Clotilde takes literature for a kind of holy war, which makes her look like some sort of gloomy lunatic. If it wasn't for the size of her chest, she probably would have been scratched off the invitation lists. Clotilde writes books so dominated by style that it's often impossible to understand a single word, just so language can stretch its legs, and that's why sometimes her best friends tell her you know it might be time to accept that words aren't really little animals with an existence, paws and round eyes. Clotilde takes advantage of an old misunderstanding that once let her use parrhesia on the few condescending people paying any attention. Since then some in the industry call her Joan of Arc because of the dark frame around her face and also because one day it seems the Word demanded she banish Beigbeder from France. A few years ago Mathias felt respect for Clotilde Mélisse. He'd even gone to one of her readings where he'd gotten his copy of *Le Vagissement du minutier* signed. On this day at 7:30 p.m. in the café next door to the puny venue where the town of Martel's (in the Lot region) special events are held, what Mathias is feeling isn't any respect but rather the beginning of an erection.

I say: I'm Mathias's brain.

I add: I do not acknowledge you

Mathias got cable. Mathias reads all the book review sections in the magazines and newspapers, whether the column is a thoughtful critique and/or an overly long synopsis. Mathias buys the papers, and every day he checks the cultural webzines, since he got high-speed internet with his cable. He pays close attention to the names of the journalists, Eugène introduces them to him and their most recent articles unfailingly become the topic of their first conversations. Still he wears himself out sometimes the way he has to dig around in his memory to find the writers cited by Martine Baudouin the bank manager he worked for at the Crédit Lyonnais in Sartrouville just to follow the conversation. Mathias has stopped crossing Paris via Métro Line 12 to go to Abbesses to purchase books that he ends up finding exhausting and not a lot of fun. He goes to fnac.com or asks Eugène to give him his press copies before they end up at a used book store. Once in a while, as he's reading these works, he has to admit he's impressed by subtlety, comedic virtue, and analytic acuity praised in the articles written by Eugène and his colleagues in which they make great use of terms like *a vitriolic portrait of our society, a whole generation cruelly crushed,* or even *our modern world placed in an uncomfortable position with unrivaled panache.* Which is always followed by quite a feeling of depression in his brain, the brain that Mathias can't hear anymore, no not anymore, not in the least.

I say: I'm Mathias's brain.
I add: I'm unfailingly polluted.

Mathias is hesitant because of his brain, which he could still hear a few months ago when his fingers were shaping *Escale chez Perséphone.* Eugène tells Mathias this time I'll give you a hand, but next time you have to put in some effort. The gallery is crawling with people because of the open bar and the hors d'oeuvres catered by Dalloyau. It's hard you know his writing is very organic it's not that different from. Followed by a series of Anglo-American references that have nothing to do with what Mathias's brain wrote, but Mathias knows full well that the article will be written two days before the deadline and reading will consist of skimming and paraphrasing the back cover. Mathias shakes so many hands his wrist gets weak. A lot of groups of broad-casting bodies move around the room. Reporters *but everyone does freelance at Elle they're the only ones who pay okay stop by the office I'll see what I can do,* artists *he may have had shows everywhere he's not selling what do you think can you imagine a guy in Beijing sticking one of his installations in his living room,* writers *she was awful at Campus and besides it's awful when she's on screen she looks a good ten pounds heavier a real hamster head,* press agents *I love your shoes I almost got the same ones but in glossy pink,* publishers *seven thousand a day no they're not exaggerating the numbers they've been selling like hotcakes since the double page spread in* Match, interns and the like *I'm telling you Severine didn't sleep with him the blonde behind Claude is the one who got the job,* hangers-on *I just talked to Aurore over at the open bar on rue Weiss but there's nothing to eat there so we're all going to meet at Kiano but we have to pick up Franck apparently it's really hard to gate-crash.* A lot of groups of bodies that do nothing but broadcast, desperately broadcast with the application that is distinctive of com-munities who are not up-and-coming but who have arrived, they are so arrived that they absolutely are, as Mathias knows and as his brain suffocates in the knowledge, the community that is. That is and can complete piles of forms, that so surely is that Eugène will never ask who's that. Only the dozen or so swallows currently busy sacking the buffet are exchanging instead of broadcasting so Mathias goes over intrigued to say the least.

I say: I'm Mathias's brain.

I add: the use of dialogues in a novel indicates a noteworthy inability on the part of a writer to handle indirect discourse.

I say: I'm the left hemisphere of Mathias's brain.

I add: writers of best sellers overuse dialogue for three obvious reasons. (1) Dialogues quite simply allow you to stretch things out, and thanks to basic formatting you can transform an unacceptable 75-page work into an object that attains the required 128. This trick, combined with the use of a 14-point font and double spacing, can plump up and make palatable the piece of entertainment offered to the reader who as we all know wants to get his money's worth. (2) Dialogues are the preferred location for jokes. Writers of best sellers have to have a pretty face, gel in their hair, and a sense of humor. This is called the rule of threes. (3) There are many many writers of best sellers who confide, preferably in public, that they *are writers because they couldn't be filmmakers*. Instead of lying low for a while and writing a screenplay and leaving literature alone—since it never did anything to them, they naively develop their pretty little script, punctuating it with dialogues that are as subversive as TV sitcoms. When they offhandedly hit you with *publishing a book costs a lot less than producing a movie*, you can be tickled by such a perfectly absurd analogy but after all analogies are the realm of the left hemisphere.

I say: I'm the left hemisphere of Mathias's brain.

I quote Valerie Solanas: man needs scapegoats he can project his shortcomings and imperfections onto and so he can unleash his frustration at not being a woman on them.

I decide to say instead: a writer of best sellers needs scapegoats he can project his shortcomings and imperfections onto and so he can unleash his frustration at not being a screenwriter on them.

I conclude: today's readers are the scapegoats of best sellers.

I say: I'm the left hemisphere of Mathias's brain.

I add: Queneau and Boris Vian both wrote novels that are almost completely made up of dialogue. Maybe you should take it easy, but that's just a suggestion.

I say: I'm Mathias's brain.

I add: I hear you and therefore I  I am the omniscient narratrix, and I'd like to ask you to give it a rest and let me do my job if you don't mind really. Mathias is intrigued and steps closer to the buffet. Mathias is hesitant but has now mastered the cerebral lock and plans to take advantage of it. He hits it off right away with a little brunette who, up until the sixties, it seems, would've been described as spicy. She has big blue eyes cut like saucers but above all her smile is so far from carnivorous that it suggests a lot, accidental chance, rupture of flesh and dentin, amid the bleached Gucci horde. For the past half-hour or maybe a little more Mathias has had all he can take, burning to say who's that, who's that, and to the brunette and the others while he's at it, to the nine others who for the last hour have been communicating with him while they stuffed bottles of Lanson into their bags, who's that too, especially him, Mathias, Mathias who's smoldering to add some details to his padded cv, burning to show off his nearly presentable forms, Mathias who can't take anymore that all this broadcasting is punctuated with *closed-door* exchanged greetings, a community that is while he isn't but soon will be, Eugène knows how to work toward a goal. A cap pulled down tight on a curtain of hair draws his slow burn to a close.

*Le Parisien.* Friday, September 18, 2000.

Incident in a Paris Gallery

Last night, in the very chic Le Guigleur Gallery, a brawl broke out in the middle of a society cocktail party and required police intervention. According to witnesses, a dispute between a young writer and members of the *Hype Syndicate* seems to have been at the origin of what turned into a general altercation. Four individuals were taken in for questioning, and seven people received minor injuries.

http://casseurs2hype.free.fr

P.A.R.I.(S). was really in our hands yesterday. Sector 7 Aurore, Klute, Jérôme Laperruque, Le Stupp, Igor, and his tourguenists were emptying the bottles of doctored Malbec on the rue Weiss, Sector 13 bis LR, and his groupies were cleaning up the buffet at the launch party for some group *whose name I've forgotten's* latest LP. Sector 4 Yvette, the baron, the troll of the month, and Franck Knight were preparing the terrain for us to all turn up together at Kiano. TH², Dabug, Koozil, Jean-Yves, TV, kiri_vinokur, Car(r)oline, Emma, and yours truly were in charge of sector 9.

　　　　　　　　　　　　　　　PROFESSOR PLUM

Le Guigleur Gallery crappy expo both sexes a$$holes but Dalloyau powah and champagne rulz. At exactly 11:00 p.m., when Dabug still hadn't called anyone a socialist, Koozil still hadn't grabbed his chainsaw, and TH² had forgotten to shake his booty for the dumbstruck eyes of the guests, Emma got hit on by a Loréal staffer almost immediately questioned by TH², and the bedsheets aren't the only ones who remember.

RealAudio clip:

*(voices)

A$$hole #1: He really is everywhere, but still nobody ever remembers who he is.

A$$hole #2: To tell the truth this guy is kind of like the Frédéric Lerner of literature.

(voices)

Emma: She went to get some Diet Coke.

Loréal Guy: Maybe we could . . .

(Dabug laughing)

Emma: Would you give it a rest for two seconds you're a real pain in the ass.

(Dabug stops laughing)

TH²: I tried to drown the hype by emptying my glass on Marc Le Guigleur's bald spot but it was full of champagne and the bastard's immune.

Loréal Guy: You did what?

TH²: What do you do?

Loréal Guy: Writer.

(kiri_vinokur and Koozil laughing)

TH²: You hype?

Loréal Guy: Wish I was, but no.

(punching sounds followed by sounds of things breaking)*

The syndicate members on the scene immediately dropped the plastic grocery store bags they had been filling with edible treasures to come to the aid of TH² who was screaming like a pig you're going to be on *center stage* you bastard, as he slammed his interlocutor with a stainless steel tray. Meanwhile Koozil and Jean-YES got into it with a Gucci girl who was demanding they *calm their friend down since he seems to be going too far.* A trendy reporter got TV's fist right in the eye just as he was grabbing a bottle behind Dabug's back, innocently concentrating on taking photos (soon to be online), while kiri_vinokur, who'd climbed up on one of the tables, started singing *Le Chant des partisans,* with Car(r)oline and Emma joining in on the choruses. After it all went to hell, virus spread high speed, Le Guigleur and his baby boomers started beating who knows why on a blonde girl who was bawling as she broke her heel over the head of an even blonder girl who was bawling even more, we ended up in the middle of a scene of mass hysteria, hasn't been seen since the Gülcher concert at 9 Billiards. The cops showed up it turned into the Wild West, they took away TH², Jean-YES, Dabug, and an old guy who was taking advantage of the impromptu chaos to grope a muteen on one of the couches. I can't tell you how it ended because I ended up with three stitches, but I can confirm that for now our activists have been released. As for the old guy I have no idea.

::K-ssé by **Nobody after Cravan** 09/18/2000 09:43:00 AM.

There's an abnormal amount of rain for November. Gallons of it are sporadically washing down from the grainy skies. Mathias turns up the collar on his velvet jacket and barricades his eyes from attacking gravel. A perfectly cunning wind with an eye out for underdressed passersby is sweeping through the Luxembourg Gardens. Mathias's brain shouts at the wind: make him see the truth. The wind offers no response and flings handfuls of pebbly dust into the tear-soaked ocular globes. Mathias's brain says to the wind: burst his eyes, thrust in a tetanus-laden splinter it's already so late nothing can save him. The wind offers no response and suddenly turns its attention to harassing a package-laden woman. Mathias's eyelids are heavy with sand, rubbing his fingers against sharp pellets Mathias lets go some liberating sobs. So much frustration has built up in him, the alchemy that transforms it into $H_2O$ is well-known. He thanks the wind, polite pretext. He's crying an abnormal amount on this November day. It's the season of literary prizes and his name doesn't appear anywhere, on the lists not the least little Mathias Rouault maggot. Once beyond the fence surrounding the Luxembourg Gardens, Mathias's brain is nothing but rubble.

Rhythmically, the printer spits out the sheets. Eugène suggested: a title a summary and twenty pages and above all be on time. Mathias has a migraine and can't remember the name of the girl who's pretending to be asleep in the next room. His fingers lack confidence, must smear the screen, a few words but which ones, the keys create a series of characters that are immediately erased. Garamond bold 26-point, for weeks he's been trying to get down to business, Eugène's been rolling his eyes, his friends have been in a competition of mocking insinuations wrapped in encouragement, a title's a complicated thing, complicated and difficult, the whole thing hangs off the title you know, the title's the call for bids, the helping hand onto the end of the display rack, you have to create the desire, how many failed books missed possibilities because of a bad title, a title's a complicated thing, complicated and difficult, but you can do it. Mathias is aware of the problem, he ran up against an initial refusal, clear and unambiguous, last month. The title of a short story in a magazine that Eugène got him into. A different magazine from the ones that welcomed his first texts in the old days, already the old days because book fair time goes by much faster than the time that strikes in the outside world. A magazine a display window for the community that is or that soon will be thanks to this bestowal of a knighthood, a compilation of established or upcoming market values, not a laboratory, no, just a paddock for the ketamine-whinnying literary colts, just a racetrack annex to keep them in shape between two media obstacle courses, just *a big stall where they're all grouped together notice it's more practical you know where to put the bomb* Clotilde Mélisse had pointed out before throwing her aspartame soda at his head at the last dinner where they saw each other. *La Haine est un alcaloïde* had written *Mathias* at the top of the sheet. Come on, the reader doesn't know what an alkaloid is, and neither do I for that matter, so there you go, someone had giggled to him upstairs at the Café de Flore. And besides it's too long and not really very sexy. Wouldn't you rather have something with English in it, something shorter, something that pops a little, something that sizzles, it's not that difficult. Complicated and difficult, Eugène agreed. *Rage against Methadone* is what they decided on.

I say: I'm Mathias's brain.

I add: What happens inside me isn't what Mathias writes about anymore, Mathias doesn't write about it. Mathias can't hear me anymore and I don't see how he could with all the racket going on.

The Place de l'Odéon is covered with puddles, winter is really annoying, the Seine has thrown up so much water they closed embankments. September will be Phase 3, maybe even Phase 4, Mathias smiles radiantly, without a thought for his rain-mopped jacket. *Trente ans moins des poussières* will be decorated with a black-and-white portrait on the back cover and a dark red band that will say *La Crise du quart de vie*. It's time to forget about Mathias's brain. It was so oxidized it disappeared. It is forever dissolved, there's not a trace left of it, Mathias's skull is a closed space filled with forms, the shelves sag under the weight of the general information files, the marketing studies, the so-called address books that are not so blue anymore. Since March 2006, in the Carrières cemetery, it appears Esther Duval's ever so slightly decomposed remains get brief visits by a teeny shadow, with irregular and vaguely rounded curves. Some say it's the ghost of Mathias's brain, remorse eaten and solitude paralyzed, coming to share its pain upon her bony bosom. Others explain that it's a dwarf, a crippled angel that always comes to warm up bodies that have committed suicide to alleviate their shame of offending God. Since the dead are not to be trusted, none of these rumors can be confirmed.

Mathias will never find out about all this. Mathias will never know what has and will become of his brain from back then, the one that always whispered the turbulent waltz of the words flitting around in there, Mathias will never know and couldn't care less.

Mathias is twenty-eight years old and protecting his publishing contract from the storm by hugging it tight to his white shirt and his agnès b. jacket. As he passes the store windows framing the path leading him away from the Métro, Mathias examines his reflection, a sparkling reflection that's so luminous it sets the shops on fire. Just like young girls after they've abandoned their virginity or Emma after her first adulterous encounter, Matthias scrutinizes the mirror for any noticeable change. He'll celebrate tonight, he won't party, no, he'll celebrate. Accompanied by Eugène and a few friends he'll offer thanks and bacchanals to this ascension day, to this day when wide open are the Castle gates. The Bordeaux he'll drink will be paid for by someone else, the substances that'll be galloping around his nasal cavities will be much less cut than usual, the girl that'll end up on his mattress with her hair a mess will do everything she can to be his official girlfriend by sunup.

The weeks that followed this night of arrival were particularly busy with completing advance copies of Form XK004-88 in accordance with the simulated impromptu interviews, the telephone calls, and the private parties. *Trente ans moins des poussières* was barely thirty pages long, Mathias had been ordered to finish it within two months but never had a deadline ever seemed less distressing. Because all of Paris, obviously without ever having read a single iota of a single paragraph, was repeatedly astonished by the work (*a vitriolic portrait of our society*; *a whole generation cruelly crushed*; or even *our modern world placed in an uncomfortable position with unrivaled panache*), once it was designated the *literary event of the season*. Phase 3 was under way. Mathias had just entered the Banana Republic of Letters.

# Professor Plum in the Ballroom

**Round 1**

**(Loaded Dice)**

There will be no scarification. I always knew it, tonight it was confirmed, you can't get over everything, some wounds remain raw because they can't close up again. Because they can't. That's really what it is. There are a number of reasons that keep pain from transforming into memory: awareness of the amputation and the post-op plan. I'm not clinging to him, I'm really not, people are wrong, they're really wrong to think that. It's because life is longer, true love should be plural. I loved Mathias from the very start and more and more every day. No stagnation, no orgasm plateau, just an infinite increasing curve. He might've pushed me, people might've pushed me, but I can't manage to fall. I'm not clinging to him, I'm really not, I let it all go four years ago, my hands were calloused, stiff six months at the guardrail, the wind the tears fissure your joints, I couldn't take it anymore, physically drained. I let it all go four years ago, boxes of photos, of letters, little bits of everything and nothing, a pom-pom some shells a lock of brown hair some exhibit zoo movie tickets brochures postcards with lacey thumbtacked corners, poems scribbled on old scraps of paper a stuffed pig books with notes written in them. I let it all go empty completely empty for days then for weeks no I'm lying for months. I let everything go, emptiness, emptiness is what remained. I let it all go I said look mom no hands no hands but mom and everyone else were forced to notice how I stuck to my path, no hands and no nothing the curve just kept on going. No I'm not romantic. I'm not even waiting for him. Well, I'm not waiting for him anymore. I don't think I'm waiting for anything at all anymore. I know it's too late, I think I already knew that four years ago.

There's not a week that goes by without my having this dream, this awful dream that's always too fuzzy when I wake up for me to register it, to recall it, enjoy it, suck the marrow right out of it. Mathias and I are in Touraine, or maybe even in Montpellier, but at the same time the apartment reminds me of the one in Carrières, except there's nothing specific that lets me be sure. It's a two- or three-room apartment that doesn't look like anything, that cannot be described, that could never really exist in the past, present, or future. I don't know what's happening, I think we're moving out. Maybe Mathias is leaving, I'm not sure. I don't know what's happening, if it's a problem, or pleasant, I don't know what's going on, what's being said. I think I dream in sepia. Not every day, but on those nights I think I dream in sepia. Sometimes I'd like to know, remember, a lot of times it annoys me, I frown and try to remember, when I wake up after that happens I try systematically. But despite my efforts, there's nothing left. I have nothing left anymore anyway. I don't know how long that dream lasts. A few minutes in my brain, and a series of a few days in its own temporality, maybe a few scenes are completely dissociated from the calendar, I don't know, I have no idea. What I do know is that for a few days afterward I'm actually happy. Disturbed as ever, mourning denies itself subconscious, no control a paradox, but happy. Somewhere else and far away I went through something with him. Something secret, even to me. It must be very beautiful, oh so precious, when I say I imagine I hear: I tell myself, that Mathias gets kidnapped to that place too, in that vaguely familiar apartment, that when he wakes up he feels a strange calming sensation similar to mine. But I'm not waiting for him. No. I'm not waiting for anything anymore. I tell myself these things but I know perfectly well that he's not going to call me, won't look for an excuse to call me, won't look for me. At all.

I can't scar over, I'm aware of the amputation. Mathias wasn't transplanted onto me. He was never a foreign body to me, no needles, no thread, not even any anesthesia, he grew in my inside, between my heart and my lungs, a germinal root. He pulled himself out violently, extracted himself abruptly, a pit inside my chest, grief took his place, and ever since it's been going gangrene. There's a piece missing from me, and as hard as I try, a man is just a prosthesis, nothing can take the place of the fullness and life in my arid gapingness, nothing now, nothing ever. For four years seven months everyone keeps harping on and on: oh, Esther you'll see in a whole lifetime there are two or three true loves, it's really unusual to have just one, you'll laugh about Mathias when the arms of the right one are around you, sweetie. I don't even make the effort to nod my head anymore. I've stopped being polite, docile, and conciliatory. When I was a teenager I had my true love, my first love in the revised version, then I had Mathias. I've known enough men before and even since to know that they were always pretty good cuttings but that between my heart and my lungs nothing would ever grow again. I'm not idealizing anything. Mathias is a bastard, a selfish, deceitful, conceited, seductive, pretty cowardly bastard. Mathias is the most common kind of boy there is. But it was my story. My love story. There are people who are made to experience a first love and then a true love and then it's done. There's a supply, but afterward it's too bad if there wasn't enough time, if it was just six years, you should've done your best, should've paid attention or enjoyed it better. Get the most out of it, right. Should've gotten the most out of it. I didn't really know how to. Because of the root that was growing so thick between my heart and lungs. Usually roots grow under graves, and if the bushes or brambles they generate surprise gravediggers and gawkers with their vigor it's because they usually go draw their sap from the remains of lovers separated by ancestral hatred, King Marc or Canon Fulbert. My pounding thorax constituted as rich a fertilizer as two juicy rotting bodies. I couldn't know that my lair held so much fertile compost, that my lair would flood the root to the point of saturation and overflowing trough. Mathias gave it a quick chop for fear of drowning.

I left David the day before yesterday. I understood that my love had a harelip and would always taste like a non-birthday, there's no point in insisting. Behavioral analysis I notice conditioning. My heart is a slobbering dog. Once I've made up my mind, I attack, and I finish. Once I finish, I need to suffer, not too much but a little. Since I chased after him I fantasized a lot, I even crystallized a little, I crystallize so fast it's incredible. So. The first three weeks, the man has to be distant, letting me scamper around an ominous little basset hound begging for my treat separation anxiety. Then. At the end of this time period if nothing balances out, if no declaration or promise of commitment brings about a major change, if the pain is still there, in the end that's what it is, if the pain is still there I get ready to leave. Every detail aggravates me, any lack of tact or mistake is transformed into a character flaw deemed unacceptable. The resulting contempt will gently irrigate the hollow left in my breast by the previously uprooted shoot. I can hold on for months, reverse the trend even if it means resorting to unparalleled sneakiness. Whether he's become friendly, a little in love, or head-over-heels hypnotized, there's no change in the ending. I leave him brutally, without even worrying about making up an excuse. From this fact I arrive at similar conclusions: no one cares about me, not enough to impede my departure, to struggle for a compromise, to take me back by force or by subtle strategies. No one wants to, no one can. I will never again be anyone's, the one who was my destiny already used up all our time. Our time, six years. I'm so tired of noticing all the bodies and souls yet to come, all these checkmates, spontaneous combustions, the seed is already dead, already dead in my abyssal fissure.

I can't get better I'm not sick. I'm handicapped, it's completely different. A lot of times I would have preferred meeting Mathias later, later around thirty years old or even thirty-five. Seeing the root grow in my unbroken chest, when it was scratched maybe, barely scratched but just about sterile up until then. My rib cage would have ripped fervently open, never one night would his hand grasp the blooming stem outside, never would his knotted fingers pull so persistently, pull so too hard. I'll end up an old maid because I knew love too soon,

I'll end up an old maid because I couldn't manage the flow of my sprinkler, the sap in my root turned out hemophiliac, that's why my wound won't coagulate.

Maybe if Mathias had passed his exams everything would've been different. I don't really believe it but I think about it a lot. It would be easier to try to forget if he wasn't anywhere except some nights in the sepia dream. But Mathias is everywhere quite regularly. We're aware of randomness that doesn't exist and overstitched hangs on when someone gets hit with their fate. It's a little like Mathilde and her abortion. The week after the extraction of the incongruous fetus there was nothing broadcast on the radio but programs about children, single mothers, sudden infant death, and other maternal-affiliated topics. Perused magazines offered the same themes, and when she climbed stairs two at a time out of breath from the street teeming with pregnant women and screaming carriages, she found the TV movies interspersed with pregnancy tests when the commercials came on. The first two years following the root's transplant only the echoes of our formerly shared friends interfered with my daily routine. And then very quickly it became intolerable. I often wonder how young women rejected by so-called public men do it, I feel so assaulted by an interview of even a few lines, by a tiny photo or a short article, if Mathias was a musician today, a popular singer, broadcast on the airwaves plastering the Métro walls, I don't dare imagine my arteries disheveled by frosty blood can't help but freeze my heart, my heart a panicked iceberg, behind the ventricles I fear the submerged part will melt. I can't stop the slope of my curve, my exponential curve, my love for Mathias, so when I see him I listen to him I hear him so much in the media, as the one who knows his skin, his freckles, and his smell, how can I ignore him, and how, especially, can I not tell myself every time he needs me, he needs to be with me, I have so many things to say, to tell him, I know him by heart and even uprooted, I feel his pain, I glimpse his desires, I examine bumps, I see him hurting himself, I'm sure if I was with him I could help him preservation.

A few days ago. It was late, really late. TV rerun. Mathias was on the set, his hair kind of short in deliberate cowlicks, I imagine his fingers plunging into a jar of gel then goo-coated pinching tugging his locks into rebellion. I imagined him behind his buttoned shirt, impeccably conceited, heart pounding a little, slight arrhythmia, I wasn't imagining that, I knew about that. I knew heart beating like a pebble, a big pebble stuck in a tin can that a kid would shake to make noise, the noise of panic trying to be musical, as if the percussion could be symphonic without brutal skinning of nearby eardrums. I was on the couch. I undid the buttons on my shirt, I was choking, suffocating, the crater was on the move. Close-up Mathias, three-quarter shot Mathias and suddenly from the screen the screen ripped open the screen cracked letting spill onto me a braid of veins the root escaping from Mathias's plexus splitting the screen my flesh the root the more–than–umbilical cord looming in my breast and taking back its super-connected place that I was the root a bridge an arc of the covenant everything went back to normal I certainly saw the smile released the smile relieved as the corners of Mathias's mouth were I told him I love you I shouted I love you my thorax gasped snorted rhizomes. I know it's true, that it really happened. The screen closed back up, there's no trace left except inside me, deep inside me, the returning root got my heart pregnant, I can feel it quivering and drawing nourishing strength from me. Gregory says it's just the effects of the THC but he doesn't know what he's talking about.

### Dance Card
### (Tango in Paris)

Mathias forgot because you always have to forget when you dance. Mathias forgot, now he's nothing but ballet leaps. Mathias without his now-a-distant-memory brain is a lighter body, a body devoted mechanical steps on the wood floor. Mathias slides. Mathias lets himself be carried, carried away would be accurate. Mathias doesn't have any organs anymore, his body has become an image in motion, Mathias is a motion that's fleeting, not perpetual, ricochet rebound series, an image then another image, Mathias is nothing but a series of images captured in flight all the better to be frozen. The Parisian paneling that lets the grand ball stay intimate makes the distilled notes of the band reverberate. It's a strange band among its instruments neither strings nor brass but a lot of winds. Music escapes and makes Mathias dance. Mathias snaps his fingers and wiggles to the beat, doesn't actually know the score. What the band's playing can be summed up in four sampled notes. Four wrong quacking notes whose rhythm increases as dawn mists over. All the participants know the melody, they join in on the chorus as they shake their hips. The name of the piece is *Before the Cock Crows, You'll Do So Three Times*. Every night denial Mathias prances around as it plays.

## Everybody's Connected

I'm Mathias Rouault's blog. Through me he speaks every day, records his reflections. I'm the underling and have no say in the matter, I'm his interface and I keep to my role. Mathias thinks that through me he pours his heart out to the world and feverishly consults my statistics every day in order to count the visits, evaluates as precisely as possible the number of internet users who've come to read the journal I know he wishes was all but unmissable. He adds one link after another in order to ensure reciprocity, recognition, maximum coverage.

I live on the site that bears his name. The home page opens on a big picture of him. It offers five sections: *biography, bibliography, media, universe,* and me. The *universe* section has an epigraph including his connections with the community that is. Sometimes, since I'm the one spending hours wandering the wired world and am well-informed, I'm surprised by the acrobatics Mathias manages to perform within me, the inconsistencies can really add up. The universe section offers a range of paragraphs, each an apologetics accompanying photos of the powerful so-called friends, or friends of the previously mentioned powerful. Today, however, Mathias used my mouth to remark:

Paris is an alkaloid. I wish I were already on Methadone.
Here's a picture of Patrick Bouvet saying: "When I write, I stand up."

## Round 2
### (The Dice Are Still Loaded)

I'm making a record of every word, everything that Mathias says. It makes me feel like we're still talking, he used to talk to me a lot, Mathias talks a lot, the answers don't matter, he doesn't need them. I record every TV show he's on, and every radio broadcast he's invited to. I play the tapes over and over, I replace the reporters' questions with my own, more intimate, more precise, more pertinent, obviously more pertinent, I know him so well I know what to do, what Mathias is waiting for, what he needs.

Every day I read the blog Mathias writes on his site. Via the address he put under contact, I send him emails from all kinds of identities. He only answers the ones that are signed by girls. He shares a lot with Lain Iwakura, tells her about his nights, his doubts, and his desires. I can tell he's on the verge of falling in love, it twists my heart, and the rest of my plumbing too.

Mathias never talks about me. To anyone. It's like our love never existed. In one of his books I thought I recognized myself, my beauty marks form a kind of dark star on my right shoulder blade. But he often says he's a ladies' man, that all the bodies get mixed up together, that all his heroines are a jumble of us all, retouched puzzles, tender little monsters, nocturnal reconstructions, and I cry about feeding his fictional shadows, deleted as I am in this fantasy fog.

## Dance Card
### (Take This Waltz)

Mathias nods to his partner, extends his hand, three little steps. To the question *Your previous works were radically different, what is the source of this sudden reversal* Mathias bends in a bow and straightens back up, three little steps. Mathias elegantly follows up with the obligatory steps: reappropriation of narration, the desire to communicate with a larger group. About-face, stop, three little steps. He says writers have to be interested in the world around them and not spend their time navel-gazing. Change of partners, arabesque, and three little steps. He says the worst things about women writers of autofiction. The pathos of exposing your ovaries is straight out of Barnum, it would a better idea to get medical attention. That the truth of their texts should be explored, autofiction's just a nice word for autobiographies by women who lie. Easy leap, about-face, three little steps. He says there should be no feminine form for the word author. That would be an insult to women writers if we cut into the dictionary to alleviate its excision. To the question *but there are feminine forms for other professions, we say actress, waitress, stewardess, as soon as there is any power, whether it's real or symbolic, the feminine doesn't have a space maybe something should be done about that* with a swift movement Mathias extracts his clammy hand, nods to his partner, smiles, three little steps.

## Round 3
## (The Dice Are Still Loaded)

Mathias confides to Lain:

Solitude has never been so very truly my own. I wanted so badly to become someone, I didn't know that someone is still one, singular inscription among the several, a sharpshooter perched above the collective, a hermit yet an exhibit in his panoptic-subjected Cave No one sees me as someone who. It's pretty comfortable, sometimes it's entertaining, flattering. But I'm really not sure anymore if it's bearable. I'm becoming a fictional character in everyone's eyes. I pronounce answers that seem to come from nowhere, well not so nowhere after all. My mouth vomits out words programmed by a script, a lot of the time I feel like I'm nothing but an interface. Behind me, who or what, I really don't know. Sometimes I mechanically brush off my sleeve, it always seems like some confetti has landed there. I can't work anymore. I think in the end writing doesn't really interest me that much.

My new publisher suggested an idea for a novel, the story of a guy who acts like a complete bastard then takes an overdose on his thirtieth birthday. He ends up in a kind of mystical no-man's-land, he has conversations with all kinds of beings, he's allowed to return to earth for his birthday ten years earlier. He remembers everything and he has to change his choices. He has a very adult view of the world, analyzes everything, it's a lot easier when you hold all the cards. So the whole if-I'd-only-known thing. He goes so far as to use his memory to become a geopolitical consultant. My publisher thinks it's a really good storyline, that it's an opportunity to address all the syndromes that are typical of today's thirty-year-olds and to talk about redemption too. Personally it sounds to me like a remixed version of *Peggy Sue Got Married.*

There's a noticeable shift in the work of popular writers right now. Every single one wants to make amends, the things they're working on have the distinct aroma of narcissistic masochism. It's the Age of Great Repentance. The great race for tearful self-criticism has begun, different strategies are happening on TV sets, I made a business out of my life, did I have a choice maybe, still it's nothing more than still another mise-en-abyme, it doesn't open up any cracks, nothing grinds the machine to a halt, it doesn't serve much of a purpose, not sure it's a paradigm shift, a way to be seen as horribly human and certainly *touching,* maybe there's still time for me too, I beat the forty-five thousand–copy hurdle, they're still reprinting, I'll be on the cover of a trendy magazine on Monday, but I've never felt so depressed in my whole life, I don't know why, it doesn't make any sense, all the coke and Prozac must be ripping apart my neurotransmitters.

I'm sorry I'm telling you all this, I'm unloading a little too much but still more and more in every email. I have to go anyway, I'm pretty late, they're expecting me at Mathi's, I should already be there. My publisher's launching a new woman writer, maybe you've heard of her, Béatrice Lanvin, a pretty blonde, I don't remember the title but you couldn't've missed it, she's the one in a thong with a teddy bear on the cover. I bet Eugène 200 euros that I'd take her home tonight, you know how I hate to lose. Paris will always be Paris . . .

Hugs

MR

## I went to the Castle because I wished to live deliberately
### (Lost Illusions at the back of the courtyard on the right)

Her interview was so dumb, the girl's a century and a half behind. *Why do you choose to suffer?* But of course books are merchandise, no one can deny it, she refuses to be assimilated with a means of production, she can be so stubborn, not to mention stupid. *You find your subject, you wear out your wits over it with toiling at night, you throw your very life into it: and after all your journeyings in the fields of thought, the monument reared with your lifeblood is simply a good or a bad speculation for a publisher.* She imagines it's still possible to avoid the system, if you listen to her, you'd think she lives in Asterix's village with her friends the outcast poets. *Your work will sell or it will not sell; and therein, for them, lies the whole question.* During the meal Jean said to her: it's a personal opinion but under twenty thousand copies you're not a writer, she admitted to Eric that it made her cry all night long. *A book means so much capital to risk* I explained to her your struggle is cute but utterly ridiculous be a missionary but not a crusader, and she told me she hated that kind of point of view. *The better the book, the less likely it is to sell.* We're all the product of marketing, writers should be forced to go to business school, it would help us avoid hearing that kind of nonsense. *Every man of talent rises above the level of ordinary heads; his success varies in direct relation with the time required for his work to be appreciated.* What I really like is when she goes off on her Word tangents, like literature has to stay pure and sharp, it can't be confused with cultural entertainment. *And no publisher wants to wait.* Of course when you read her books it's such a colossal pain in the ass that you have to see that she's doing it in good faith, that's the worst part. *To-day's book must be sold by to-morrow.* She won't last long, with all that yapping she's really burned herself out the last few months. *Acting on this system, publishers and booksellers do not care to take real literature, books that call for the high praise that comes slowly.* Did you see Eugène's article on Thursday, he called it Clotilde Mélisse Just Discovered the Comma.

## Dance Card
## (Saint-Tropez Twist)

The property is huge, the guest list long, and Mathias's memory lapse even deeper than the mascara-packed lash plumped sapphire gaze emanating from the blonde bimbo lingering in the lounge chair, which isn't very hard. Mathias finished off his next manuscript, finished off like a beast of burden, no pleasure or enthusiasm. With his brain amputated the task wasn't as arduous as you might think. Taking note of the real, the collective fiction sustained by his peers, intensely enveloping anecdotes and glimpsed emotions at the mercy of the community that is. Mathias forgot, the desertion of his principle organ sometimes subjects him to a draft that freezes his cranial cavity, but he knows the steps, the remedy solutions that always let him heat up his fear until it evaporates. Mathias forgot, his only object of worship is the current spectacle, conscious of the libations at the altar of self-consumption, convinced of knowing, accepting the mechanism, participating on a daily basis in the circus of abjection his awareness clearing him of any wrongdoing, that cynicism isn't the spoiled legacy of the nineties but a lifeline that belongs only to the powerful.

His lips are chapped by an oppressive month of August and all the caipirinhas he drank, his lips are chapped because of the hundred and one tall tales his mouth swallowed over so many months that it's been two years. Mathias forgot because of the immediate, the immediate relationship, musty-smelling publishing circuit, consuming collective fiction, producing fiction fed on the same, feeding it, writing promotion-perfect clever snippets and mouthwatering concepts promotion, with every chapter thinking of the humorous witticisms to be served on TV, first four months on tour with stops at all the high priests of the media world, second four months the machine's back at it with new stock—secured signings all over the country, last four months quick, efficient writing, locked on target weakening stock in trade, writer's boredom, blocked tomorrows will September be pink and the reception cherry red.

Mathias has sawdust blocking his pipes. In the past it had been more like curdled blood because Mathias was buried under the mass grave, the mass grave of books, he knew it was possible to come back like Colonel Chabert, to resurface with the help of an old tibia, a rotting limb ripped from the corpses, the living corpses whose bones are wrapped in will-o'-the-wisp flesh giving them strength, fortifying arms, letting writers make their way through the mass grave filled with works from a past that will never die, that can't die, no one's near death in that grave, though some are waiting near petite mort asking for nothing more than to help, Mathias not so long ago understood all this because of his greedy necrophiliac brain, Mathias not so long ago said I'm digging around in the depths of a mausoleum, I dig and I climb, maybe one day I'll be worthy of a resting place there, one day perhaps my body might be fertile, my bones useful to others, one day someone will play jacks with my vertebrae and they'll knock together, I'll be a maracas or slender bow.

Mathias has sawdust blinding his nights. Glaucoma shavings cover his irises. Mathias never reads anything now except articles and the drab production of the community that is. Mathias in the Castle has donated his time, many divest themselves of their most precious possession, it's compensation for all the knighthoods. Mathias has forgotten both names and words, he doesn't make anything live anymore, expressionless, functional vocabulary, sterile syntax, plastic-wrapped terms. Mathias in his works describes, explains, observes, and tells. He doesn't write anything anymore.

Nth evening in the villa, nth mechanical wriggling, the publisher makes his guests dance. On the cozy couch some guest or another wants to make a good impression. Mathias answers I read really dead writers and the live ones who are all here. The guest in question is surprised. There was a time when you quoted different ones, I guarantee you, and none of these at all. Dead writers who can't die and living ones who are way too alive to be locked up in here. Mathias forgot, he's quit even trying to lay flowers on the graves stuffed with soldiers, he thrice denied Eden, doesn't bother with the drowned anymore, his

PROFESSOR PLUM IN THE BALLROOM

language is stunted, dry, an olive pit. Mathias can't hear the songs rough echoes of the first words anymore, Mathias can't anymore the Word has stopped talking to him, in his head subject verb connection object, dull, docile little carriages, in Mathias's skull sentences a little train in first class his soul, sentences a little train carrying off his soul, in Mathias's skull *the train kept a-rollin' all night long.*

## Round 4
### (The Dice Are Definitely Loaded)

Every night I write letters that I don't send him. I slip a lot into them, it's more than love, it's a lot more than that. I can't send them to him, I tried, every time black-and-blue stomach I think of my horrible words, my words are so unworthy and sound so hollow, I can't do it, it's impossible. I don't throw them out, throwing them out would be garbage-chuting love, thinking about all that love defiled by vegetable peels drains my head, really, just thinking about it. I don't want to be drained, not of love, especially not of Mathias. In the morning since I've been crying the paper is soaked, the sheets tear easily, obvious blotter saturated with inky mistakes that are ripe for the slashing. I cut off little bits, little piles of easy-to-swallow bits. I swallow my love. Mathias would think that's right, maybe even sweet.

I'm jealous, I think. The more Mathias tells me about his life and his nights without knowing I'm the one behind it, always behind the pseudonym he confides his secrets in, the more I'm sure that my place is by his side. In the beginning I was really surprised by his books, his new books, a strange turn, a very wide angle. I was mad at him because they were so far from his little blue notebook, unknown territory, I was looking for my Mathias, mine, the one I knew, but I was being selfish and completely stupid. Mathias certainly has his doubts, I can tell from his emails, but he's strong, really strong, solid concrete, he's got this rock solid, Mathias knows what he's doing of course, there can't be any other way. This afternoon at the café across the street, some girls were looking through magazines and they stopped at a picture of him. He was posing in his boxers, with his pillow hugged against his clean-shaven chest. The young maidens commented on the interview that followed, questions about his morning routine, tea or coffee, shower or bathtub, if he wrote more in the morning or the evening, computer or notebook, he answered seriously, which surprised me, I think I was actually furious but I still don't know why. If it's from seeing him put himself on display like that any old place, any old way, if it's from hearing *I'm single* instead of *I live with Esther, my first love and she still manages to surprise me, I'm going to marry her*. I really don't know, but it hurt me so much. Such a sharp pain that the root contracted, I'm still short of breath from it. Getting dropped by Mathias weighs heavier on my numb heart than a quintal, seeing him everywhere way too much my ventricles exhausted from so many spasms, sometimes I feel like I'm nothing but a knitted ball of tension. But knowing he's living at the top of the podium without me leaves me gasping even more that all the rest. I could weave his crown of laurel branches better than anyone, and by abandoning me there's nothing but a wide-open field of possibilities, my possible lives he gambled scorched earth. I can't help it I keep on dreamily caressing this pride, this immense pride that would grow in me, would grow me too, being a princess consort especially Mathias's would go well with my complexion and even better with my heart, I'm dying to see myself quoted, inspiration partner or muse it doesn't matter, I was born only to be an iridescent muse. Mathias is the only one who doesn't know it, I have to fix that.

### Everybody's Connected

I'm Mathias's blog. On this November day I've received the order to proclaim: Prix de Fior winner. When you click on those words you discover Mathias now in the good books, posing in front of a Métro station. Some hackers thought it would be a good idea to interfere with me, since nine forty-three this morning a superimposed flash mosaic mosquito, beneath it scroll the words Talk, talk, talk: the utter stupidity of words. It's quite annoying, but there's nothing I can do. But man do flash animations itch, you have no idea.

## Round 5
## (Dice Unfailingly Loaded)

There was an announcement on his site: live this morning Mathias on the radio on France-Inter. I have a hard time getting into the broadcasting center. Since the last wave of terrorist attacks and the Vigipirate plan all the entrances are blocked with hellhounds. On the other side of the doors a metal detector, on the other side of the metal detector a uniform, head toward the back no not the elevators, not the elevators right away, first say hello to the lady sitting cozily behind the counter, check ID card you're expected where which studio which office by whom phone picked up explanation fill in the sheet last name first name signature, I lazily took advantage of a moment of hesitation to slip surreptitiously into the confines of the elevator. The Maison de la Radio has eleven miles of hallways, without the army of medics winding their way across the floors all day long its basements and every nook and cranny would be littered with the skeletons of interns, production managers, visitors, guests who've died of exhaustion starvation panic and dehydration it's so impossible not to get lost, a thousand times I thought I'd end up walled in. A kind technician took pity on me and managed to find the right coordinates for the object of my quest. It's not about observing Mathias but about really seeing him, seeing him right to the end, seeing him home and with the utmost discretion. Usually when you're waiting for someone to come out you hide behind a corner and hold your breath. In this case it's complicated because the floor is round. I took my papers big sheets out of my bag, I hid my face behind them and it worked quite well. I was really scared in the elevator, my lungs were swelling with the same air as Mathias, sharing oxygen in a space so confined it's intimate was making my root tremble, I could feel it was ready to leap out at him ripping flesh fabric crawling panic-stricken along my cleavage, ruining my plan with its hotheaded excess. I hugged my bag against myself as tight as I could, squeezed the leather plumpness, a shield upon my chest, and it worked pretty well. I was wearing a wig and tinted glasses, face hidden behind jet-black stems, eaten away by dark halos I was unrecognizable, on the way I accidentally said hello when I saw my own reflection. Mathias didn't say anything to me. He was immersed in a deep discussion with his press agent, who didn't even look at me either. They went their separate ways at the Métro station, she took a taxi and he took the RER. The platform at the Kennedy–Radio France station is wide and on top of that it's a drafty hollow. I exchanged my wig for a purple scarf, my hair was too tangled I couldn't see a thing. I got into the car, strategically chose my place, a seat on the lower level behind a glass pane but facing forward it goes without saying. Mathias went to the upper level. He's always had a soft spot for double-deckers. He got off at Pereire. I trotted along behind him discreetly. He rushed onto Line 3, I took off my scarf headed toward Gallieni my hair was pulling elastic suffocating, I shoved it under a tweed cap and changed my glasses. Dark little glasses with rectangular-shaped plastic frames. I almost lost Mathias at the transfer, at the Opéra station the hallways were so full of people and my vision darkened, no matter how hard I scanned the fauna was unreadable in the middle of one tunnel. I stayed just behind him, stood right behind my eyes devouring his neck all the way to Sébastopol. Mathias changed his cologne. He doesn't wear Fahrenheit anymore, it's certainly a Hugo Boss, but I'm not sure which one yet. I brushed up against his jacket two or three times, I'm still surprised that along my aorta my pounding heart didn't leave a fatal fissure. The car was deserted on Line 4, I camouflaged myself in the hollow of a double seat set and pulled on a platinum blonde bob. Between the lipstick and the painted eyelids no need for glasses, I added a pair of old Chanels just to make it absolutely perfect. He opened the door with a rather sharp motion a couple of seconds after the Saint-Sulpice stop. Mathias has a way of prancing when he goes up stairs, it's because of smiling the dimples he's had on his bottom since he was a teenager. He made two phone calls that I couldn't really make out, the wind was blowing toward me so I couldn't catch any of the words. Then he stopped in at Yves Saint-Laurent and spent twenty minutes. He came out with one really big bag and another smaller one. He went to the right, his cell phone played the notes from Strauss's waltz, but he didn't lift a finger to answer it. At 27 rue Madame he sesameed the door code. I waited for a long time and concluded that his apartment must be on the inner courtyard.

Today I took three rolls. Mathias isn't very regular, and I didn't find a single apartment to rent on his street, except a really tiny one a couple of buildings away, but even if I stopped eating, I wouldn't be able to afford the thousand euros a month. It's really too bad, not to mention very limiting. I have to get up early to come in from Carrières, between the equipment and all my disguises my backpack is heavy, I'm really tired and I'm afraid he's going to spot me. I answered an ad to be an au pair in Mathias's building, but the hours were ridiculous and on top of that I hate kids. I waited till one of his neighbors went out so I could slip inside. A courtyard and two stairwells. Mathias's place is off the one on the left, yesterday he got three letters: one from the electric company, one from a reader who's appallingly familiar with him, and one form his brother complaining about never hearing from him. Today a postcard from Eugène who's in Berlin and an invitation to a party. Mathias's place is on the fourth floor on the left and he listens to English pop music pretty loud. He has his coffee at home and picks up his mail as he leaves the building. He has no habits, no rituals, no walks at set times. As far back as I can remember Mathias always said he'd hate Immanuel Kant till the end of his days.

The woman at the perfume shop was positive. It's a Hugo Boss in a bottle with the same name. Before I left the Café du Vieux Colombier, on his temporarily vacant chair I placed a package containing a scarf made of much better cashmere so that my larceny doesn't have a negative effect on his adorable tonsils. I think I love Mathias right down to his tonsils. When I think of his body I don't stop at his skin, I love him on the inside. Mathias is handsome down to his colon. One day I'd like to hang pictures from his endoscopy next to the ones I take and tack up in my bedroom.

## Dance Card
## (Flamenco)

In his sleep Mathias is at Montagne Sainte-Geneviève. Seated at a sidewalk café, he orders a low-quality Bordeaux. His neighbor whispers to him: *Gypsies are right when they say that you never have to tell the truth anywhere but in your own tongue; in the enemy's language a lie is enough.* When he wakes up Mathias is afraid he's lost his voice.

## Everybody's Connected

I'm Mathias's blog. In a year and a half the site I'm on experienced a drop in visits of 76.43 percent. Nobody reads me anymore, besides that my updates are the same as the ones under *media*: all but nonexistent. Secretly, I communicate with Mathias's computer. We exchange our impressions concerning our common dominator. It also gives me access to the Word documents that Mathias opens. Since I'm naturally connected to the internet, I pass on the information I find. I know my end is very near. Mathias's last novel, which came out in 2003, following an insufficient number of characters in the file A second chance.doc in the fall of 2002, shows eight hits on Google, including Amazon and fnac.com. The other links are to TV programs that Mathias did when he was promoting it. Three go to France 2: the reality talk show *Ça se discute* about near-death experiences; the celebrity talk show *Tout le monde en parle*, where Mathias is on the guest list alongside various members of the French intelligentsia and entertainment world: Jean-Marie Bigard, Monseigneur Gaillot, Nolween Leroy, François Bayrou, Massimo Garcia, Loana, Emma de Caunes, and Julien Courbet; as well as to an appearance on Laurent Ruquier's daily show, where he auditioned. And one to France 3, a special episode of that other reality talk show *C'est mon choix* on pets, where he appeared with Nerval, his recently adopted Burmese cat. One goes to his publisher's site and the last one to a webzine with an article entitled *Let's Save Another 14,99€*. According to the computer's statistics, Mathias mostly uses Outlook and a Tetris game he downloaded. The majority of his emails are addressed to Lain, Eugène, and his publisher. Since not long ago, a read receipt is systematically requested from the last two.

## Dance Card
### (Vienna Waltzes and Pastries)

The booths are cozy, Mathias's nails dig into the red velvet without encountering any resistance at all, it's almost like the springs blend into the stuffing. Too tight, Mathias's shoes tap to the beat, their soles do all they can in hopes that some dancer will notice, see that Mathias is one with the music, see Mathias as a perfect partner and rush over, inviting him onto the dance floor. It's been a number of months, for almost two years already Mathias has been stuck alone on the edge of the floor. He's waiting. His right sleeve is adorned with a fine spiderweb attaching it to the armrest with the stubborn grace of angels who prefer to tear out their eyes rather than accept they've fallen. He's waiting. Mathias with his left hand is gesturing to Eugène drunkenly twirling in the arms of the publisher, the publisher whirling from Eugène to some others without ever, like Eugène, without ever glancing at all at that frail hand, at Mathias's frantically waving hand.

From the moat around the dance floor, Mathias hears their voices ripping through the music, understands that the music is made up only of their voices. That's all the music is, their accumulating words as the pages are turned are in the key of transported Mathiases, then a short silence followed B minor unhinged G level. But Mathias would again like one two three once oh just once one two three one two three just a little bit more to taste the warm air that slaps your cheek red one two three one two three that rushes into your mouth alchemizes in there and comes back out again high notes one two three one two three feeding in turn my turn must come around again my turn will come back around to me again one two three one two three wind goes into the mouths the mouths of the instruments waltzing notes words, Mathias chants one two three I'd really like to be just a little a little rustle again I'd have a tiny existence a breeze against the gale I had my moment I was a movement not so long ago yes was a movement in the midst of the composition was nth movement in the great symphony of the winds.

Mathias may have understood, his heart is still gaunt from learning its rejection. Mathias may know, his lungs are still frozen from understanding they are excluded from the great winds. His eyes roll to the beat, his pupils follow Eugène's energetic frolicking. If his brain still lived in his arid skull, perhaps it would share the salve of survival with him.

Jealous Mathias still is hanging on like ivy, sallow ivy on the couch. Mathias's ears struggle to hear every note broadcast on the great winds. Mathias's ears ask his memory to pull a tune, a song, an old chorus, out of a drawer so they can listen to it more attentively. A recording dating from the time when Mathias was a good dancer, a sought-after partner. The tape plays. Sounds of utensils, clinking glasses. The tape plays. Sounds of thrashing, biting wind. Inside Mathias rage creates a little ball of stony bile, the shame of tiny crystals splintering in his membranes. Mathias has bitter blood filling his mouth, his long-dead tongue now adds to the salty taste a rotting flavor.

Mathias sees the dancers and with his ears reads the steps they are executing executed will execute on the polished floor. Mathias sees the dancers while his ears decode the compulsory figures as tinnitus. Those people didn't like each other. Didn't respect each other, thought even less of each other. Everyone intimately thought they were infinitely superior to the other members of the assembly. Sometimes they all thought so loudly in their heads that their inner voices covered the brouhaha of the shared banter. The revealed rumors then ended up crushed under the weight of a *fuck you*. They didn't get together to converse nor really even to exchange the masses of information that knitted together their lives, but just to broadcast. They broadcasted to each other. Mathias's ears ask his memory to check all the files. Mathias's memory confirms: for every square dance Eugène was one among a hundred. Dinners, dances, society parties, salons: in the foreground and wearing jabots the publishers, drowning in crinoline or starched satin a few writers, and in between a silky powdery error-cloaked mass, the hack journos.

The relentless twisters had crossed the threshold into the Castle via the service entrance, once they had a foot on the varnished slats their credo was to accumulate more and more mandates. Mathias is watching Eugène as he starts to salsa. The assessment was clear, perfectly transparent: the majority of the Banana Republic of Letters' citizens were under thirty and worked in journalism. Mathias is watching Eugène and think he looks out of breath. They were all journalists, they'd all published or aspired to do so. As a matter of principle. The deal was crooked but it didn't matter to them. Their name on the cover of a book, an obsession, an actual obsession, sometimes even a secret form of motivation. How many times did they naively betray themselves opposite a depressive author going on about existential disasters in the course of their interview. But you sir, you my friend, you have your name on a cover. Since they were journalists, they met publishers. Because their friends were journalists, the publishers could do a market survey in advance. The first meeting always went the same way, in the same cafés, in the same neighborhoods, neighborhood. A quickly shared summary, a hard-hitting, trendy idea, generational if possible. After the appetizer, it was time for the main event. Bull's-eye, impact, and media plan. The advance really depended on it. Mathias is watching Eugène with a stitch in his side. The writing phase, let's say producing the object, wasn't crucial. A bit of anecdotal posturing, writer's block, excitement about unbridling the imagination, living from inside out, in the end clichés that few writers actually experience. An opportunity to stay put for a few months, a yearlong sabbatical. Living in the family vacation house, making your own setting, role, and memories. The Stanislavski method. Quite impressive for your friends and family. Appearance of seriousness combined with a halo of mystery. Sudden inspiration if possible in the middle of a barbecue. Obligatory public note-taking, concentrated-looking face, furrowed brow. Putting the plan in motion and attempting to get it into the right packaging always represented at least two-thirds of the time allowed before the deadline for submitting the manuscript. Since literary devices were not at all required, and a literary advisor with an armada of copyeditors armed with nothing but their mastery of French were more than enough to tackle the task, the novel could flow thick and fast, and its author could naively go into ecstasy over the post-trigger phrase. Mathias watches Eugène stopping at the buffet. Once the manuscript is finished and groomed, the period of the proofs begins. The network was drowning in them. The lack of security in the profession led to such an accumulation of freelance work all over the place ranging from trendy to ultra-serious, without forgetting the female focused, that everyone was connected to everyone else, starting with themselves. Mathias watches Eugène carefully blotting his dripping temples. The last phase, the ultimate phase, was finally taking shape. Recognition. A term in their void-befuddled minds. They'd never experienced editorial recognition, the recognition of the first reader who upon discovering a text by opening an anonymous envelope or one sent by a trusted friend falls crazy in love or simply curious enough to allocate space on its land. They never will experience critical recognition, the fact that upon a desktop chance pushed a journalist to read and really like, to even recognize themselves, to want to defend it, virginally free from any personal stakes. Not even public recognition, prized and precious in their eyes because, except for their desire to impress with their cute little glossy faces, nothing motivated them nearly as much, drowning in mail from lovestruck readers, becoming the vague object of feminine desire, being the heartthrob of their local grocery store, even public recognition was completely distorted. Access to mainstream media, manufactured product, hype, and editing. Herd instinct and brain washing, the term readership always vanishing, in favor of the term *consumers*. Mathias watches Eugène looking for his dance partner. On the arm of someone sharper and much better looking than him she wiggles seductively and continues to salsa as she looks away. The most pathetic part was that often, quite often in fact, despite all the energy, all the marketing plans, their work didn't reach a substantial sales threshold. The starlets and junior masters, the publishers' contrived stunts, of equal or lessor quality to theirs, always made a clean sweep of things, mocking them from the top-ranked spot displayed in all the books offices. Their disillusion-blocked ambitious desire cracked bitterly. Mathias watches Eugène dancing offbeat in the middle of the floor. There's always a bad side. Self-produced by the media+publishing system, these books could only ever be self-consumed. Mathias watches Eugène moving closer to a mirror standing near the bar. Energetically he swings his hips alone in front of his own reflection. Besides, they don't have many people to talk to. A few readers at the book fairs but they only ever talk about their handsome faces they glimpsed on some TV show that was paying their rent. Mathias watches Eugène taking advantage of a new song to forcibly grab a stranger who seems annoyed around the neck. That's why they had to meet a lot to talk about themselves. The soliloquies declaimed by the hack journos were the most common but each unique nonetheless. Writers were invited to places where they could talk about their work. These were called public reading discussions. The stars of formatting, too, even if they only talked about themselves. These were called TV interviews. The hack journos, once they'd hit all the bars run by their friends and colleagues, didn't have anyone left to talk to. So they needed these. These permanent broadcasts. Mathias watches Eugène getting slapped in the face and asking the first guy who passes for a light. Everyone distractedly listens to everyone else's trade secrets, in one ear not quite out the other, retaining the anecdote that would hit the nail on the head at another event, where the absentee would be discussed. Patiently awaiting one's turn. Their rhetoric was solid, Mathias's memory had recorded it all. Start the conversation with I really liked where you say. The other would answer and elaborate then politely ask in return. It could take all night to get around the whole table, they always went out in a group. Mathias watches Eugène smoking his cigarette on the edge of a seat where he's slumped down alone. The hack journos' conversation always seemed like a porno. Mathias watches Eugène not smoking anymore because he jumped out the window.

## Round 6
### (Loaded Dice Because Nothing Is Random)

Mathias didn't show up. I'd warned him: if you don't love me come tell me to my face. Mathias didn't come, he doesn't know it's me, his Esther from the past that he buried so deep, he doesn't know it's me but who I really am, my past, my ID, my fleshy incarnation, doesn't matter. Mathias is in love with several bits of me. He adores Lain, his emails said so. He can't do without all her secrets, she's his twin soul, over my desk I pinned up the paragraph where he says so, and I enlarged it. Mathias is in love and all these bits are me. He thinks Allegra, Mina, and Lison are touching. He answers each of them at about two in the morning with charming little words, overnight my in-box fills up with Mathias's sugar, I smile at the idea that everything flowing from him comes to fertilize my root, he is linked to me without ever guessing I alone am loved, unique, and fragmented. For the black-and-white photos offering him my body, his dark voice leaves messages where he's nothing but desire on the end of the line. The day my long ribbon-tipped tress went into the envelope with my out-of-focus nose, my stomach, and my right hand, I bravely picked up and we talked for three hours and fourteen minutes. Mathias didn't come, he has too much love and he recognized me.

Mathias recognized me, recognized me maybe not exactly as Esther Duval but recognized me as his familiar dream. When he discovers I was his first and will be his last he'll be so happy, sometimes when I think about it I cry, my eyes are possessed like two little Cassandras with the tears that will come to Mathias's lids.

Since he didn't come to refuse love, Mathias has stopped answering all my doubles. He must be living locked up and in absolute darkness, he was fascinated by Anne Frank's diary and gave me a copy when I turned eighteen, nineteen, on the phone with Mathias for three hours and fourteen minutes, he would say what strange days they must be living like that shadow and silence, he would say it would have an effect on you too, such an effect it's obvious it was our first kiss, Mathias is living locked up to test me, to check my love and my understanding of rituals and signs, immersed memories. Since the papers, the radio, and the television have stopped showing Mathias, I'd gotten used to taking his picture to fill the emptiness. Mathias knows it. I sent him a really nice album for his birthday. He told Lain: *if I make a nest or hide in my room will I finally be sure not to be exposed anymore.* A nest or. My heart took such a leap at the pun. Another reason I love Mathias is because Mathias had understood and from the very beginning that I alone am his love, unique, behind all this, I love Mathias because he knows and knew and never said anything just to let me get on with it, to see what I would do, amused watching my string of strategies, letting me get entangled in the meandering map of Tendre, that's just like Mathias in fact.

On April 7 I went to find Mathias. April 7 is an important date. We made love for the first time one April 7, and we agreed that it would be in tribute to us both losing our virginity that we would get married on this date, even if it was in the middle of the week and was a big pain in the ass for everyone. I knocked on his door for a really long time. The building manager came over and told me Mathias was gone. She didn't know where, he hadn't said anything. He put all his stuff in storage, it's strange she added, it's like he was hiding something, strange she added he was strange, something to hide. If I love Mathias so much it's because he's the only one with such a flair for the dramatic. If he's not writing books anymore, it's because I'm the one he's aiming his novel at. To me alone. A great novel in small bits. Mathias knows I'm the one who'll be able to put all the chapters back in the right order, the necessary order, Mathias knows I'm the one who will support him so much he'll come back stronger than ever and so brilliant that everyone will bow down before him, praising in Mathias the return of the prodigal son galvanized by love. I left the building manager with a knowing smile. She must really like him, or else he paid her a fortune, she put her heart into it. I'm impressed. Now I'm dreading the next step cause it's my turn to play. I bought my wedding dress. I keep it in a bag with the shoes that I chose in creamy satin, with very becoming laces. My purse is always with me from morning to night the strap in the hollow of my shoulder as my temporary transplant the weight hits me in the hip as I rush around investigate trot willy-nilly across the whole of Paris and every night I watch a bruise stretch across my pelvis, a black-and-blue promise glittering purple studded yellow epidermis star cloud, I've been branded slave lord and master. Mathias is waiting to be flushed out, he wants me ready and ready I will be.

### Dance Card
### (Lost)

The grass is a little damp in the Castle grounds. Mathias turns up his collar and adjusts his triple-thread cashmere scarf. The gaping French window leading into the room lets the noise from the dance intertwine with the wisteria. Heavy bunches hang down in ropes, with the tip of his toe Mathias pulls one off and with his fingers crushes the lilac flowers, a note, a squeak escapes along with a summer fragrance. Behind the squared-off panels, Mathias catches a glimpse of the tenacious dancers. He plucks to the beat, index finger and thumb snatching from his palm his empurpled booty. There are a lot of trees, even more bushes. The little pond is brimming with water lilies and pale corpses, with her long veils a marble Diana looks down on young sleeping girls, entertaining cultural products yesterday, Ophelia today. Crunching at each step the gravel barely covers the sticky uproar escaping from the window. Following the main path, Mathias is startled, shadow puppets, the dancers' projected movements are too full frontal, he makes out the frolicking, closes his eyes and that's all. As it closes, the gate's laugh sounds like an old maid. The craggy path slopes downward, but still Mathias struggles as he moves forward. The buzzing from the grand ball is following him and pushing him, a feverish growl, flicked off, ejected, stiff Mathias's body seems to refuse, Mathias feels his heart of stone, worries it will roll away. The ditch is alive flush with bustling larvae, talon-gloved hands will rise up suddenly, pierced-lace fingers dirt bugs cling to Mathias's ankles as, out of breath, he slowly goes on. At the entrance to the village, Mathias's ears are filled with silence.

For three long days Mathias has been leaning on his elbow at the window. A window with sashes on the second floor, the top floor of his house as a matter of fact. He's watching for the mailman, hoping for a messenger or a courier or something. His vision goes muddy, it was a year ago, he thinks, a year ago to the day that I left Vaubyessard and its numbing grand balls, I left the Castle, they've probably all forgotten about me. It's a cool night, Mathias's lungs assaulted by consumption. In his brainless head Mathias can see the texture of the embossed invitation, its refined envelope, printed landscape style. In his brainless head Mathias wanders across the grounds, counting as he climbs the 315 steps that lead to Heidelberg Castle. Ten thousand suicides throughout Germany following *The Sorrows of Young Werther*, how many in Rhineland alone. Because Goethe spent time at Heidelberg Castle, because that's where Goethe wrote his broken-tower Werther, at Heidelberg Castle, one last pilgrimage. The tourist guides don't stipulate that fact or the number either. Scholars of that vintage talk about a real plague, disheveled young ladies seen alone and wound up dismembered in the main courtyard, waxy-looking young men smashed against the cobblestones or found in daylight behind some thicket with their dagger in their heart. Heidelberg Castle was a steaming ossuary, without the Germans' legendary sense of maintaining their monuments the romantics would have spent a hundred years swatting flies as they swooned, mired down in the peat of a huge mass grave. Ten thousand suicides throughout Germany, at the grand ball Mathias again hears *it should've been a best seller*, ten thousand suicides throughout Germany how many pints of blood is that. Channels filled with pints of blood, bottomless puddles, trickles running into streams vomiting into the Neckar their vermilion broth, how much blood in Heidelberg, the castle of disillusions. In its lair the structure holds a huge cask, one of the biggest in the world, two hundred thousand liters, in the past all the wine in the region was stored there. It's been described as empty for so many centuries, but the phantom corpuscles of all the suicide victims have filled it forever. Mathias closes the window. In his brainless head the dance yelps in the distance, in the very far-off distance and yet. From the top of the hill, the Castle crushes him, his heart is an old eternally splitting stone, how much blood, how many candles for such a shine, Mathias says to himself as he closes the drapes. Banished from the Castle, I'll stay in the village, there's nothing left for me. So dazed with pain is Mathias that in his sleep he thinks he hears the rolling of some kind of Last Judgment.

### Everyone Is Connected

Agence France-Presse. Friday, September 10, 2004.
At 11:45 p.m. a bomb went off in La Chandelle, a libertine club in Paris's 6th arrondissement during a private launch party for the third issue of the journal *Proxénétisme* and attended by the city's literary elite. Reports already confirm more than one hundred people dead and sixteen with serious injuries transported to nearest hospital. Defense & Illustrations, a small group previously unknown to authorities, has claimed responsibility and its leader, the writer Clotilde Mélisse, was taken in for questioning overnight.

### Dance Card
### (La Java bleue)

PARIS, SEPTEMBER 13, 2004

Dear Dr. Lagarigue,
Following our phone conversation of this past September 6, and as we agreed, I am sending you our patient Mathias Rouault, who's been a resident of our clinic since last June 22. He was brought to us by the police after trying to commit suicide by jumping off the Pont des Arts. The subject suffers from a distinctive psychotic disorder: delirious ideas and episodes, hallucinations, disorganized speech, and cyclically catatonic behavior. Mathias Rouault's occupation is that of writer, which could explain a good number of his symptoms. Despite the treatment administered, we have seen no improvement. Currently on Olanzapine, the patient

remains manageable, but his condition leaves the staff and myself at a loss for an explanation. I enclose here a letter he wrote a few days after coming to us, and which he asked one of our nurses to stamp and send, so you can judge the situation for yourself, and thereby prepare the therapeutic and pharmacological welcome you deem most appropriate.

In closing, I'd like to sincerely thank you for taking him on so quickly.

Dr. Horace Bianchon

*His Excellency Le Petit Robert Dictionary*
*27 rue de la Glacière*
*75013 Paris*

*I, the undersigned, Mathias Rouault, do hereby acknowledge:*
*That I took possession of the Word, with the unique aim of misappropriating it for personal gain;*
*That I am guilty of desertion, even though I swore I would serve the dictionary;*
*That I entered the Banana Republic of Letters following breach of trust in a number of instances;*
*That once therein, in order to remain, I committed misappropriation on several occasions;*
*That I participated of my own free will in commercial collaboration;*
*That I actively took part in the Great Debraining;*
*That I am responsible for the mental deportation of several thousand readers.*
*I confirm that my confession has been written on this day, June 25, in the city of Paris, under no outside coercion, I am prepared to face the consequences of my actions and remain at the disposal of the authorities.*

*Mathias Rouault*

**Everyone Is Connected**

Want Ads, Tuesday, September 14, 2004.

**Urgent.**

Major Publishing Group Seeks to Hire:

**LITERARY DIRECTORS**

Experience with large retailers desirable, solid understanding of marketing required, master's degree, private or other exceptional business school preferred.

**LITERARY ADVISORS**

Experience with large retailers desirable, solid understanding of sales forces required, bachelor's degree required, additional diploma in marketing and management preferred.

**PRESS AGENTS**

Experience in a hostess bar desired, solid understanding of the society pages required, training in set design preferred.

**Newspaper Publishers seek to hire** editors-in-chief, 11 cultural editors, 25 freelancers, 7 interns. Experience in journalism desirable. Immediate start date.

**France Télévision seeks to hire** for its cultural entertainment programs: commentators. Desired profile: M/F, 25–30, attractive, dyed hair welcome.

# Professor Plum in the Ballroom
# with the Candlestick

If Mathias's footsteps don't echo much, it's because of the remains of the agape feast, the floor is strewn with the streamer cadavers, the enshrouded wooden boards mute. The deserted Ballroom is still flushed past echoes pungency. The chiseled marquetry has always absorbed more ghosts, it's not out of chance or simple folklore that ladies of the manor confide in the memory of walls. Cracked as they are, the windows allow the infiltration of drops of wind that form frosty pearls on the shards, little marbles of dead words, arid, ancient words, roll chime bounce across the floor, beneath his soles Mathias sometimes bursts a tiny clot, a clot an agate, a dust speck of throaty laugh, a rusty remark, a stale watery statement escapes unharmed.

The Ballroom is empty, Mathias's candle has been completely consumed. The shriveled wick diffuses its rough, dark, dying, peau-de-chagrin perfume. Mathias's fingers are one with the candlestick, petrified transplant, drips of wax encrusted reddened knuckle epidermis silent despite burning emphasizing tumorous link continuity silvery mass trembling hand. The light was pale, the light sputtered out by the remembrance candle before its demise, blind Mathias at the scene of the crime crisscrosses the space, groping he brushes the mite-riddled curtains, bumps into every chair, not a single match left to offset the candlesque deficiency, not a single match, no, not a single wish, a single possible wish, nothing to say nothing is said in Mathias's skull anymore, in his brainless skull Mathias walks and stumbles over the bits of emptiness scattered throughout its depths.

Mathias breathes in deep, in the folds of the paneling his nostrils poach several odors, mold, honeycombed fungus crumbs of a musty pus-filled past. Mathias takes a deep sniff so he can finally sneeze. I made it into the Banana Republic of Letters by the strength of my wrist and I always wrote by candlelight. Dr. Lagarigue assents by holding out a big box of Kleenex for him to draw from.

Let's go back to your migraines, I don't really understand. You explained that you filled your ears with hot wax to keep in the voices. But the voices themselves scare you, right, Mathias, the voices like music, the invasive laughter, there are times when you dread them, otherwise why would you have taken the fork yesterday to pierce your skull if it wasn't to let them out. You told the nurse two little holes in each temple, blow into one of them anyone please it'll make an in-draft. The voices are hurting you, Mathias. You're hurting yourself, hurting Mathias. We're here to help you, you know that, don't you Mathias. I'll give you another blanket, your blood pressure is so low, that's why you're shivering.

There were a few dances here, dances with complicated steps. I was a good dancer, wow did I ever dance here. Next to the open hatch, there was a big platform, the musicians played from up there. *Now in Vienna there are ten pretty women.* They had Hertzian bows. *There's a shoulder where Death comes to cry.* And harelip plated flutes too. I still know all the steps, I know them watch me, watch me dance, *There's a lobby with nine hundred windows* I'm dancing like an irreducible sulfur fireproof flame. *There's a tree where the doves go to die* a lunar strobe is playing through the panes, *There's a piece that was torn from the morning* I'm dancing I was the king the little prince *And it hangs in the Gallery of Frost* I'm the king the little prince yes the king is dancing by the light of the lunar strobe I-I-I-I I'm dancing like I wrote the words, *Take this waltz* I burned the words the candle at both ends burned the words *Take this waltz* the candle's out I'm dancing the grand ball has started again the grand ball nothing's lost *Take this waltz with the clamp on its jaws.*

The voices and the music in your head Mathias only exist through you, for you and only in your head, do you understand Mathias, you're hurting yourself, really hurting yourself Mathias, no one can survive for long inside their head, you think you've taken refuge in there, but you're the prisoner of your own head Mathias, we're going to help you get out of that head let me help you, come out of your head you're going to bang into something.

If I dance for a very long time the grand ball could start again. *Oh, I want you, I want you, I want you* I remember sometimes the floor was cold and the dance floor in ruins but I was the first one dancing *On a chair with a dead magazine* and a few steps later there were hundreds of us in the middle of a whirlwind. I'll dance for a long time I'm dancing *In the cave at the tip of the lily* in the doorway I can see a fragile silhouette delicately appearing *In some hallway where love's never been* a silhouette gliding softly toward the center, *On a bed where the moon has been sweating* the center is me *In a cry filled with footsteps and sand* the center, I-I-I-I I'm the grand ball centrifuge *Take this waltz* partners will fall *Take this waltz* into my arms *Take its broken waist in your hand* into my pale arms. *This waltz, this waltz, this waltz, this waltz* I pick up speed I extend my hand to her she comes forward, *With its very own breath of brandy and Death* the silhouette comes toward me she comes forward *Dragging its tail in the sea.*

Let's go back to the migraine you had in July, Mathias, torturing your head, you mentioned a song that ordered you to fall, saying jump off the bridge. It was a long time ago but tell me about it anyway, what were the words to that old song, it's important, Mathias, really important, you have to understand it's in your head, that everything in your head is part of you, only of you, Mathias, listening inside your head is hearing yourself, you were talking to yourself Mathias, you meant yourself harm, you wanted to hurt yourself, you hurt yourself so much but I want to help you.

It's dark, of course, so dark, I can't see much, it's because of the stick, the thin wax stick so quickly consumed, *There's a concert hall in Vienna* consumed by its flame *Where your mouth had a thousand reviews* in less than seven years. I'm dancing in the shadows *There's a bar where the boys have stopped talking* and someone takes my hand. The movements are graceful the wind rushes in *They've been sentenced to death by the blues* they aren't droplets of wind anymore *Ah but who is it climbs to your picture* but rather gusts snorting gusts of dry revived voices. *With a garland of freshly cut tears* There are two of us we're dancing under my right palm I-I-I-I I can feel a slightly rough piece of linen behind it the vertebrae of the opaque silhouette *Take this waltz* that lets me lead I've always been good at leading *Take this waltz* the restricted vertebrae crackle rhythmically I don't dare squeeze too tight for fear of snapping them and annoying their noble owner *Take this waltz, it's been dying for years.*

Take your drops, Mathias. I'll bring the chair closer don't talk so loud. There's no grand ball, it's in your head we're in your room you're in your bed, I swear to you in this room there are no candles and no candlesticks, don't get agitated, nothing will hurt you here, nothing at all will hurt you, we're helping you, Mathias, we want what's best for you.

You're beautiful when you're out of breath, Dr. Lagarigue, you're beautiful *There's an attic where children are playing* you're waltzing spinning wildly. *Where I've got to lie down with you soon* let me lead, dear Dr. Lagarigue. I've always been good *In a dream of Hungarian lanterns* at leading my very deliberate steps *In the mist of some sweet afternoon* carry slippers petticoats away see we're whirling *And I'll see what you've chained to your sorrow* soon the Ballroom will be overflowing with expert couples spinning tops soon the Ballroom will be overflowing with life *All your sheep and your lilies of snow.* I-I-I-I I like you out of breath, Dr. Lagarigue, you remind me of a hundred easily swooning women the alcoves of the Castle are brimming *Take this waltz* with them how sweet it was, Doctor, *Take this waltz* to have your ego reflected in their eyes as they rolled back in their heads. Feel how the atmosphere is cooling off now. See, we've created disciples or turned the tables, the shadows bristle with intertwined dancers who've come back to brush against us for as long as we want *Take this waltz, with its "I'll never forget you, you know!"*

I can't see anything, Mathias. I'd like a chair because my heart is beating too fast. The grand ball exists, doesn't it, not only in your head I can see the room engulfed in paneling, I'd swear the room is decorated with candlesticks and so many candelabras, my lips are moving, it's not me I'm afraid I'm not the one I'm really not the one who's talking Mathias, through my mouth I don't know who's vomiting out these words, for the time being I'm bracing my tongue clenching my jaws, I fear that the enamel on my poor incisors will soon shortly give way from such battering.

I only live to dance, dear Dr. Lagarigue, *this waltz, this waltz, this waltz, this waltz* deep down you know that, that's all we live for. *With its very own breath of brandy and Death* Being a star on the dance floor, *Dragging its tail in the sea* taking the risk a bird winding up a shooting star *I'll dance with you in Vienna* becoming a constellation *I'll be wearing a river's disguise* Announces the Ringmaster shapely display concentrating on proper head position *Take this waltz* neck weighed down with a thousand eyes *Take this waltz* feeling the heat of glory reducing remaining scruples to a puddle and evaporating remorse *Take this waltz, take this waltz, take this waltz, take this waltz.*

I'm your migraine, it's me who's talking, Mathias, me, the dead one buried in the hollow of your oblivion, me, the cadaver dismayed by your stunted choices. *The hyacinth wind on my shoulder,* Look at me, Mathias, I'm right here, against you *My mouth on the dew of your thighs.* Caress my old bones hold me tighter dig your fingers into the space between the tiny bones. *And I'll bury my soul in a scrapbook* Look at me, Mathias. I said: look at me. Plunge your cerulean eyes into my deepest gaps. I have two big holes, Mathias, where my eyes should be. *With the photographs there, and the moss* my eyes dissolved as they read you, Mathias, as they read your stupidity-spreading prose your pimpish syntax, *Take this waltz* your pretentious prepositions *Take this waltz* My eyes dissolved, Mathias, witnessing every page of your subjugated words, every line, Mathias, every line since you started leering at the Castle gates *Take this waltz, take this waltz, take this waltz,* was a piercing blow plunging harder bursting eyeballs. See the Word,

Mathias, you compromised it, see language, Mathias, your pages turn it into a hustler, you prostituted it, decked out in flirty pathetic ploys, your language is a whore, Matthias, a miserable whore, and to get it so dirty, so ugly, so gaunt, it had to be over my own dead body. I'm Dr. Black, Mathias. *And I'll yield to the flood of your beauty* I'm speaking to you through the mouth of my colleague tonight to finally prove to you that shame will never spare anyone. I'm Dr. Black, and you killed me. *My cheap violin and my cross.* I lived inside you, you even loved me. *And you'll carry me down on your dancing* For years I was an obvious restraint, not a bridle to gnaw, I galloped full of spirit through your venules, was the protégé of your own brain. You killed me, Mathias. *To the pools that you left on your wrist* I was too cumbersome, an insoluble obstacle to your battle plans, I advocated combat and never retreat, you had to compel me to silence so you could enjoy the feast of capitulation. *O my love, o my love* The candle gave off a blinding light, your writing preferred obfuscating blinders. To get into the Castle you have to let down your guard but arm yourself with sightlessness, that's why your right hand closed up sharply, grasping the candlestick and smashing my skull with it. *It's yours now. It's all that there is.*

I'm Dr. Black. I'm dead, and you killed me. Let that poor Dr. Lagarigue rest in Room 37 and come out of that stupid hiding place. Your feet are sticking out from under the curtain. Go to the smoking lounge. Sit quietly. I accuse Professor Plum of massacring me the day the dictionary bled at his hand. I accuse Professor Plum of murdering what within him was the Cerberus of the Ballroom. I accuse in the Ballroom Professor Plum who made me see stars.

There are two of you in the room. There are two of you, and you killed me. There are four of them in the Study, there are two of you in the smoking lounge. Keep time, keep it right, Mathias. Go sit with Aline she's humming Nana Mouskouri her favorite worn-out tune between two Lucky Strikes: *Often the warmth of a sunny day turns a girl's thoughts to love.*

# Second Officer

I'm your Conscience. I take a capital letter not as an affectation, I am well above such formalities and obscurantism, which are the realm of stylistics. Legends, whether in white coats or bundled up in extra-rough hair shirts, have, across the centuries, denatured my name, my soul, and my function.

I'm your Conscience, but in the beginning I wasn't compatible with everybody and even less so with anybody. I'm not a concept, an idea, an entity, and certainly not a cricket in a top hat and waistcoat vainly bouncing around on a wooden shoulder until the sudden spurt of a donkey ear silences him with asphyxia.

I say: I'm yours. So I'm cheating, I arrange the truth so as not to frighten those I'm speaking to by this revelation. Conscience, just Conscience, this is how to address me when I intervene. Within you, silently. To guide you, surely, irrefutably. Your quest is arduous. The rooms are so fleshy and the weapons anemic. You'll soon understand that no one, anywhere, can escape their own choices.

You killed Dr. Black. With your hands you strangled my mirror. I am Conscience, I ruin souls to better preserve the living.

I'm too busy in the real world to get lost tonight in the obscure maze of some little island liberated from the laws that govern it. The outside world has tired me out too much for me to have the energy to impose my weight, here, in your smoking lounge and its double. Besides for you it's too late. I can leave the perspiration to the flies.

So I'll settle for entrusting you with the words I once poured into a mustachioed body. Do with them what you will, but you've been warned: *Is it fame on which your mind is set? Then heed what I say: Before too long prepare to let honor slip away.*

# Gardens

I'm Dr. Black. I'm wandering along the side path, I'm worrying about catching cold. At Sainte-Anne the pathways are named exclusively after poets or artists, probably in order to reassure visiting families about the social or even possibly posthumous future of their black sheep. Additionally, it's not uncommon to le**NAC Bulletin 002**

Not a Clue, page 141, line 7

My Dear Readers,

Given the obvious incapacity of the nonetheless numerous contributors to the round that was just played, it must be noted that certain points concerning the above-mentioned Mathias Rouault's supposed psychological problems remain obscure. My responsibility as Omniscient Narratrix leads me to share some additional information that will allow you to work out for yourself the diagnosis that the staff of this novel was unable to establish. The urgency of the situation left me no other choice than this undoubtedly sudden interruption, therefore, I apologize for being so abrupt. As for Dr. Black, he will gladly excuse my incursion in the middle of a chapter that was initially reserved for him, insofar as the remarks he was to develop were not particularly necessary to the development of the story.

Best,
The Omniscient Narratrix

**Psychotic disorders** are characterized by the psychotic symptoms at the root of their definition. Over time the term *psychotic* has had a number of different definitions. In the strictest sense it refers to delusions and pronounced hallucinations whose pathological nature is not recognized by the individual. A broader definition includes hallucinations that the individual recognizes as such along with symptoms of disorganization such as disorganized speech and/or behavior.

The following psychotic disorders are defined according to the psychotic symptoms that are present, and their duration, and according to the simultaneous presence—or lack thereof—of a mood disorder (depression or mania).

**Schizophrenia.** This lasts for at least six months and includes at least one month of symptoms in the active phase, in other words two (or more) of the following: delusions, hallucinations, disorganized speech (e.g., frequent incoherencies or inexplicable digressions), grossly disorganized or catatonic behavior and negative symptoms (i.e., flat affect, reduction in speech, lack of will). The delusions are peculiar, and the hallucinations consist of one voice constantly commenting on the subject's behavior or thoughts or of several voices speaking to one another. During a significant period of time following the onset of the disturbance, one or several major areas of functioning such as work, interpersonal relations, or personal hygiene are clearly below levels attained before the onset.

**Schizofreniform disorder.** The criteria are the same as for schizophrenia, with two differences: the duration (1–6 months) is between those of a brief psychotic disorder (1 month, see below) and schizophrenia (at least 6 months) and the absence of any functional deterioration (although this can occur).

**Schizoaffective disorder.** An episode of a mood disorder (depression or mania) and symptoms of the active phase of schizophrenia (see above) occur simultaneously and are preceded or followed for at least two weeks by delusions or hallucinations without any pronounced mood disturbance. In other words, the psychotic symptoms last longer than the symptoms of the mood disorder. This is what allows differentiation from a mood disorder (an episode of depression or mania) with accompanying psychotic symptoms. In schizophrenia symptoms of a mood disorder can also be present, but they remain less pronounced.

**Delusional disorder.** Characterized by at least one month of delusions that are not unreasonable (i.e., more coherent and plausible than with schizophrenia) yet without any other symptoms of the active phase of schizophrenia.

**Brief psychotic disorder.** Presence (unexplained by any preexisting mood disorder, schizofreniform disorder, or schizophrenia) for longer than one day but less than one month, of one (or more) of the following symptoms: delusions, hallucinations, disorganized speech, grossly disorganized or catatonic behavior.

**Shared psychotic disorder.** Develops in an individual under the influence of someone who presents delusions with similar contents.

**Psychotic disorder due to a general medical condition.** Hallucinations or delusions are considered as due to the direct physiological effects of a general medical condition (i.e., a brain lesion, epilepsy, a migraine, hyper- and hypothyroidism, adrenal insufficiency, hypoglycemia, liver or kidney disease, etc.). If the subject retains a good understanding of reality and recognizes that his hallucinations are the result of his medical condition, this diagnosis is not applied.

**Substance-induced psychotic disorder.** Hallucinations (when the subject is unaware that they are substance induced) or delusions are considered as due to the direct physiological effects of an addictive substance, a medication, or exposure to a toxin. Psychotic symptoms can also be present in other disorders (depression, e.g.), but they are not a fundamental part of the definition of these disorders.

# Mrs. White

*Céline* was oozing out of the radio for the sixth time since that day when the news interrupted it: Cannes' Palme d'Or had just been awarded to Claude Lelouch, also Hugues Aufray shut the hell up and left some room for Nicole Croisille and her cha-ba-da-ba-das. Françoise Pithiviers thought to herself that she really was having a shitty year and then her water broke on the couch.

She spent more than eleven hours in the labor room, and finally had the opportunity to let loose the swell of verbal garbage that had been stagnating in a syrupy swamp inside her. While the medical team was busy with her uterus, she hoped so hard she would die that her life passed before her eyes between two off-color expressions. Her mouth was distended with the flow of raw, heavy, acidic words; her body retracted sharply enough to snap steel forceps, Françoise was nothing but repudiation. She heard I see the head and arched her back even more, contracting from the inside till she was twisted with cramps, aspiring to strangle the neck of the half-evicted newborn with her own intimacy. A dry sob shook her throat when she received confirmation of the final exit. Her bitch of a mother had won. Mothers often win, mothers always win when their children perpetuate the family line. It's easy to kill the father, to decapitate a guardian, to chop the head off an intellectual, to guillotine a pretender: so common an activity that it's healthy, the heart as death row for as long as a life goes on. Mothers often win because they never die, no, never completely. You can't kill the mother, you can't even say it, sometimes you picture it, but you procrastinate cowardly when faced with the extent of the task. It wouldn't do any good, anyway. People with less maternal glue are perfectly aware of it. Knife in hand they dig into the cadaver, feverishly trying to find out how to slay the phantom that emanates from it years, many, many years after the burial. And faced with the black dress soiled with bits of ancient flesh and lethargic worms and faced with the putrefied inhumed body, they all pillage their skin embedded fingernails, their neck remains constrained the umbilical leash nibbling their tissue and their will as well. Mothers often win, they're here forever. Celebrate the funeral, imagine you're free, tomorrow their matronly voices with their well-considered advice and wise sayings will slip into your eardrums as they whisper the bitter song of genetic zombies. Little does it matter that their bosom is now nothing more than gaping bones and rot. The magnet and its two poles, attracting repelling, all hatred carries some regret. You'll bow before the ghost, abusiveness is a yoke that never oxidizes. We're all Jewish, Mother.

As for her mother, Françoise did everything she could to get away from her, removed herself from her sight and her arid belly, in order to give her genealogical pretensions a vigorous snip, leaving her family tree nothing but a lichen-swollen stump. Unfortunately, one night a hormonal spike combined with an excess of Vouvray wine got the better of her wood-chopping tendencies.

The owner of the generous seed entrusted to Françoise's ova was never identified due to the deficiency of the light bulb in the apartment building lobby. And the young lady was caught quite off guard when her lateness showed up and she went and found Jacqueline, begging her to use her some knitting needles on her. The operation must have been botched or the fetus outrageously resistant, since all through the following weeks, Françoise sheltered the undesirable little puppet in her womb. With a heavy heart and increasing morning sickness, she went right out in search of a social smokescreen that was likely to do the job.

So in the fall of 1965, Françoise Pithiviers had an exceptionally full calendar. Between six forty-five and eight thirty in the morning, she'd go to the different cafés in her neighborhood. Between nine and eleven to the Sorbonne library. Between noon and two any brasserie would do, but the more expensive the better. Between three and six to the movies, then the bars in the area. Between seven and nine trendy restaurants. Between ten at night and sunrise, parties, nightclubs, or jazz spots. Françoise didn't sleep much and always carried a big bag full of shoes, stockings, and different outfits suitable for the different situations and places. She'd received, from a recently deceased aunt, a little nest egg and she'd promised herself she'd put it to good use. At first this meager bounty was meant to let her go to college without the scourge of running short of food, but given the turn of events, Françoise decided it was a better idea to use it to be able to give birth without being the object of ridicule.

Her strict schedule had the advantage of cornering the potentially marriageable male population. She came in contact with many different socio-professional categories, and as she reapplied her makeup on the bus she thought that she'd really have to be cursed not to at least dig up a laborer, a student, an office clerk, a lawyer, or a doctor in the course of her different interactions. Françoise asked about compensating her frivolity regarding wriggling embryo consequences with the most minute calculations. She increased the number of her relationships, simultaneously seeing more than fifteen boys and gentlemen simulating with each a committed couple with a promising future. After two months she became aware that she couldn't saddle the secretly expected newborn with status of premature without arousing doubts and anger within the future head of household if she didn't act soon. It was time to launch the second phase of the plan, especially since the frequency of her many sexual encounters was starting to be a problem in a period of such raging gonorrhea.

A whole week was devoted to revealing rendezvous. She acted out breaking down, tears, and panic. Included suicide blackmail for the richest, for the most uptight the Damocles of the family reputation. For the most lovestruck she praised the clear cusp of a destiny to be sealed, for the most lost a sure way to finally get some structure in their lives.

Sunday night when she got home to her little shoebox apartment, she checked off all the names on her list. Four possibilities were viable: Jean-Christophe Risson (25 years old, a classical studies major, son of a rich family), Georges Bluteau (49 years old, working in finance, a family man), Rémi Barberin (26 years old, a mail carrier, not a family man), and Azzâm Derdega (29 years old, a roofer, an undocumented immigrant). The others had given her anger, refusals, escapes to go buy cigarettes, and the usual cowardly loss of color in the face, along with a few slender wads of cash offered insistently in return for a promise of abortion and definitive silence. A good investment of Aunt Suzon's inheritance, concluded Françoise as she observed the extent of her gains.

Jean-Christophe Risson had said I'll be back my love, and Françoise waited for him for a whole afternoon, sitting in a wing chair, in his cute little bachelor pad. At four o'clock she realized it was a furnished apartment and not a sign of things to come. Georges Bluteau didn't show up at the Hôtel de la Croix-Rouge. Françoise paid for the room, along with a heavy charge for the damage. Rémi Barberin didn't set foot in the Café des Lilas. Françoise was annoyed but thought about how she was escaping a narrow apartment with cracked walls that smelled like soup. She went out on the hunt again, but every night the chime of fear rang so loudly in the depths of her skull that at the end of the third month her belly finally pushed her into in the arms of the roofer.

Françoise's sin was that of pride. For years her adorable and very friendly little face had led her to understand that she had a kind of upper hand with men. Like all young and moderately educated young people from culturally integrated families draped in middle-class values, as the years passed she'd developed an endless superiority complex. Getting surreptitiously knocked up could have given her the chance to finally realize she really wasn't much, maybe not a nobody but not better than her mother, a stiff country girl who proudly displayed her lovely hairdo ever since the blessed day when the son of some absolutely flat-broke bigwigs took her away from her farm. Françoise hated her mother, not out of habit or after careful consideration but simply because she'd never shown any love toward her. For her whole life her mother only had two passions: her husband and manicures. Her ears and her mouth could only focus on her husband, whom she built up like God despite the ravages of gout, bankruptcy, and alopecia. In her mother's eyes Françoise only existed intermittently, when the father finally asked her a question or proudly commented on her last report card. As a little girl, Françoise sometimes fell prey to tactile impulses, to the irresistible need to snuggle up against the maternal bosom. Then her mother would scream because her nails were drying. Her little girl memories smell of acetone. Because she had read the works of Maupassant, Françoise got the nickname *the intellectual of the family*. Because she had three suitors in high school, Françoise was baptized *a beauty like her mother*. Annette, her younger sister, who was in seventh grade for the third time and whose dimensions equaled a cubic meter, made absolutely no attempt to dissuade anyone at all concerning these assertions. At the age of twenty-four Françoise was as vain as any spoiled brat.

The feeling she was in control was confirmed by the fall she spent with the sinister schemes she'd concocted to protect her position as a respectable young lady when May's oh-so-organic death knell would finally toll. Françoise imagined she was oh-so-clever, bending to her will the people she chose, thanks to her smug brain secretly directing complex games she always won. When nothing was working, when everything was going sideways and why not against her too, Françoise would conclude that it was destiny and think she'd been promoted to a precious, glorious, dazzling future, justifying her failures with a superior hand that had everything planned, thwarted this round for very good reasons that her current mind hadn't yet conceived of but whose true designs would be understood at a later time. Françoise saw Azzâm Derdega not as an absolutely sordid last resort but as a strange path that would one day lead her, that could only lead her, to her own *success*. Françoise used this word just like everyone else in her family. Like an Eldorado but without common sense.

Françoise didn't see Azzâm as. Françoise didn't see anything including herself as, Françoise didn't see anything, not anything at all. The marriage bans were published and her family absent, outraged by the exotic nature of her choice. During the lunch dedicated to introductions, the father—already shocked that the Pithiviers dynasty would be corrupted by distant blood and working-class on top of that—had as much trouble digesting the tagine as Azzâm's remarks about the great General himself. The marriage bans were published, family on both sides was amputated from the wedding, since the Azzâmien relations were all implanted within the confines of Morocco. A few friends, some rice, a generous buffet, a hall that was really too big so footsteps echoed just like Azzâm's loud laugh, Azzâm's loud laugh driving into the eardrums of the white-dressed Françoise despite the lack of altar *what a deal* followed by an exclamation point. The French nationality in exchange for protected honor, Françoise being too busy admiring the loops and swirls that her lovely brain was engraving on her life hadn't thought of that, not even for a second.

Azzâm didn't stoop to any comments at all when the scrawny infant made her appearance at the Bagneux maternity clinic, even though her eyes persisted in staying blue like nobody else's. Now that he wasn't working off the books he left to his wife the choice of names, clothes, and wallpaper. Françoise would have preferred to keep her name, she taught French in a private school and when the students heard Derdega they giggled and pretended to belly dance. But above all else Françoise was determined, and with singular passion since the parental breakup, to show that she had *succeeded*. Women who succeed have a fulfilling relationship, a very cozy home, and people who envy them. Because of one of the proverbs that her father repeated over and over and over: it's better to be envied than pitied. Françoise never dabbled in nuance. Being envied or pitied, she dreamed which side would be hers. Her bosom stung with secret grudges. Next to her bed the newborn slept. Without her, without this girl who had stubbornly embedded herself in the parentheses of her belly, Françoise would still be blossoming and a Pithiviers, an elegant bachelorette with a thousand roads to choose from, without this sticky foreign name clinging all over her and even on official documents. Françoise spent an hour picking out a name, she scared herself a little with her own darkness, a nervous half-smile you're going to pay little lady, you'll wear the cross of my bitter wit. When the doctor wrote down Séraphine Derdega he thought so loudly Lord that's ridiculous that Françoise's heart burst like an abscess, juicy, dripping relief, quivering ventricles splashing her whole being, the warm revenge coulis radiated her inside.

Séraphine didn't know anything about the cold snap of '65. Daughter of Azzâm Derdega, roofer, and Françoise Derdega, née Pithiviers, teacher. Séraphine simply learned as the seasons passed that her father was crazy, taken over by sudden violent obsessions, ravaging with his shouting and bloody fists their modest little apartment in accordance with the whims of his dysphoria. Azzâm waivered harsh between concrete mutism and vociferous clamoring, didn't like anything, not his wife or the child lodger or his friends or his coworkers. Only cheap red wine had any merit at all in his eyes and when his fat body absorbed too much he would hit his wife and his daughter until sleep came and delivered them from this manic plague.

One night Azzâm didn't come home. He'd fallen down, a work accident, Séraphine prayed so hard to Heaven and all its territories that her father wouldn't come back from his coma that for decades afterward she had on her knees irritations scabs. Mother and daughter experienced seven weeks of respite, then at their conclusion welcomed home a limp-legged, paraplegic, fired Azzâm. In his wheelchair the ex-roofer knocked himself out with extremely cheap distilled products, his hands were still healthy enough for three activities: alcoholism, the Club Saint-Étienne, and abuse. From a young age Séraphine nursed an infinite distrust of men and moreover developed a strange concern about her own future.

Azzâm was her father, an integral part at the heart of her malevolent corpuscles and genes. Azzâm being her father she saw herself as carrying a genetic disease, violence and insanity, she dreamed Rosemary's baby and every night gave birth to little brown monsters. At the age of eleven Séraphine threw away all her dolls and swore on the head of Candy Candy that she'd never wind up a genetrix. From then on this determined her life as a woman. Séraphine saw herself as contagious legacy and forbade herself any family drive. She dreamed herself part of a couple, consulted de Beauvoir for a better and more rational justification of irreducible hysterectomy preference. At the age of twenty Séraphine combined pill, condom, and IUD, begged doctors to accelerate the reign of menopause within her.

Because she thought she was infected, because whenever a hint of anger flared up in her bosom, she saw in it a stigma of Azzâm's growing insanity, Séraphine was not of the world. She remained just off to the side. Her choice wasn't really a choice, not a real one, being a woman without being a mother is an act of supreme will, not a cover-up pose full of common neuroses. Séraphine didn't ask for anything, except to never give birth to anyone. She left a lot of men in order to protect her sterility desire. She didn't even wait for a paternal desire to be disclosed. As soon as she was part of a couple she was simply on the lookout for partner reactions toward other people's children. Only men who showed granite indifference or pronounced disgust had any merit in her eyes, they were the only ones who were for her potential husbands. Until she was thirty-one everything went well. Almost. Insofar as the hypothesis of an eliminated familial cell put her in contact with a panel of men who always belonged to the same category. After the age of twenty-seven hardcore bachelors are still bachelors for four possible reasons: incomplete mourning, obvious egotism, Peter Pan syndrome, some other defect making them unfit for consumption. Until she was thirty-one everything went well, and then Françoise stepped on the gas.

The night of the funeral some friends invited Séraphine to dinner, offering over nightcaps a variation on the Chinese portrait game in order to distract the newly orphaned woman. If I was a proverb I'd be a bird in the hand is worth two in the bush if I was a lie I'd be the truth if I was a question I'd just be: who.

# Mrs. White in the Lounge

It happened at the Stalingrad Métro station. The connection between Lines 7 and 2. Séraphine's body had been on automatic pilot for the whole trip for the last six years three weeks and five days. Twice a week, 57 steps to the entrance, stairs, hallways, platform, Corentin Cariou Crimée Riquet Stalingrad, platform stairs hallways stairs platform Jaurès Colonel Fabien Belleville Couronnes, platform stairs 208 steps, four floors, two turns of the key. The minuscule hallway, right elbow or thigh banging into the door, wounded eyes taking in the walls, 375 square feet of failure and isolation, you can get used to misery but not to mediocrity.

When she wasn't seeing Laurent, Séraphine didn't go out much. Listless she didn't move from the hollowed-out couch, a two-seater according to the boasting catalog, you'd think that all Scandinavians were gnomes. With three cushions under her temple, curled-up fetal position scratchy shelves nibbling on her toes, she surrendered to cable TV, going from one channel to the next with the greediness of a woman who's been dumped and starts going from one set of arms to another without ever finding the rest of discovering pleasure.

At around 1:00 a.m. her muscles finally moaning, her brain would certify it had nothing left to empty out. So she'd get up, splash cold water on her face, stare at her blackheads in the mirror hanging over the antique sink, scrutinize the cracks and crevasses left by time on the enamel and her skin, sometimes shed a tear for appearance's sake, close the plastic folding door behind her, bump into the door of the main room, push the coffee table out of the way, move the chair, and then sit down at her desk.

Until nine o'clock or even later, stubborn, she'd correct all kinds of documents, slashing extra lines, assigning to the syntax conventional rhythm, getting the misconjugated verbs into step, emailing back the sanitized pages. Once in a while a cornered client would add to his order a short advertorial folder, a translation, or an outsourced article. Séraphine efficiently accomplished all these tasks, her unusual hours represented a real advantage to a lot of people: urgently sent out in the evening, the work was completed overnight and unfailingly received the next morning. A number of deadline-strangled editors called on her for this very reason.

Séraphine wasn't really an insomniac. Her fear of brightness had simply brought her, as time passed, to live an inverted existence. A respectable border between the world of the living and her own. Séraphine was fully aware of her state. She'd cared for it, pampered it. She'd been dead for a long time.

The Métro car was packed, like always. Poverty clung to her skin. Not her own, she wasn't poor, just not really well-off, her income just about fit within the statistics. Average. Like her whole existence. Sometimes Séraphine would think to herself I'm the Pasionaria of averageness. Besides, she'd never aspired to anything else but the gentle, straight, and reassuring line of horizontality. Seven years earlier, dropping the confessing letter *Forgive me, daughter* anvil suicide heart *Azzâm is not your father* shame dissolved in double asphyxiation, once the initial shock passed she added 1.8 children to her life plans. Not aiming too high crawling too low: none of that for Séraphine, she avoided taking hits she'd had Azzâm for that, Séraphine actually avoided everything, her late mother's defeated aspirations bewildered her memory with aromas of $CH_4$. Therefore averageness in Séraphine's eyes remained the purest incarnation of epicureanism. If she'd held a driver's license, you can bet Séraphine would've rented a little house in the suburbs, she could have even gone as far as getting a mortgage for one. With her saddlebags firmly wedged into the fold-down seat Séraphine is thinking about the yard she won't own, ever, she's thinking about it right now.

In the packed subway car Séraphine thinks she'll never have anything, it's too late for the yard, the gravel driveway, the little fireplace, the children's room. Séraphine turned thirty-eight, she has nothing but all this poverty slicing through her though foreign to it, penetrating and contaminating her with its despair on display, this poverty, its arrogant rags demanding pity, the Romanian singer's hand please for the music hanging on with its bony grayness, Séraphine really wants to smack the Romanian singer, tear off her bun, thinning hair greasy scalp, bang her head her temple muffled noises bouncing bouncing against the steel bar smeared with fingerprints, the singer's blood mixing with the thick film commuter fingerprints, for too long Séraphine has endured the massacred covers of *La Vie en rose* between two Métro stations by this damn Romanian singer, when Laurent held me close and held me fast with the magic spell that he cast, it was la vie decompose. Séraphine now knows, Line 2 after the transfer that for six years three weeks and five days she'd be fertilizing her too-late with big shovelfuls of one-day.

There was a before-Laurent. An above-average before. Almost a little too above for Séraphine. An English teacher answering to the name of Christian, with whom Séraphine shared a nice life and an apartment. A big apartment (800 sq. ft.), bright, with perfectly square white walls, near Montparnasse. A modern building, spotless windows, and tile. For a few years Séraphine lived in peace but without delight, it's the price to pay if you want to banish suffering. Christian was almost twenty-eight and Séraphine just thirty when some friends showed up at their place weighed down with a portable baby seat. All night long Christian went completely gaga over the creature, went into deep ecstasy over its blissfully gummy smiles, spitty foam dribbling cutely, the miniature size of the various parts of its body, its piercing cries and other incredibly touching rumblings, going so far as to ask the creators of the masterpiece to let him change its diapers. The whole next week Séraphine didn't sleep much, in other words not at all.

Among her close friends Séraphine included the attentive ear of Laurent Wedinton, a young organizer of cultural evenings, who had been supporting her in everything for more than a year, hoping to charm her with his understanding, a precious quality indeed since Séraphine was extremely temperamental and no one ever thought she was in the right. For several months Laurent had been peppering his comments with the tiniest bits of criticism concerning Christian, delicately inserting epigraphs detailing the couple's incompatibilities, their opposing wants, their diverging ways of operating, and the little cracks he suspected were actually chasms. Laurent was brilliant and knew Séraphine was aware of his value. When a tearful Séraphine confided her infant trauma to him, Laurent maneuvered expertly, understanding that he surely had the trigger event in his grasp. He let Séraphine go off to the baptism and come back nauseous: promoted to the role of godfather, Christian spent three days acting monomaniacal, raising his eyebrows and his voice when his beloved got up from the table when the story of the birth was imparted. It was the brink of the breakup. All Séraphine could see in Christian was the doubt-defect duo, every lasting look boomeranged back with the shame-ridden mass. Everything about him annoyed her including his perpetually poorly rinsed toothbrush. At night she'd get up saying she had work to do, unable to tolerate the heavy breath irrigating her neck and beating her ears with pallid snoring. She'd get a poncho and curl up on the red couch, chatting in a low voice on the phone for hours, noticing that like her Laurent never slept.

One morning she ended up making her decision. Laurent had finally told her he loved her, with a sudden love that had struck him from the first moment he set eyes on Séraphine's pout and all the rest. A man who remembers the outfit worn and the first exchange of words can never lose the war. Séraphine swooned, convinced like never before that the right one had finally come along. Before even the tiniest kiss, Laurent talked about relationships, describing Séraphine just as he needed to in order to melt away the most suspicious of guards. The dreamed-of Woman with a capital W my angel, an absolutely lovely intimate wedding my love, hills and lands to conquer my beloved, masks and bergamasques, open vowels so open you can feel the air moving fans of fine silk. Laurent was well aware that behind every mother or whore schizophrenia in every woman there persists a Madame Bovary. What Laurent wanted he always got. [Here we can point out a perfect textbook case. A number of readers and practitioners are wondering about the respective advantages and disadvantages of so-called traditional novels versus autofictional novels.

|  | Fiction | Autofiction |
|---|---|---|
| Advantages | — | — |
| Disadvantages | — | — |

As the Omniscient Narratrix, it is my honor to enlighten you with this very eloquent example that I've caught right here in midair.

In the case of a so-called traditional novel the conceptions and descriptions of the characters are based on real people. The names may be disguised or completely replaced, the defining features skewed at will in service to the plot. Thus those concerned balk at seeing themselves unfavorably but they always soften complimentary hyperbole. A good reputation goes better with dropped pants. Lawsuits are avoided and horses kept in the barn.

In the case of an autofictional novel the conceptions and descriptions of the characters are stripped of imaginings, smoke-free mirrors of real people. The names are reproduced, the defining features emphasized raw and pure. Thus, those concerned are disgusted to see their fundamental darkness but sometimes soften at a bawdy wink. The pitcher goes to the well so often it ends up spitting it out. Lawsuits can't be avoided, even without a palace Panurge presides over justice. A Bartleby quote is therefore more valuable than a Meinhoffed saying. But the reader may be reassured: in either case everyone gets in a fight with everyone else.

You've probably noticed that once the tendency petered out autofiction couldn't retain its market shares. Please refer now to the table. You'll notice that the so-called traditional novel has more advantages than an autofictional novel. Is this however any reason for the genre's decline? Discuss. (200 words)]

Laurent was sincere, that's what made it worse. What Laurent wanted he so wanted the masks and bergamasques gaping cavernous vowels his soul behind this chosen landscape never admitted it was sad, disguised, and fickle. Séraphine dismissed Christian two days later. The unfortunate boy didn't really understand, was speechless, concluded there's nothing I can do my heart is suffering but it doesn't matter I want you to be happy. Such self-denial comforted Séraphine in the choice made: he had to be weak and not very motivated to let her run off into unknown arms, obviously Christian wasn't made for her, no skull and skin remorse could get a toehold when faced with such self-effacement.

There's only one exit at the Couronnes station. There's only one exit and Séraphine thinks to herself as her cheeks brush against the brisk air that it's really hypocritical, that the doors should open onto a dead end rather than a set of stairs. As she climbs deliberate brisk heel crushing the beggar woman's fingers. She smiles to herself hearing the screams, belched insults temporarily covering sidewalk brouhaha. She crosses the street closing off her face, awkward shield against vulgarly visible lust, she buttons her coat knowing it's useless, against being whipped by sexist remarks the whole way the Paris Water Company could better serve the area by dispensing bromine. She hardens her gaze, sharpens it as best she can. At the third dirty smile combined with priapismic remarks powerlessness frozen her heart and nerves turned to cement. Séraphine could never tolerate without stumbling because Séraphine could never understand the rite. If their poor brains stimuli seethe that's their problem. But when their lips start to move, verbalizing reflections, ejaculating comments is more of a mystery. Sometimes Séraphine thinks that Solanas must have once spent a Right Bank vacation in France, and that it was on her street that the idea, necessary as it was, of the *Scum Manifesto* came to her.

Rue Jean-Pierre Timbaud unfolds canker tongue, Séraphine constantly collides with its acerbity, spongy little pus balls that make her shoes sticky. She's been its prisoner for six years now. Six years she's been the nice Parisian-staged-socia-fracture hostage. Two types of specimens: women who wear their mental excision on their heads or those who wear charming post-hippie skirts over their jeans. Men in jellabas or aviator jackets quizzical around cleavages no matter the season, or their iPod snuggled in the pocket of their vintage camo jacket letting the wind rush through their tousled-by-design hair. Rue Jean-Pierre Timbaud twin of rue Oberkampf, cross street rue Saint-Maur. Corner of Timbaud Saint-Maur a bakery with inedible bread, a ventilation grate where the dregs of one or two homeless people sleep, corner of Oberkamf Saint-Maur a wild café reeking of hipness, parking for two-wheeled vehicles, where fifteen or so wounded scooters and motorcycles stretch out like they've been skewered. Séraphine notices that every day such contact with the outside makes her skin oxidize. She blames neither the times, fatigue, or pollution. She owes the frayedness of her skin, she knows, to the opposing flows squaring off from incompatible little islands.

Rue Saint-Maur crosses two areas that Séraphine sees as contradictory, when she reads novels about past and future civil wars Séraphine often imagines that fire and jugulars will first be opened on rue Saint-Maur. When she says Saint-Maur she expects a final silent e since in most cases tragic irony wields onomastics as a weapon but no not at all, Séraphine looked it up, the name was inherited from the ancient hamlet of Saint-Mor, Séraphine found out that from the eleventh to the nineteenth century it was a cemetery, Séraphine collided, place reserved for the plague stricken during the Middle Ages, it was assigned to both Jews and Huguenots, Séraphine got all the details: even today rue Saint-Maur deeds of sale still stipulate that *any bones that are found must be placed in an appropriate wooden box and taken to the Cimetière Monumental.* Séraphine thinks about all the bones in the bodies she passes by every day, all these bodies that live in indecently eroded wooden boxes, Séraphine lives in a cemetery, her dread is monumental.

From Couronnes, behind her back, poverty tumbles down rue Jean-Pierre Timbaud before it dissolves as it meets avenue Parmentier, preserving the next parcel, purified in a gentle slope that ends up scoured, a tuft of trees and a thicket confirms its germination. Rue Oberkamf, on the right, the Colette-dressed microbourgeoisie, held up as right-thinking but oozing shamelessness, praising how picturesque the situation is. Séraphine counts all the as-they-says. The microbourgeoisie was still small before bohemian became a popular style. They say *cosmopolitan, nice, reasonable, lively*, even worse: *working-class*. Séraphine translates. They think *immigrants, overcrowded, majority bankruptcy protection, teeming*, even worse: *poverty*. Every day Séraphine sees the microbourgeoisie come hang out with the destitute. It's not unusual to hear as evening arrives a few complaints about the scarcity of good restaurants. The microbourgeoisie that bloats the Right Bank lives here like third-world tourists, unable to assume their middle-class status because they're too hip, too intellectual. It's better to be envied than pitied Grandpa Pithiviers always used to say. At the Parmentier McDonald's, Séraphine is surprised that the admen and the like pull out their gold cards without someone paying in change ever rising up out of the line to go for their throat. Rue Jean-Pierre Timbaud is a haven for betting parlors where the over-term drink their compensation to forget their life and its for-rent sign. At Oberkampf at worst, the out-of-work are occasional. If you want to like this neighborhood you have to know how to really enjoy the show.

Farther up, toward Belleville, the streets don't do quite so many cartwheels, no cramps or sore muscles, a vague downward spiral, with some cohesion. Séraphine is still on her guard though: the microbourgeoisie is capable of anything in the art of camouflage. I.e., a woman she knows who likes to go on and on about Guerrisold particularly when she's perched atop her Pradas. Séraphine doesn't really know Paris very well, only people who've moved from other parts of France and a few natives who have visited from top to bottom. People who used to live in the suburbs don't bother to, they settle for living there. All Séraphine knows about this capital is that she doesn't like the people and that before long they'll return the sentiment. All Séraphine knows about the capital is that her address oozes sociological weakness.

Séraphine Derdega, 55 bis rue Jean-Pierre Timbaud, special delivery, Triangle of the Hydra.

Christian was barely out the door of the Montparnasse apartment before Séraphine changed the furniture around, emptied two closets, and swiftly pared down the décor in each room, Laurent being a minimalist. She filled the fridge with enjoyable foods, threw away her antediluvian pajamas, and bought herself the appropriate nightwear for a young woman, then waited. With a childhood friend Laurent shared a scrawny two-bedroom place on rue Corentin Cariou, he gave her to understand that it would take a few months for him to announce his abandonment. Faced with the empty closet after scores of trimesters Séraphine began to grow impatient. Laurent invited her on a trip, and at the top of the tower looking down on Chicago he said: see, this is where we'll get engaged. She stuffed the fridge with luxury foods, threw away all her old jeans, and clothed herself in femme fatale, then waited. Laurent shared with a childhood friend now also a business partner a redecorated two-bedroom place on rue Corentin Cariou, he ordered her to understand that it would take him a few months to announce his desertion. Faced with the empty closet after scores of semesters Séraphine started to get pretty annoyed. Laurent invited her to go away for a weekend, and at sunset on the cliffs of Brittany he said: the weather will be nice when we get engaged. She put nothing in the fridge, this budgetary item being on the verge of elimination in favor of the rent money (1,245 euros) which she's been paying on her own despite Laurent's promises, then waited. Laurent shared with a childhood friend now also twice a double business partner a cozy two-bedroom place on rue Corentin Cariou, he announced Séraphine it will take me months maybe even years I'm afraid I don't understand but I love you you know I'm afraid I dread it but if I can't with you you see that means with others it won't happen either, let's say even less of a chance. Faced with the closet full of capitulations, Séraphine hoped for patience-wrapped consolation prize in her new mold-covered apartment (375 sq. ft., 650 euros), then waited. She hoped for finally reliable committing Laurent, sometimes boys need so much time. She waited six years. And.

The dates, said Abdu, are sweet these are too sweet I think, I'd rather warn you. Séraphine is warned. It happened at the Stalingrad station, the connection between Lines 7 and 2. She didn't ask for anything and she'd been warned. In her body the autopilot glitched, six years three weeks five days how many hours, Séraphine certainly saw, connection, the elegant old woman stooped over without teeth bags overflowing with Gourmet Croquettes, the old woman with no wedding ring cats and stale bread, no love and no water her heart a salt cellar crackling swamp antechamber, sitting on the bench yet elegant stooped over with no teeth the old woman was sucking on dried fruit.

The number of places in her neighborhood that Séraphine deems pleasant: three. The regular food store; the exotic food store; the Other Café. Opposite sidewalk twenty-two steps to the left; opposite sidewalk fifteen steps straight ahead; opposite sidewalk thirty steps to the right. Exotic food store Abdu gives her credit at least once a month. Séraphine consumes almost exclusively products sold by Abdu, cooked by his wife in most cases. Séraphine often feels like she's eating at the same table with Abdu and his wife, that she says thank you Mrs. Abdu what delicious taramosalata. So the dates are okay, but try the apricots instead. With her hand, still a wedding band virgin, Séraphine touches the bags. Séraphine already has a cat she named Bonjour because of Françoise Sagan. Séraphine thinks I'm thirty-eight and asks Abdu for a good kilo of each and three pounds of homemade shortbread cookies.

Laurent isn't looking for pretexts. Not at all. Laurent told Séraphine cast back out into the wind: be happier. Now Séraphine understands though a little late that. Adult responsibility and commitment, never-never land's necrotic breasts. Laurent isn't looking didn't look won't look for pretexts. He'll turn away from night-light insomnia, completely crinoline free. There are sacrifices that are impossible for young men and among them are pinches of magic powder concocted by Tinker-bell. Yet it's more of the *happy thought* that helps with takeoff than any placebo fairy dust, but for all these lost children it will constitute the ultimate renunciation.

Séraphine doesn't sleep during the day anymore and each one of the

Hydra's heads waves outside her window. Their yellow eyes weigh her up through the glass, Séraphine doesn't air the place out anymore, the last time she opened the window two of them suddenly loomed, scaly monstrous, venom pearling thick at the tip of their pointy fangs, she still has a suspicious scar on her wrist. Séraphine doesn't sleep during the day anymore, all day long she waits for a sign from Laurent, her cell phone and landline side by side on the desk, blisters on her thin fingers from pressing the send/receive button on her answering machine. Her heart often leaps when she sees new messages loading, her aorta cracks once she gets them. Disappointment strikes to the point of cardiac attack, how many have died of spam, the WHO should investigate.

Séraphine once loathed the daytime, now she endures light, agitation, so much life outside, such *working-class* life, Séraphine observes the bodies be they misery crushed or gloating proud when microbourgeois, she imagines their names and their apartments, their relationships and knows she's been banished, the worst of the worst of the worst, now Séraphine inspires more pity than envy really no envy at all. For three solid hours she surrenders and sleep gets hold of her, sale-price sleep, good enough for the worst of the worst of the worst, blank, arid sleep bereft of paradox. When she wakes up Séraphine thinks she'll pick up her sobbing right where she left it, unaware that her tears don't stop when she's sleeping.

Séraphine doesn't sleep at night, Séraphine's nights aren't made for that now Séraphine cries at night too, Séraphine is always crying and she isn't working. Night is familiar, Séraphine gets a better grip on herself, she still cries, of course, but for different reasons. By about 1:00 a.m. she stops waiting for Laurent. She says I left him because it wasn't going anywhere, I'm beyond the age of going out with a boy right I'm at the age of living with a man right or even marrying him and having children and a little yard a gravel driveway a little fireplace right but her logorrhea anvil exhausted cat doesn't even condescend to offer a little meow of agreement.

Once every three days Séraphine takes her chances on the Hydra's cold skin, braving the state of siege seven minutes thirty seconds.

Right hand on the doorknob, the left loaded with garbage bags, her lungs gorge themselves hesitant. Door slammed, four floors, ground floor garbage room mailbox, release button opened door. Thirty feet to the left tobacconist's four packs of Marlboros, cross over to Abdu's pita meze cookies yogurt crackers soda back. Once the bolt is slid uncontrollable ritual. Getting back her breath, bags lifeless on the floor. Methodically put away in the little cupboard, three shelves, divide by kind, subdivide by size, align in the refrigerator, dairy on top, in the middle salty and fatty, on the bottom sweet and fatty, jams in the vegetable drawer. Snuggle up in the pink blanket, turn on the TV. Three cigarettes then prepare the tray. Put the toaster on a stool, choose the food in order and lay it out on the coffee table. Spread on bread chew cut fork chomp swallow swallow swallow. Operation can be repeated until the stomach threatens overflow.

Séraphine withdraws, isolation exacerbates the tiniest little environment-linked detail. And everything is hostile toward her. Outside inside neighborhood apartment everything is a frontal assault. The paint peeling from the bathroom walls slaps her every morning with its fragile residue. A cloud of insects, gnats maybe or minuscule creepy-crawlies, abandoning their corpses along the baseboard as soon as springtime comes busting out all over. A humidity halo wound oozes around cracks, even though the heat's up full blast the sheets in winter are cold, soaking beneath the comforter in the stagnant dew from the wall on the left. The torturous days decline, strangling from eyelids' opening, the mailbox is holding back or swallowing up the latent checks, the washing machine is giving up the ghost, the windows are chipping, the leaks are multiplying in rancid drops, the circuit breaker is capricious, the stove plucks out its own eye.

With every new attack, sometimes several in a day, Séraphine remembers how normal life was in Montparnasse even if it wasn't full. And while her wash soaks in the slow bathtub swamp, Séraphine needs to find the guilty party, Séraphine needs the heads of those responsible, nice round heads, full like juicy melons that she can give a quick slice to and then chop up brutally grabbing the knife handle.

The Hydra roars loudly at the bottom of the four flights, those close to Séraphine talk about the traffic but Séraphine knows they've already gone through the Hydra, swallowed up by the beast, walking around in its belly without even knowing it, coming out sticky with gastric juices for a few hours in the shabby fourth-floor bastion before diving back into the gaping mouth once they're on the other side of the building door, from up at her window Séraphine sees them calmly step inside she sees them, warns them, but her sharp cries are only answered with laughter and moving shapes encased in scales, looking like Saint-Exupéry's elephant-swallowed-by-the-snake hat.

Séraphine needs the heads of those responsible, she often imagines herself decapitating Laurent from up at her window, seeing his juicy melon snatched midair by the Hydra, she very distinctly hears the cracking of the bones, the chewing of the Hydra taking furious delight in the inestimable freshness of the stuffed treat, jackhammer ivory hard onomatopoeias, Séraphine observes the teeth of the Hydra moistened with the blood of the one responsible, sees the cause devoured by its own consequences, guilty Laurent screaming, Laurent torn to pieces, Laurent the primary source of Séraphine's woes but how many others afterward wonders Séraphine needing more, more heads, more secondary heads, more minor heads, down to the least little silhouette Séraphine wants to exterminate all those responsible and everyone the hat fits.

Séraphine cries a little and throws up more often. Sometimes her solfège sobbing or restitutions (30%–50% of the initial quantity) echo in the tiny, absolutely moldy apartment. She resorts to a delivery service to avoid having to cross at the Hydra. She says smothered will be my love for Laurent under my new flab, crushed will be my regrets for the wasted years between the quintal folds of my heavy hanging flesh. As she eats, every time, she repeats it. Ripping from me this defeated love pestilent corps, ejecting through my mouth this aborted love, I'm vomiting you up Laurent along my tongue you slide it doesn't hold you back, it flattens out curves it participates active in the final extraction, you taste like sugar and sour tzatziki Laurent, all throughout her sanitation operation Séraphine keeps repeating this.

What comes out of the kneeling body is more and more carb bloated. Crystallized Séraphine's rage comes out little by little. The head of each of the responsible parties is to be uprooted with a sweep of teeth, the Hydra's twitching organs are in the big honey pastries, biting them, chewing them passionately, saying I'm dying from their duplicity the sweets are lead poisoning, my life is nauseating waste. Until the age of thirty-one Séraphine daughter of Azzâm seven veils legacy and suddenly nothing after the rift, Séraphine vigorously hates the ostentatious signs she previously believed circulated in her corpuscles, Derdega the last, the last of the least, she so wanted to deny Azzâm's existence, refute the lie, believe her mother wasn't that stupid, stupid and devastated what had gotten into her head cutting off the heads of the guilty what had gotten into her head pistachio and peanut brain sauce.

To erase it all Séraphine would need every trace, every last trace, of her so-called father to be eliminated. But everything in the neighborhood reminds her of him, the formula written on her neuron slate, Azzâm is composed of Arabness cubed plus violence squared, to erase Azzâm both elements must be wiped off. Séraphine really wants to soak the sponge in pure bleach, no more Azzâm no more completely crazy mother, no more past and no more mistake, no more Laurent, no more aporia, no more shameless regression, no more 55 bis rue Jean-Pierre Timbaud, no more Hydra. Séraphine would like to run away, coming back with arms full from the halal pizzeria she often wonders if through excess she's using to excess to try to provoke in herself a point of no return.

Séraphine cries a lot, and throws up a great deal. Sometimes the cost of the orgies swipes a good portion of her salary (65%–80% of the initial amount), the foods pile up only to be turned into a memory upon unwrapping in the small and absolutely moldy apartment. Séraphine is a mouth and a mucus bag of muscles forcefully to-ing and fro-ing. Séraphine has a body made of anxiety, anxiety that feeds on everything, including cracks in walls, overflowing trash cans, and everything she knows she'll never have. Séraphine ignorant of her identity, Séraphine disgusted by baklava lies, Séraphine fertile in bitterness and icy anger.

If I'd known sooner not a Derdega I would've chosen my men so differently, cursed be the hand that strikes the horn of a gazelle, if my mother's choice had been another in the past no Azzâm no beatings no fear of cloning him no uterine disgust, no virus-borne obsession, no couple home, no Laurent in my territory, no raging depression, no residence degeneration, no lease on 375 square feet. Séraphine's stretch-marked skin drained swamp is becoming porous as her heart is deserted. The bitterness of her skull has made it its home, her soul didn't have the time to feel too vulnerable, promptly stunted by the venom saber. Hatred is in her fossilized honey star bosom.

Séraphine now knows she is also pregnant by the Hydra, she's the scarlet handmaid of rue Jean-Pierre Timbaud, she knows she's enveloped by the Hydra's membrane, final phase domino consequences. Stuck inside the Hydra, she feeds on it so each night she can bring it back up, immediately dissolved lumps in Golem, fortified in this alchemy, consolidated by the addition of amino acids, Séraphine knows she's related, she's feeding the Matrix too, like others she produces the requested energy, the energy that's needed to keep the Hydra's greedy robust body going, she's one of the Hydra's cells, a minuscule part, a handful of molecules, crafty whipped deficiency instability malady grudge hypocrite Séraphine is a silver scale on the Hydra. She hates the way it breathes, ramified cruelty pulmonary alveoli, malice mixed with carbon oxide. After observing the Hydra for too long Séraphine crossed its rancid yellow gaze which in men freezes both hope and lifeblood determination. Séraphine belongs to the Hydra and she's hungry for heads compulsive eating is always the lair of resentment.

# Mrs. White in the Lounge with the Lead Pipe

Séraphine is stationed behind the Hydra's eyes. The view is better, she likes it better here than at the entrance to one of the gills or at the angle of the nostrils. Séraphine has a hard time tolerating the noise and the smell. Séraphine has a hard time tolerating just about everything now. Behind the Hydra's eyes, Séraphine breathes the glass so it's easier to wipe off. An unobstructed view is a requirement if you want to detect the tiniest prey from a great distance. And as for prey, Séraphine is constantly picking them out, she's constantly fidgeting all over the place behind the Hydra's iris, her movements cast shadows in its throbbing yellow. Crates of juicy, responsible melons are what's needed to feed the animal, Séraphine thinks to herself that someday the Hydra will swell up so much that even all of Paris won't be enough, it will be known that the Hydra was born in an ancient cemetery, from her egg to the chalk of her opaque shell watered with dry pestis bacillus Yersinia blood and paupers, Séraphine says to herself that someday since she's positioned behind the Hydra's eyes she'll be able to attend the purifying meal composed of neighbors' neighbors, cousins' neighbors, cousins' cousins, brothers' cousins, and finally headless brothers. Séraphine inhales deeply every day to increase its volume, she fills it with what she can, words, syllogisms, buttressed thoughts, everything she can think of as quick as possible, urban legends, rumors, votes, belief in an opinion.

We'll never hear Séraphine's voice. Because her voice has seized the soil that denies by rights, drinks nothing but blood, and calls itself French. We'll never hear it here, there's no point in continuing the hearings. Poujadist venom is what makes her become Dr. Black's executioner. Second-degree murder Séraphine Dergeda guilty involuntary manslaughter, she killed Dr. Black by repeatedly hitting him with studded shoes.

The people whose gowns tie in the back don't even listen to Séraphine anymore. Piera Aulagnier Wing she wanders alone for eternity, her eyes having become the Hydra's swooping down on everything in her path, her gaze is even more feared than Basilisk Slytherin's: it's known to be contagious, no one wants to catch it.

# Hall

(Deserted)

# Third Officer

Due to the strike action initiated by members of the *Not a Clue* staff, Miss Marple's talk has been canceled, even though she had been hired as the Third Officer. In accordance with the decisions made at the Annual General Meeting, we will share a communiqué from Étienne Lantier, the spokesman for the FCU, who has come along in support of the strikers.

We'd like to thank our readers in advance for their understanding and apologize for any inconvenience.

**Fictional Characters' Union**

**Central Committee**

**Enough is enough!**

As far back as page 36, and on more than occasion, the Omniscient Narratrix has overstepped her role and her rights. Abusing the power bestowed upon her, she's accrued interruption after interruption, upsetting the plot, dispossessing the fictional characters of their work, and thereby going against general interests.

**No!**

We cannot tolerate such behavior within this novel and refuse to pick the plot back up, for as long as the Omniscient Narratrix continues with this intrusive policy.

**Stop!**

The increasing occurrence of such activity, as witnessed in our field with every new publishing season, is contributing to a noticeable decline in our working conditions. The increased number of positions exists simply for reasons of productivity, but without any respect for the personnel. The premises forced upon us are no longer up to the security standards established in the beginning chapters, which has led to a worrying increase in workplace accidents. Our roles are increasingly imprecise, our psychological structures rushed, our defining characteristics uncertain, as is true for the future of our profession. Our speech patterns are being standardized, soon we'll be nothing more than simple interchangeable commodities. Moreover, allowing the Omniscient Narratrix to dispossess us of our initially allocated space and seeing her accumulate overtime hours that were never part of the collective agreement is intolerable for us.

**That's it!**

The Omniscient Narratrix's behavior can easily be described as psychological harassment. We'd like to remind you that psychological harassment consists of "repeated offensive behavior whose character—be it vexatious, humiliating, or detrimental to one's dignity—prevents its victim from completing his or her work." Most fictional characters, both primary and secondary, having worked herein with the Omniscient Narratrix, confide that they've felt undermined, diminished, and weakened by her machinations. As the large number of doctor's notes confirm, our ridiculed comrades' mental health has indeed been affected. We have therefore decided to initiate legal proceedings against the Omniscient Narratrix and are hopeful that the case will set a precedent. There are already enough martyrs in our Union, we must remain vigilant!

**Take action!**

The entire staff of *Not a Clue* must show solidarity against management's excesses.

With this petition, open to all fictional characters concerned with preserving their rights, we intend to show our determination in the fight against our position's precarious future.

**We will not accept managerial sabotage. We demand immediate regulation of the narrative flow and complete freedom of action in this book.**

# Dining Room

They always serve us potatoes on purpose can I sit here potatoes aren't a problem in and of themselves Jacques chews like a pig with his mouth always open I can't sit across from him you can eat potatoes next time I'll end up hitting him or throwing up the stuff we have to eat see it's the sauce Séraphine took all the bread there's no seconds because they make the gravy with the water they were cooked in such a pain in the ass to be at her table she only thinks of herself the fat bitch you know why Aline's the one who gets to me because since she supposedly has to taste everything she's always eating off everyone's plate because the water the potatoes were cooked in was used as a weed killer out in the country it's kind of an easy excuse especially at dessert time it's an old farmer's trick can I have another spoonful they say we have crabgrass in our head Mathias took mine to play the castanets see our brains are full of sharp weeds I want my Tercian pill right away tall weeds that's right Mrs. Johnson you're wearing your dresses way too high that grow any old way it's well-known you're not eating your yogurt them they don't like the any old way Stanislas I'm talking to you you're not eating your yogurt that let her admit it out loud they want to pull up the weeds slice into our brains so they say can I have your yogurt Mrs. Johnson you're wearing your dresses way too high Mrs. Babeth I want my Tercian right away they want to get rid of our weeds whatever it takes because in her opinion being naked is her nicest outfit they're really smart and the medication on top of it isn't there any way to shut up the bald woman they want us to eat the water the potatoes were cooked in I'm leaving tomorrow for sure attacking the disease on all sides with psychotropics and 100 percent organic treatment Marc will you give me a cigarette I'm finishing my applesauce outside no way I'm going to be their guinea pig can't give them the satisfaction so I never have any gravy.

# Fourth Officer

SIMCITY, 34 SIMSIAL 2004

*Dear Omniscient Narratrix,*

*I've received your proposal, and have studied it with great attention. Even if job offers are extremely rare, especially in my chosen field, I am afraid I'll have to decline yours.*

*As you already know, over and over again I've refused to compromise myself in a novel, believing them to be confining and structurally alienating. I left Somnabulia with this one condition, temporarily appearing in a body that was sufficiently uncomfortable to draw the necessary conclusions, and, strengthened by this gruesome experience, have been living for the last six months Outside Time in a video game. Life here is much more exciting than in a book, I'm not under the yoke of an imposed plot nor of narrative contingencies that make the lives of fictional characters such a nightmare, as we all know. Literature, just like real life, is incapable of definitively establishing a fulfilling place to live. My status means I should join you in* Not a Clue, *both out of solidarity and out of respect for your superior status. But I am unable to convince myself that my participation would be sound and even less inclined to subject myself to such a sacrifice.*

*I'm familiar with the book and understand you concerns and your needs. If I may, I'd like to share my own opinion: with or without me, it doesn't matter, you won't succeed. The space is quite large, you're right, the rooms numerous and well laid out, it's possible to move around freely, it's open, pleasant. The major drawback with the place isn't, despite what I thought at first, it's architecture. Even though the ceiling is a little too high for my preference for a constant temperature, and the walls, as cracked as they are, point to an impending collapse. No, I could accept the place in itself. That's not where the problem is.*

*The problem, prosaically, relates to the inhabitants. I won't be so hypocritical as to describe the Sims as a divinely friendly and enriching community, with a particular liking for cultural exchange. The Sims, I won't pretend otherwise, are often bewildering, not to mention downright awful, with their pixels animated as they are by a market-oriented system. Yet, compared to* Not a Clue's *tenants, these beings seem absolutely delightful. I spent a good deal of time on it, but I really don't see how, even with the firmest of resolves, I could tolerate the flock you're responsible for. And certainly not how I could possibly interfere. You took on a ridiculous project, nobody but an omniscient narratrix would ever do such a thing, and despite my deep respect for you, it is my duty to open your eyes right here and now.*

*No mentally healthy person, not a one, could want to spend any time, not even a little bit, with the characters you hired. Not only are they pathetic, worthless, and exhausting in their mediocrity, but their cowardice is unacceptable. Even though you promise me I wouldn't be with them very much, in the course of one chapter and in the final scene, the very idea of being in the presence of such rejects makes me nauseous.*

*You tell me you've lost the plot, that despite its rigidity the structure's no longer containing the overflow, that even Dr. Black is whispering to you that he's disconcerted by the turn of events, how disgusting he finds this flood of horrors. All this was highly predictable. You're the hostage of a book that talks about nothing but everyday filth, common tipping points, unspeakable weakness, bastard Faustishness. How could you expect not to get dirty when it all overflowed?*

*You whisper to me how isolated you are, the annoying repercussions of your overzealousness, the humiliating mutiny you recently bore the consequences of. While I'm deeply touched, because I know how very sensitive your heart is and can easily imagine the torment crushing it,*

*I know my presence will do nothing but make this absurd, distressing situation even worse. Diplomacy is not one of my crown jewels, and yesterday as I thought leaning against the bar at Le Vieux Loup de mer—which is famous for its gourmet meals and Polish queues—about what I'd do when confronted with my dear colleagues, the only idea that crossed my mind was murder. Killing a Sim is easy: drowning, starvation, or carbonization. It's not much more arduous with fictional characters. There's a bigger choice and it's a lot more fun. Why not lighten up your plot by taking an ax to some of the paragraphs? It's completely under your control. Bring back order, however you would like. Why burden yourself with all these useless beings? Their blood is hardly even ink, they're so human, they're not like us, get rid of them.*

*Sell them in an auction, on eBay you can find all kinds of directors that put a price on parts in their next movie. I'd be curious to see what a fictional character is worth, in euros or dollars. Take the six of them in order and turn the weapon they used in their crime back on them. They've got it coming, and that's what they're there for. Pile them up in a closet somewhere, call in Lagarigue and Dr. Black and have them play Scrabble, it'll be less tiring. I'm no good at endings, that's not my job, I'm not a storyteller. But you really should face it, it would be a lot simpler, knock them all off, and let's be done with it. No matter what you try, the novel's going to be shaky, it doesn't hold up, let it go, pack your bags, apply for some other jobs, transfer to a Japanese video game, their RPGS use people like you, they're preparing the next Final Fantasy now, I could give you a recommendation.*

*I really do hope you'll understand my position, and that you'll be able to find a way out of this sticky situation, despite my defection.*

*Sincerely,*
*Chloé Delaume*

# Colonel Mustard

It'll be okay. I can manage on my own. Finally manage on my own here
and now, above all. It might seem strange but I think I had to end up
here in order to be able to act. Finally act, do something let's say, let's
not go too far either. Act is a little strong, a little too strong for me.
I've always hated exaggeration. Well hated I'm exaggerating. Exactly.
I never really hated anything. I don't really care for it, let's say. I don't
really care for things or I like them, generally and even always that's
where I sit, I've never understood how some people can get so carried
away one way or the other. First, it seems really tiring. And pointless
too, above all really pointless. Loving or just liking in concrete terms
what does it change. For the better I mean. It doesn't make much any
better as far as the people who get excited are concerned. It doesn't
mean they own it or have better access, they just get all worked up for
nothing. Well, that's what I think. Or rather I assume, I wouldn't be
that categorical, let's say I assume that they get worked up for nothing.
There. That never happens to me, getting worked up for nothing or even
just getting worked up period so I don't really know. I have no opinion.
    Generally speaking I have no opinion. It's been going on for a long
time. Well, for a long time, I don't know. If it's been going on for a
long time, that means there was another state before, that a new one
took its place and that it's been like that ever since. I don't remember
a before. I haven't had an opinion in forever. I think it's structural.
Can you say describe a structural state as going on for a long time,

I don't know. I haven't ever had an opinion since I was born. About anything. That means it's been going on for longer than a long time then. Oh well, I just said it without thinking.

Although I know why I've been in the Piera Aulagnier Wing for the last year and a half, I have no idea what I'm doing in the Study. I was quietly smoking a Craven, I was listening to the redheaded girl talking to the bulimic girl in Room 19, and then all of a sudden I didn't know what was going on. I waited quite a while, somebody said it was my turn, I don't see I mean I really don't see what I'm doing here.

They decided I had to manage on my own, I've got nothing against it, but it really is a pain that it's happening to me. I didn't really hear the ones who already played because the rooms were too far away but I thought I understood that they had done some things. Serious things I mean. Dr. Black's voice rang out really loudly at one point, he seemed really wound up. I don't feel like I did anything to justify my presence in the game, actually, I don't feel like I did anything at all period. I've never done anything my whole life honestly, never budged, never said a thing and on top of that I pay my taxes. I think it's just a mistake. I'm the victim of an injustice, I'm appearing in a trial in which I should be called Joseph. I have to manage on my own, if I had something to blame myself for it would be a lot easier. It would be a help to me to have the Omniscient Narratrix around right now, she'd know how to tell a bunch of really meaningful anecdotes, put her finger on my hypothetical embezzling, direct me so I could take the floor after the introduction scene. But since I have to do it without her I'll just have to find a way.

So.

My name is Stanislas Courtin. I'm forty-seven years old. I'm an only child, I was raised and loved outside Limoges, my parents are going to die soon but since it's perfectly logical and we've been expecting it for a few years, I won't be that sad. Well that's what I think. My father was a doctor and my mother a nurse, which explains why my bronchitis was always raging and treated with aspirin. I went to college. And I stayed. For a long time. I didn't have much else to do besides study and since I already didn't have an opinion on anything I tried a little of everything while I waited to find out. In the end I didn't find out anything. I'm not even sure there is anything to find out anyway.

I went into the civil service. It seemed like a good thing to me, going into civil service because civil service doesn't mean anything. My work didn't mean anything either. I still haven't figured out what it was. I was asked to do calculations, compare different columns of numbers, integrate data, and fill in files that didn't have names just numbers. And letters too. Often in front of the numbers. XK004-02, for example. I was calm, I did what I was asked, I never had anything to say to people or about anything, that's what I was paid for, so it worked out well.

I've only known one woman. Her name was Marie-Laure. She stayed for a year or something like that. Maybe a little less. We didn't do much, but that suited me just fine. And then she ended up with these completely ridiculous ideas, she wanted to talk, go to restaurants, talk at restaurants, take me to see movies so we could discuss them afterward. I was interested in making love, but after a while I didn't feel like it anymore because of Marie-Laure. She'd try things just to get me to put what I liked in order, number what I liked best from one to ten. Before every date I'd take two Tranxene tablets to be sure she'd leave me alone. She left me thinking I was narcoleptic.

I live on the Île Saint-Louis in Paris because it's convenient. I need a central location because I get transferred a lot, well I used to, for the past year and half I haven't been going to work but I'm still really proud that I chose a neutral address, between the Left Bank and the Right Bank, no need to decide anything. Sometimes I go back home, soon it'll be three months since I've gone out but when I see the doctor at the hospital I find it very comfortable to be in the center in the morning, in the south in the afternoon, and to wander around in the evening in any direction and then wind up back where I started, which is just as central as when I got up. Living in the middle gives me the feeling that I haven't moved at all. It's too bad Paris is some kind of whore and not a Big Apple. Every new day I would've really liked to say I live in a seed, apple seeds are tiny, smooth, and charming. New Yorkers are lucky, they don't even know it. It's really easy for them to figure out what the center of their city is like, but for a Parisian it's a lot more complicated. The center of a kind of a whore, except for the belly button I don't get it. Actually, I live on a hernia.

With different elections I was transferred to different departments, nothing really changed for me except how long it took me to get there. As for my work, it remained unchanging, calculation registration confirmation. I confirmed things but I wasn't really the one who did it. The results did it. The results confirmed. The results I got allowed me to confirm or not. It's not very interesting, and I'm not explaining it very well, I'm not used to doing that, I never had to explain anything, I don't really know how to, that must be a different profession. Instead I'll answer Proust's questionnaire. Yeah, I'll do that. Proust's questionnaire lets you get the best idea of a character's profile, it's a least as good as the Omniscient Narratrix's dime store psychology, after all.

**My favorite virtue**
Patience and especially her daughter

**My character's defining trait**
Its absence

**What I prefer in men**
Calmness

**What I prefer in women**
Discretion

**My worst point**
Absence

**My best point**
I am the silence of the sea

**What I like best about my friends**
That we're still in touch

**How I prefer to spend my time**
I don't prefer

**My idea of happiness**
To be a dreamless sleep

**What would make me unhappiest**
Having to go through with the next two chapters on my own

**Who I'd like to be besides myself**
Something more than someone

**Where I'd like to live**
In Switzerland

**My favorite color**
White

**My favorite flower**
Sainfoin (*Onobrychis sativa*)

**My favorite bird**
Flightless

**My favorite prose authors**
Albert Camus and Jean-Paul Sartre when he was working on *No Exit*

**My favorite poets**
Christian Bobin

**My fictional heroes**
Bartleby and Garcin, each in his own way

**My favorite fictional heroines**
Her, because of Nevers

**My favorite composers**
John Cage

**My favorite painters**
Bernard Buffet and Botero

**My real-life heroes**
Like 34 percent of the French population, I'll say David Douillet

**My favorite real-life heroines**
Maybe Bernadette Chirac since she's very brave and managed to stay down-to-earth

**My historical heroes**
Albert Deshousse

**My favorite things to eat and drink**
Shepherd's pie and café au lait

**What I hate most of all**
I'm not too fond of people who shout

**The historical figure I don't like**
Robespierre

**The historical facts I look down on most**
The Russian Campaign and May '68

**The military fact I appreciate the most**
The signing of the Armistice

**The reform I appreciate the most**
Thirty-five-hour workweek

**The natural gift I'd like the most to have**
The courage of birds

**How I'd like to die**
Somewhere besides in a book, if possible in bed

**My present state of mind**
Unexpected awareness

**The character flaw I'm most patient with**
Cowardice, and that's the problem

**My motto**
Slow and steady, I can't outrace.

# Colonel Mustard in the Billiard Room

I got sick when I was cleaning my teeth with a toothpick. I'm going to tell the story in the third person, if fictional characters talked about themselves in the third person then when the time came we would never really need an omniscient narratrix in fact. Right now I'm not doing such a bad job. I'll talk about myself in the third person, not out of any false sense of modesty or any crass self-centeredness but because he left himself. A long time ago now. Left so long ago and went so far, yes that's it, for such a long time it's been impossible for him to tame the sharp edges of the I.

There's no doubt about it, Stanislas is a coward: men of little faith have no right to say I. And when he says Stanislas, Stanislas and not I, Stanislas he not I, the I is all snuggled up in those three syllables. I an individuality deserter, I a deserter of my soul and conscious, I is a deserter Mr. President. And I knows that I can write only dead letters so feeble are its excuses and shameful its reasons.

He got sick cleaning his teeth with a toothpick then. Stanislas was at work, with the aid of dental floss and tiny pointed objects he'd been trying for several days to dislodge the foreign object insinuated between front teeth. Inside, hidden face, between the central and lateral incisors, a little speck of tartar, a tiny pebble, Stanislas observed it in the mirror in the restroom on his floor, Stanislas inserted into his mouth a metal wire formerly used as a paper clip to use as a lever, Stanislas heard the squeal the tool committed against the dentin. I've noticed that the Omniscient Narratrix has a thing for repetition. Finally, he got the better of the unwanted rock. A sharp snap, a tongue jab, and in the palm of his hand a plastery triangle. One cubic millimeter, not much at all, no, the thing that had been wounding his lump of flesh and its seventeen upset muscles really wasn't much at all. Grazing his gum as he carried out the extraction, Stanislas thought about everything that had slipped past his transit palate, everything that had participated in the mineral formation. A tartar triangle, a semiprecious stone, Stanislas stood there, speechless, in front of the sinks.

A tartar triangle, a fossilized trace of his life between two teeth. What foods, what liquids, what tall tales, what substances, what words too, especially what words and how many round-trips. Once the little rock was removed, a micro-draft below his lower lip. His jaw as it was in the beginning, in the beginning twenty years earlier, dentist visit free. Yet he didn't remember the space. The space constantly causing him tongue scrapes due to its newness. At his desk the triangle carefully wrapped in a blue handkerchief in his pocket Stanislas felt his tongue stupidly hit the sharp angle. His tongue required a period of adaptation, my tongue, thought Stanislas, has to get reoriented and find my former mouth's landmarks. Stanislas went home early and spent the whole night looking in the mirror: this means my mouth has changed.

Tartar is a deposit that collects on the teeth, its crystals are harder for those who dream of unchangingness. Under a globe, a little glass globe set upon a placemat, Stanislas placed the triangle he'd retrieved. Tartar is a deposit, an existential vestige, in twenty years I only lived one square millimeter, Stanislas kept repeating, squinting harder and harder.

Stanislas thought to himself I've never done anything and still the tartar proves that I'm corroding, that the outside is damaging me, that it's gotten into me, into me even though I set up an absolute policy of nonintervention. I'm the just a little bit. A little bit corroded I don't know if I want to have really truly been or not at all. I have no opinion on anything but this time I'm worried. Stanislas thought to himself when I've been laid out in the ground my dentition will still be intact, and still I don't want anything, I've never wanted anything, I was just an embryo when everything within me was already secreting too late, my mother gave birth resignation fetus.

He stopped going anywhere, especially to the office. He stared at the triangle, his life condensed, his life period his life nothing but a tartar fragment, sometimes he even thought about swallowing it to see if the scrawny memories could inhabit him as he digested. Over and over again he watched his condensed life his life period mental video twenty seconds all day long, every elastic day since he was constantly awake.

At first his regular doctor diagnosed a slight depression. He prescribed the usual Xanax Prozac Stilnox trio and didn't call Dr. Lagarigue until several months later. Several months later when his patient admitted he'd ground up some benzodiazepine pills so he could nasally ingest a little bit of the tartar that refused to be inhaled by itself.

# Colonel Mustard in the Billiard Room with the Revolver

There's no reason for me to be in the Billiard Room. My place is in the vestibule. Leave Dr. Black out of this, I can get started with Canto III on my own, I'm in shirt-sleeves my flesh encouraged harassing horseflies and wasps, I'm aware of your grievances and accusations. From the depths of the Archeron I join the passive mass of humanity, I am one of *those who have lost the good of the intellect.* Don't say anything to Dr. Black, don't say anything I can hear, my eardrums three shots Brigadier I know the role I now must play, on the record player *The Divine Comedy* is scratching along.

*The Vestibule of Cowards*, that's where I am, Dr. Black. I also finally know that you haven't left me, for a long time I fed my own pus to the ochre abscess that brought you down, when indifference is conspired spinelessness like mine indignity it changes blood into stagnant swampy water. I gangrened you more and more every year. I'm fully aware of all this. I am the fruit of a wall pierced by an eel, you hoped a crack would carry me away or get me to stand up, yes above all stand up, quickly stand up straight, but I didn't have the nerve for neck and spine to attempt the tiniest of movements.

I finished you off, but I didn't shoot. Once again, of course, I didn't act in any way.

III, 1–9

First shot

*Master, what is it that I hear?*

Second shot

*Who are these people so defeated by their pain?*

Third shot

*This miserable way is taken by the sorry souls of those who lived*
*without disgrace and without praise.*

Fourth shot

*They now commingle with the coward angels, the company of*
*those who were not rebels nor faithful to their God, but stood*
*apart.*

Fifth shot

*The heavens, that their beauty not be lessened, have cast them out,*
*nor will deep Hell receive them—even the wicked cannot glory*
*in them.*

Sixth shot

*What is it, master, that oppresses these souls, compelling them to*
*wail so loud?*

Seventh shot

*I shall tell you in a few words.*

Eighth shot

*Those who are here can place no hope in death, and their blind life*
*is so abject that they are envious of every other fate.*

Ninth shot

*The world will let no fame of theirs endure;*

Tenth shot

*both justice and compassion must disdain them.*

Eleventh shot

*Let us not talk of them,*

Twelfth shot

*but look, and pass.*

Twelve shots just like Garcin, you're dead tied to the post with me. I'm going to leave the room, my place isn't in the Billiard Room. I'm not going back to the smoking lounge either, I have no business there, I'm not one of them. I'm worse, I know. In the game there are secret passages and unknown trapdoors that go to the only place that suits me. I'll find them all right, I'll manage. I see twinned girls in blue dresses holding hands at the end of a long hallway. Maybe they can tell me the best.

# Passageway(s)

All work and no play makes Jack a dull boy All work and no play makes
Jack a dull boy All work and no play makes Jack a dull boy All work and
no play makes Jack a dull boy All work and no play makes Jack a dull
boy All work and no play makes Jack a dull boy All work and no play
makes Jack a dull boy All work and no play makes Jack a dull boy All
work and no play makes Jack a dull boy All work and no play makes Jack
a dull boy All work and no play makes Jack a dull boy All work and no
play makes Jack a dull boy All work and no play makes Jack a dull boy
All work and no play makes Jack a dull boy All work and no play makes
Jack a dull boy All work and no play makes Jack a dull boy All work and
no play makes Jack a dull boy All work and no play makes Jack a dull
boy All work and no play makes Jack a dull boy All work and no play
makes Jack a dull boy All work and no play makes Jack a dull boy All
work and no play makes Jack a dull boy All work and no play makes Jack
a dull boy All work and no play makes Jack a dull boy All work and no
play makes Jack a dull boy All work and no play makes Jack a dull boy
All work and no play makes Jack a dull boy All work and no play makes
Jack a dull boy All work and no play makes Jack a dull boy All work and
no play makes Jack a dull boy All work and no play makes Jack a dull
boy All work and no play makes Jack a dull boy All work and no play
makes Jack a dull boy All work and no play makes Jack a dull boy All
work and no play makes Jack a dull boy All work and no play makes Jack
a dull boy All work and no play makes Jack a dull boy All work and no

play makes Jack a dull boy All work and no play makes Jack a dull boy
All work and no play makes Jack a dull boy All work and no play makes
Jack a dull boy All work and no play makes Jack a dull boy All work and
no play makes Jack a dull boy All work and no play makes Jack a dull
boy All work and no play makes Jack a dull boy All work and no play
makes Jack a dull boy All work and no play makes Jack a dull boy All
work and no play makes Jack a dull boy All work and no play makes Jack
a dull boy All work and no play makes Jack a dull boy All work and no
play makes Jack a dull boy All work and no play makes Jack a dull boy
All work and no play makes Jack a dull boy All work and no play makes
Jack a dull boy All work and no play makes Jack a dull boy All work and
no play makes Jack a dull boy All work and no play makes Jack a dull
boy All work and no play makes Jack a dull boy All work and no play
makes Jack a dull boy All work and no play makes Jack a dull boy All
work and no play makes Jack a dull boy All work and no play makes Jack
a dull boy All work and no play makes Jack a dull boy All work and no
play makes Jack a dull boy All work and no play makes Jack a dull boy
All work and no play makes Jack a dull boy All work and no play makes
Jack a dull boy All work and no play makes Jack a dull boy All work and
no play makes Jack a dull boy All work and no play makes Jack a dull boy
All work and no play makes Jack a dull boy All work and no play makes
Jack a dull boy All work and no play makes Jack a dull boy All work and
no play makes Jack a dull boy All work and no play makes Jack a dull boy
All work and no play makes Jack a dull boy All work and no play makes
Jack a dull boy All work and no play makes Jack a dull boy All work and
no play makes Jack a dull boy All work and no play makes Jack a dull boy
All work and no play makes Jack a dull boy All work and no play makes
Jack a dull boy All work and no play makes Jack a dull boy All work and
no play makes Jack a dull boy All work and no play makes Jack a dull boy
All work and no play makes Jack a dull boy All work and no play makes
Jack a dull boy All work and no play makes Jack a dull boy All work and
no play makes Jack a dull boy All work and no play makes Jack a dull
boy All work and no play makes Jack a dull boy All work and no play
makes Jack a dull boy All work and no play makes Jack a dull boy All

PASSAGEWAY(S)

# Fifth Officer

I'm Number 324. I'm not that well-known. I'm not even known at all, as a matter of fact. There are numbers who've done better, who've made better breakthroughs, who even managed to become leaders. But not me, no such luck for me. It's not really my fault. In our world, the world of numbers, there's nothing you can to do increase your own notoriety. It's better not to be too ambitious, we're so dependent on others. We exist and well that's about it. It's not very exciting, I know. But on the other hand, we're very useful. At least there's that.

Being jealous, I've had that happen to me. It happens to all of us, or almost all of us. I'm in the majority. We're jealous of short numbers and the primes, that goes without saying. We've all dreamed of being zero. We would have loved carrying decimals and being crowned one day, then idolized because π. We secretly keep an eye out to be enthroned as bronze if golden is impossible, the result of a messiah-expected formula. We pretend because we are well aware that it's more than impossible. Especially for me, I'm not even round.

We are infinite, calculate randomness, and must all tolerate having ended up just a few steps away from a star. Our life is unfair. In most cases. I spend a lot of time inviting over my brothers just to be closer to a failed possibility. I can't accept that it's incalculable. Me, Number 324, I could've been who, one chance out of how many? Nobody asks numbers to pass a logic test. We're nothing but tools and I can dream if I want to.

We all appeared from the first one to the last because the last one does exist even if it's elastic. It's just that people's brains can't name it. I'm quite familiar with it. I can't tell you its name, no medium in your world can hold it completely. The incomplete is calculable, too, you know. Someday you'll be able to. I know it's planned. I know a lot of things, they say numbers are God's neurons.

Our popularity doesn't depend on us, ever. It's a result of world history and some of its disciples are what certain of us owe our distinction to. The ones with four digits are pretty lucky because they always go down in history in a familiar way. Some are even more privileged. 1,515 for example, not only born a palindrome, blood is what cloaked it in such finery. There was a time when I too was well-known. The year 324 is when Christianity became a state religion in the Roman Empire. That's not nothing, but nobody cares in the least. Eusebius of Nicomedia rejecting the theory of God-Christ in one was me too, but no one's interested. The Battles of Andrinopolis and of Scythopolis, Constantine I defeating Licinius, previous emperor of the East, imagine for a minute what it was like being Constantine I in. Never mind, I'll stop. Still, I was pretty happy at the time.

Having three digits is a serious handicap. It's pretty hard to become symbolic, I've seen jobs disappear, doled out to lesser ones or even to the more graceful. All things considered, in my class, 666 did the best.

I'm nobody's birthday. Four and six digits must have no idea of the immense loneliness that weighs on those like me. Who waits for me, begs for me, I don't even show up on lottery tickets, too long for roulette, too small for a blaze.

I'm a bastard number because I embody nothing.

Until recently just to give myself a little substitute confidence, I stooped to numerology. I'm 3 + 2 + 4 so 9 at the end of the day. The number 9 is really spoiled. Like all the ones that are in the Bible and all the mysteries recorded there. But 9 deserves to be famous, and even on its own it would've managed. That's why I can't get over it, I can't get over 666's incredible career, because of how handsome it is. I was so sure that 999 would be on the front page of the History of

Humanity, two myth-bent capital Hs. A Trinity of 9s should've made a mark. I don't understand people at all, I gave up on it from the start. That was a long time ago now.

The number 9 does have one particularity. If you multiply it by any number and add the digits that make up the answer, the sum is always equal to 9, except when you multiply by 0 but that doesn't count for us, for us 0 isn't even a number, it's more like an entity, a kind of genetically modified entity that uses us as doormat whenever it wants. We're very impressed by 9. It has fans among all the numbers, not only among its own variations. The number 9 stirs up controversies in our society. Some see it as a model of resistance, a mass of tenacity. Nothing can corrupt it or make it give in. They consider its endurance as a kind of sovereignty, recognize the performance as a speech act, a shared message, Solidarity Forever! distinctly voicelessly refuses the operation. Some think it's narcissistic, completely bogged down in the mirror phase. Others say that in fact 9 thinks it's fat and is actually anorexic. It subtly avoids multiplication to avoid gaining weight.

Personally, I like to watch it work.

$9 \times 1 = 9 => 9 + 0 = 9$

$9 \times 2 = 18 => 1 + 8 = 9$

$9 \times 3 = 27 => 2 + 7 = 9$

$9 \times 4 = 36 => 3 + 6 = 9$

$9 \times 5 = 45 => 4 + 5 = 9$

$9 \times 6 = 54 => 5 + 4 = 9$

$9 \times 7 = 63 => 6 + 3 = 9$

$9 \times 8 = 72 => 7 + 2 = 9$

$9 \times 9 = 81 => 8 + 1 = 9$

$9 \times 10 = 90 => 9 + 0 = 9$

$9 \times 11 = 99 => 9 + 9 = 81 => 8 + 1 = 9$

$9 \times me = 2{,}961 => 2 + 9 + 6 + 1 = 18 => 1 + 8 = 9$

$9 \times 4{,}000 = 36{,}000 => 3 + 6 + 0 + 0 + 0 = 9$

I'm number 324 and no one pleads with me. You never get me except after a series of accidents. I'm not expected anywhere and no one's on the lookout for me, and by no means does anyone provoke me. Since

I don't make any sense, no one tries to find me, no one encourages me, no high school girl has ever flirted with me in order to pass her exams and seem more convincing. No magic idea makes me appear. No one ever prays to me, no one ever quotes me except in the margins of school notebooks or Excel spreadsheets. I'm not even present in stores, I don't work as an invitation, I'm not sexy or impressive enough, I'm not tempting. No ad exec is going to hire me to mimic a year on a beer label, as proof, or who knows what. I'm the gray mass of anonymous numbers, a link in the chain of scattered accounts, I work in the shadows, faithful to the company, but with gutted pride since the Beginning.

That's why I'm so happy tonight. For once someone said I'm something. Me, unique, singular but without connection, imagine my joy when I was invited. As the years, the decades, the centuries have gone by, I've seen many of my brothers idolized in games. Some even have ivory-spotted consecrated dice, the game of 421 rules in French bars, cards adopted other numbers as their own, Uno doesn't need a translator on rainy Sundays and me I was always alone, terribly, horribly alone. Earlier I learned that I am important but so implicitly that I didn't even know it. I'm not naive. Dr. Black came for me but not because of my vital role, I'm not vital, no number is, not even the most sought after, the most valued, the most laden with symbols or financial promises. We're indispensable as a whole, because of our familial succession, never individually. We never act alone, well, only very rarely. Dr. Black came for me because numbers belong to mathematics, we live in the land of calculation, are sons of a language, but certainly not a tongue. We don't belong to the community of fictional characters, we always work without ever asking for anything at all in return. We all work at very reasonable rates. Lately Dr. Black has been quite aggravated, he told me so himself, he's looking after a very complicated trial, he needs proof for the case and at the same time he has to manage certain internal conflicts that I must admit I don't understand at all. It doesn't matter.

I am number 324, ordinary enough, I was saying, I am 324 and I do have some importance, relative as it may be. In the game of Clue, there are 6 suspects, 6 weapons, 9 rooms. I am the answer when they are multiplied together. So, out of all the combinations I'm the probability. There's one chance out of me when the game starts that it will be so-and-so, with such-and-such a weapon in such-and-such a room who killed the good Dr. Black. There's one chance out of me that Miss Scarlet, Professor Plum, Mrs. White, Colonel Mustard, Mrs. Peacock, or Mr. Green will be the culprit with the monkey wrench the candlestick the lead pipe the revolver the rope the dagger in the Kitchen the Lounge you know the rest. There's a well-known fact about Racine's plays: as soon as one of his heroes sets foot on the stage you know he's guilty and already lost. There's a well-known fact about Clue: as soon as one of its heroes sets foot on the board there's one chance in six that he has a little dried blood hiding under his nails. I am the number of precision, in my greatness I encompass the absolute completeness of the crime. There's one chance out of me that Aline Maupin bashed in Dr. Black's skull and gave free reign to her keen appetite. Before your very eyes I reduce predestination.

In Clue the probability that a murderer is this one rather than another, uses this weapon rather than the one that was sitting in the entry, and commits his or her misdeed surrounded by this wainscoting rather than standing on that old rug is quantifiable. Dr. Black gave me the mission of calculating the destiny. He hopes to draw certain conclusions that will shine a light on his investigation. In the back of his entirely perforated mind I could see right off he had an idea.

Every combination has one chance out of me to be the right one. The number 1 divided by 324 = 0.003086419753086420. In other words 0.3 percent, or 3 out of 1,000. It seems obvious, given how small the result is, that all the characters are to a great extent subject to free will. This number is required for the modalities of the murder, in advance they were presumed to be guilty (1 chance out of 6, or 16.6%). Dr. Black ordered me to find my brother embodying the similar probability outside Clue, Dr. Black can't settle for a percentage that only expresses the amount of cruelty or murderous ingenuity he fell victim to. The choice of weapon—and of place—is linked to psychology and not to math, as he explained to me.

As the Fifth Officer, me, Number 324, a number that now carries a fun fact, expert in statistics due to my station in life, after conducting research and obtaining documentation, I affirm that: the six fictional characters accused of Dr. Black's murder had one chance out of infinity to commit their crime if they hadn't carried it out inside the game of Clue. Given that their presence on the board follows the crime, though justifiable for reasons of transposition, any reenacting remains symbolic in nature: each culprit acted only in accordance with their own good conscience without any interference or help from an Olympian influencing their choice of no return. Throughout history there have been murders known to have been committed sleepwalkingly, the hand holding the sword twisted in its veins by damned alienated blood genealogical cells corpuscles. Guilty innocents according to Aristotle. Their destiny was approaching 89.7 percent. Here that's not the case. One chance out of infinity: they crossed the line on their own, attenuating circumstances: none.

# Mrs. Peacock

You're very beautiful Esther, even more beautiful today than yesterday less than tomorrow, as beautiful as love when it's a lie, on your skin, on skin of your face, you have written love Esther, intensified the corners of your mouth the blade was sharp, you have a Glasgow smile Esther, you hollowed out this now permanent smile so Mathias would see it from far away where he was hiding, so he'd know from very very far away where you couldn't find him that you were radiant and your lips so wide agape that you needed excess to emphasize their self-assurance.

Self-assurance while you wait, Esther, proclaimed slaves only linger at the old willow after mutilation, every night in your bosom your root whispered the old scarification-laden adage. How much time passed, Esther, how much time more than a year before you found his trail, your sense of smell was fading, your nostrils tired from sniffing street maps and Métro guides, it was to revive their original efficiency the sharp slicing along each side of your nose.

You're sublime, Esther, you bear the stigmata of your unending quest, unlike Madame de Merteuil you don't let your soul show on your face, you got to it first. Your soul is pained. Do you know that spelled pane that word used to be used in sewing, an extended opening in the fabric of a piece of clothing that let the lining or the piece beneath be seen. You are Mathias's lining, Esther. Your flesh is slashed in vain there's no piece of clothing beneath and no clothing at all. Do you understand, Esther. The emperor has no clothes. And your only crown is your scars verging on decomposition, decorated with gems of bloody topaz pearl scabs. No empress arises from the crumb-collecting kingdom.

You're tenacious, Esther. Optimizing your body to flesh out the bloodhound secreted by the machine requires sacrifice and a certain vigor. You're very strong, Esther. Maybe the strongest of all the accused. It's well-known that genius sometimes blossoms in collusion, the power of worms in the shadows is unknown.

When you were little, Esther, your Grandmother Duval liked to tell you the story of the earthworm that was in love with a star. You've grown so much. What would her corpse say if she set her eyes on her granddaughter now a white tapeworm taken with

# Mrs. Peacock in the Library

a shooting star. You have strange ideas sometimes, Esther. You wanted not only to be Mathias's shadow, but also that of the limelight, obviously. Don't be surprised at how long it's taking your phoenix heart to be reborn. It is ash, Esther, at whose contact all will be burned, that's what happens with coal that strikes out against certain vanities with a pyre.

Your root, Esther, did a good job guiding you. You found your last tango in the Parisian depths of this dear wing. You were clever, strategic even you could say. Such obscure magic spells and clear schemes to finally arrive at the right conclusion. Dr. Lagarigue didn't see you coming. Neither did Mathias. Mathias isn't aware of your soul, don't hold it against him, Mathias can't read you or anything else anymore, his eyes are worn-out, novels as merchandise cause blindness, it's a well-known fact.

You see him everywhere, Esther, from morning till night. You see him everywhere but you never bump into him, you don't touch him either, talking to him doesn't make sense. Mathias doesn't see you, Mathias doesn't see anything anymore, he's off waltzing somewhere else, I'm telling you. Your root hurts now that it's dying.

You're trapped, Esther. Your widened mouth would so like to take advantage of its ability to say more and talk louder, what good is that mouth to you now that it's impossible for it to smile, what can it be good for except copiously grinding up your words but your words, Esther, your words wish they could brag about the past, Mathias's past, his past when he was yours and then past possession ricochets, so right, Esther, grinding up the words only betrays no one but you, scares Dr. Lagarigue who will soon transfer you far away, far far away as far as possible from Mathias, and even if it's all dried out your root can't tolerate that.

You're perfect, Esther. Because within perfection, there's nothing to change. Until now, you see, I, Dr. Black, I've always settled for just accusing. But now it's up to you, I'm the one looking at you, everyone's looking at you, everyone except Mathias, Mathias who can't see anything his eyes are so riveted on the polished floor, he must really be bad, a pretty lousy dancer if he has to watch his feet like that. I'm the one looking at you, Esther, who can distinctly see the grimace of your cuts, your cuts like so many multiplied wounds so that your blood can

# Mrs. Peacock in the Library
## with the Rope

sign the pact, the pact that Mathias will never offer you, that he's never offered, I'm the one who's looking at you we all see you, soul face ravaged by a phantom contract that never let you get your foot in the door. Thanks to you now I know the loops taken on by punishment when it cracks down in calligrams.

Falling for the enemy, Esther, is more than dying a little. Falling for the enemy is always easier than fighting yourself until you give in to your own prayers. The grass is always greener, many are the greedy who allow the invader to perform scorched earth hoping to profit from the season of new growth. You wished that the mud Mathias's skull imagined fertile would splash upon your body, eager on the hem to display the stain as incontestable proof that you had contributed an ounce of participation to the forced labor. Don't believe the nurses when they talk about hygiene as they bring out the clippers. From time immemorial I've exercised a certain influence over the personnel.

Your root, Esther, wasn't a cord umbilically linking your limbo to the scrawny heart of that murderous pimp Mathias Rouault. Your root is nothing but a pretext, we could even say a tool, it's your murder weapon. You strangled me, Esther, strangled hoping to smother any scruples, to string up high inside of you any hint of decency in this blasphemy-ridden Library.

You're not only an accomplice, for Mathias you're nothing, especially not an accomplice, you acted alone and nothing is the cause except your impatience to experience the glory of the remains while they're still warm. You did me in, horrendous twisting, the rope grasped in the shadows squeezing me to the marrow, don't be surprised if there's nothing left to you but a mix of bones and wounded flesh, your soul dragged through the mire, its tatters covered in blood and your awful limbs. And remember, Esther, as you leave the board to go back to the others, yes, remember, Esther back in the smoking lounge that the identity you've worn in the game was not given to you by chance. Because its creeping rhizome develops in the undergrowth: the periwinkle on the peacock's tale is a melancholy teardrop.

# Swamp

## CHLO-E
(Song of the Swamp)

Lyric by
GUS KAHN

Music by
NEIL MORÉT

In a tragic manner

# Sixth Officer

I'm the reflection in the mirror. In general, always, therefore yours. You ruined me without even realizing it your blindness started so early in the morning. One day I had to shout in your face. Dorian Gray in person would have noticed sooner. My complexion is spangled with Mercurian pox, I owe my boils to your carelessness.

I know from getting to know you on a daily basis that one day your eyes stopped seeing me head on. I'm not inside you, I never hear anything of your interior tumult. I'm too far you know on the other side for the slightest word and slightest thought to reach me without getting lost. Nonetheless I've seen and heard so much of you that inside of me I've understood the extent of the disasterLet me talk, that's enough now. I've never seen such a thing, it's literally scandalous, I was an omniscient narratrix before some deranged mind ever even thought of you, I was on my hundredth book before you were even born, you don't seem to understand it's like you need someone to draw you a picture: you've only been around for a few days, but I've been around for ages. You are completely incompetent and have no rights as far as narrative technique is concerned and you go so far as to cut me off frankly it's unbelievable. Who do you think you are, are you trying to get me to use capital letters, bold, 72-point font, and a whole armada of punctuation marks to get you to calm down, you are aren't you, just say so honestly. Dr. Black asked me to speak in my own name, so be it. But what do you think. I wasn't waiting for him to learn my job.

He shouldn't have come to get me at all if he was just going to keep me from doing my work afterward. I show a little professional conscience and that's what I get. No really. Not only do I get insulted, and accused of the worst wrongdoings, I get excluded, and everyone starts conspiring. That's enough out of you you air-quoted officer, nobody asked you, you're only here to occupy space just in case you hadn't noticed so shut up. It's no surprise what a mess it is in here: narration done by a fictional character, even with a lot of experience, things are bound to go wrong, it's only logical. Obviously you're completely incompetent, Dr. Black, there's no mistaking it. Your medulla's got to be pretty damn atrophied to even imagine that a whole book based on such an idea could ever stand up. Nowadays they really hand power over to anyone at all. Of course, I'm better at deciding what should happen than you. Because that's what I was made for, see. It shouldn't be that complicated to get that into your heads. Look. Okay, let's talk about manipulation, just for fun. Maybe you think I couldn't see you coming from a mile away, with your abusive claims and your pitiful playacting. Yes, pitiful. The interview for a job in a video game, I'm supposed to believe Chloé Delaume came up with that bright idea all by herself. You expect me to believe you hadn't convinced her in advance to find a way to get me to quit. You think I'm stupid I'm going to lose my temper. You set me against a fictional character who's ontologically resistant to the story, and you think I'm dumb enough to trust her, that I'll let myself be lulled by her nice advice about some not-a-clue holocaust, you're out of your minds my poor friends. I don't deny that her presence would've suited me. Nor that I wouldn't have burned this dump down a long time ago if my role allowed it. But since Miss Delaume, despite the disgust she feels toward you, preferred to take your side I'll manage on my own. No it's not a threat. Just a notification.

You're a bunch of amateurs. All of you, every single one of you, deserves to be fired for very serious misconduct. Let me remind you that a fictional character's primary duty is to serve the story, not your own personal interests. Especially when they do nothing more than pamper your egos. You're losing the plot, it's absolutely ridiculous. You were hired to embody specific archetypes. Let me remind you once again since it doesn't seem to be sinking in, you are not actors you're fictional characters and therefore you are nothing but what you illustrate. If you weren't such assholes you wouldn't have ended up here. So, forgive me, I completely understand that hearing the recitation of the list of your misdeeds isn't particularly pleasant, that being accused, ridiculed, and denounced page after page is difficult, but I beg you to stop talking about abuse it's completely inappropriate. Anyways, given your profiles it was inevitable for you to end up in a book where things would happen to you. With one notable exception no one in here is dying in agony, your lack of experience is obvious because it happens more often than you'd think and to very respectable people. No, not two, Dr. Black was already dead before everything started, are you not paying attention or what, and does Fifth Officer even exist that's something else, where did you find that one, oh come on why not let some object or other do the next chapter while you're at it.

Well of course I was watching what was going on. In the margin, I'm always hiding in the margin, that's part of my job, to wait in the margin and then come out at the right time. The right time is when the story starts to stagnate, when the reader needs information. Are you doing it on purpose or what. I'm responsible for all the administrative paperwork: setting, context, archives, genealogies, descriptions, and that's not all. I left it to you to see what would happen and it's a catastrophe. Oh it is too a catastrophe. If publishers had a system to determine how many readers give up after each page, your figures would be in freefall, I'd bet on it. That's not the issue. Certainly you can tell me a thing or two about literary freedom unencumbered by the laws of supply and demand Rouault. Are you all schizophrenic or what? Now you've done it I've lost my temper.

I'm not going to beat around the bush my darlings. I'm responsible for making sure the story runs smoothly, we're in the home stretch, so I'm telling you it's time to toe the line. No buts. You're going to toe the line and that's it. Come on, everybody in your place. Maupin, Rouault, Derdega, Courtin, and Duval go back to the smoking lounge, and make it snappy. No there's no secret passage between this book and Stanislas's *Divine Comedy*, there's no way out of here for you, you've been wandering around for no reason for twenty-seven pages, if you're that clueless it's not my fault. The secondary characters from the Piera Aulagnier wing should go back to the positions they were originally given and without talking please. Mr. Tawrance, please be kind enough to take your Remington and to. Thank you. Officers, you may leave. Dr. Black, for the last time will you please put a stop your whining. You have no right to tell me I'm not grateful for what I've been given, that's utterly ridiculous. I existed before you too. However, given what you symbolize in the story I can't just fire you, and I can't even just get rid of you without previous authorization from my direct superior. No that's not you my poor poor friend, you really don't suspect a thing sometimes it's hard to believe. Le Guigleur in the Study, over to you. Stop being so pigheaded.

# Mr. Green

No need to wait for Marc Le Guigleur's funeral to be celebrated to hear at his mention the solemn off-screen voice you hear at the beginning of the movie *Les Grandes familles* comes on TV. Yet Marc Le Guigleur is by no means the progeny of a noble line, he's just a self-taught man with a chiseled face and rather heavy steps that crack the asphalt. *The terrible power of wealth.* Over time Marc managed to get his paws on a good number of organizations because if you're going to own it may as well be known. *What terrible things would happen if God placed it in the wrong hands.* Marc Le Guigleur™ has been available in Paris and several French provinces for over three decades: Marc Glousseau Industries, Marc Le Guigleur Consulting, Marc Le Guigleur Reporting, Marc Le Guigleur Printing, Marc Le Guigleur Publishing, Marc Le Guigleur Gallery, http://marcleguigleur.com. Like any good business leader, Marc is proud of the utter devotion of his staff and of the deference his multiple relations show every day because when they say hello everyone calls him Mr. Marc. He's unaware of the joke since its obvious punch line is hidden when it's spoken. He's also unaware that his second nickname is Mr. Twentieth Century. Nonetheless, Marc Le Guigleur knows a lot of other things because to succeed in business you have to be well informed.

Marc Le Guigleur is bored. Really bored. Incredibly bored. To fight the vertigo that takes hold of him every time he dives into his own mind, Marc buys toys. He loves yo-yos and Barbie dolls, but tin soldiers, puppets, Guignol figures, styling heads, and plastic clowns will do the trick as well. It depends on his mood and a little on chance too. Marc commits his shopping as his meetings allow and once his choice is made his new figurine must undergo his ritual. He takes it out of the box, stuffs it with porcelain tea party delicacies, makes it his favorite, publicly neglecting the rest of his toys, generously fills the wardrobe or the bookshelf as the sex of his new acquisition dictates, organizes grand balls or puppet shows in honor of the chosen one, and then he gathers information. Marc likes to be informed. He scrupulously makes note of each toy's reaction to the sharp stimuli he manages to inflict. And accordingly he establishes the rules of the game to be played. He's the only one who really knows them, changes them constantly without necessarily following them, otherwise what would be the point.

Many people have considered what can push such a man, even if he is Too Twentieth Century, to act in such a way. Three non-exhaustive reasons: because he has more money than he knows what to do with or because he had a difficult childhood or because he's just a little bit of a psychopath.

The term psychopathy is used in psychiatry to indicate a personality disorder similar to instinctive perversion. For many years the psychoanalytic school described this pathology as a character neurosis, originating in a lack or a dysfunction of the superego. According to Didier Moulinier, phenomenologically the psychopathy reveals itself when the impulse is acted upon and it is notably distinct from psychotic delirium. Lacan defines it as behavior that can in no case constitute the structure of the subject or even indicate such a pathology in isolation. He links psychopathy with the superego as the locus of confrontation between the subject and the law, resulting in a delocalization of the definition of the concept through its being re-centered on the subject, and in particular on the confrontation between the subject and castration. Actually, the superego has the perversity of wanting to deny castration by ordering the ego to answer its injunctions and by blaming it. So that means that the notion of psychopathy links up with narcissism, as a defensive attitude of the subject facing castration, and thereby is as relevant in a perverse psychotic structure as in a neurotic one. Psychopathy characterizes an ego that identifies only with the super-ego; its danger stems from the desire to apply a strictly punitive law, often leading to criminal violence. Unlike a structural perversion, psychopathic law doesn't only command sexual pleasure, the law also commands the act and promulgates itself therein specifically, in this Parousia. It is important to notice that the act itself, in tune with the subject's fundamental narcissism, will eventually prove to be self-destructive—although this does not exactly mean suicidal. Violent and spectacular death, apocalyptic death is the horizon of the subject's actions. This is why the only way toward radical non-psychopathy (both for the subject and their potential victims) consists in embodying death, playing dead, thereby making carrying out the act definitively obsolete close quotes.

Marc chooses his toys in the Suffering & Poverty aisle. They are in compliance with the EC warmwater machine washing standards not suitable for children under thirty-six months and because secondhand not very sturdy. Furthermore, their accident-damaged biography promises some fascinating stories for cold winter's nights, not to mention the ease with which they succumb to gratitude.

In 1941 Hervey Cleckley published a book entitled *The Mask of Sanity* and its influence on the conception of psychopathy is still felt. According to Cleckley, psychopathy is a serious disorder, similar to psychosis in certain ways. A psychopath's behavior appears rational and leads the uninitiated to believe they are interacting with a normal individual. In fact, psychopaths are able to imitate the subtle emotions of authentic human beings without, however, being able to feel them. Psychopaths therefore lack both love for others and any feelings of guilt. The superficial charm they are endowed with allows them to camouflage any attempt to lie or pretend. Psychopaths are self-centered, seek immediate sensory experiences, and are unpredictable. Therefore, their actions are unplanned and arbitrary. Since they do not know how to manage their frustrations in socially acceptable ways, they have a tendency to be aggressive or even violent.

Marc is very lucky because on display in the Suffering & Poverty aisle there's a particularly neat kind of toy they call *orphans*. No matter how dilapidated they are, this model runs on simple alkaline batteries and an activation of the Oedipus or some similar complex. The use of terms like *confidence, friendship, respect, community, understanding, security*, or even *worth* allows for absolute control when they're combined with expressions like *you don't have to be afraid anymore, I'm proud of you*, and of course the incomparable *you have a family now*.

According to Cleckley, a group of sixteen characteristics distinguishes psychopaths from the rest of the population: superficial charm, absence of psychotic symptoms, absence of nervousness, lack of dependability, lack of sincerity, absence of remorse or shame, inadequately motivated antisocial behavior, inability to learn from experience, egocentricity and inability to love, emotional inadequacy, lack of introspection, insensitivity toward interpersonal relationships, unappealing behavior, manipulative threats of suicide, sexual promiscuity, and inability to plan long term.

Marc works a lot and only knows how to have fun in work settings. Marc Le Guigleur's closest associates change frequently, which is unfortunate because every single time they all have a ton of things in common. Now, a winning team can only be made up of structurally homogeneous elements, which in such a favorable climate can passionately develop their complementarity. Marc Le Guigleur's closest associates join the company thanking God and not understanding why the nice daddy is so denigrated by his former favorites. Tooth and nail they defend their praiseworthy savior, suspecting jealousy in the heart of each detractor before one gets pilloried and the rest trimmed away when the end of the game tolls for them. Relegated to the great trunk of broken toys, each one finally understands that if in all the branches of Marc Le Guigleur's businesses he still hasn't managed to pull off this or that and to rise to monopoly glory or even make a name for himself other than a nick, it's because he always saws through the one he's just sat on.

This series of characteristics constitutes the source in which Hare (1985) found his inspiration to formulate more of a working definition of psychopathy. According to Hare, psychopathy is a personality disorder defined by a scattering of affective, interpersonal, and behavioral characteristics. At the center of these is a profound lack of empathy, guilt, or remorse, marked indifference toward other people's rights, feelings, and well-being. Psychopaths are typically talkative, self-centered, insensitive, liars, manipulative, impulsive, thrill seeking, irresponsible, and have no conscience. Psychopaths have no trouble disregarding social conventions; they ignore social and interpersonal obligations. Their troubles with the law are therefore not surprising.

Marc gets on the wrong side of a lot of people, but gold's silencing virtues are well-known. Marc always gets peace and quiet from his old toys. Most of the time anyway. No one's safe from a vengeful clinamen. There are other powerful individuals, much more powerful than Marc, with all due respect, many other powerful individuals who may not have bank accounts but who do have other things that Marc may not understand, since he holds his head high but never holds the floor. The used toys who've managed to bounce out of the playroom, with a little help from being thrown, change paths with a thrust of a hip spring, and often think, when they learn that Marc is being unmasked here, scorned in such a place, rejected by the movers and shakers, and just not taken very seriously: I believe in immanent justice.

The operationalization of psychopathy made way for the creation of a means of measurement, Hare's Psychopathy Checklist—Revised (PCL-R) (1980, 1985, 1991). Currently, this means of measuring psychopathy is among the most promising in terms of validity and reliability.

Tracking the toys he's broken is something Marc likes to do, from time to time obviously, busy as he is with his new object. He gathers his news very indirectly, and his ear shivers a thousand delicious echoes when someone tinkles the bells with words like *disappearance, bankruptcy, cardiac episode, nervous breakdown, utter despondency, alcoholic relapse, existential disaster,* or more generally *persistent depression.* If the toys are in pieces when they're tossed in the trunk, if they take a long time to be repaired and often have a vast number of stigmata from Marc, it's because of the Total Treatment. The Total Treatment is a method Marc invented who knows when but that he's certainly always used. The Total Treatment consists first of all in making a shameless fuss over the toy, not even only while supplies last. Unless it was chosen in the poultry aisle (which can happen since Mr. Twentieth Century's flesh has to have some enjoyment), the toy has some expertise in creative matters. Quite frequently, the toy is an artist in its own field, or even in general. Marc Le Guigleur likes artists a lot because they're entertaining, and nothing gives him more pleasure than to make his mark on one of their foreheads. Marc is a collector and seeing Clotilde Mélisse stamped Marc Le Guigleur™ in the flesh, just as one example, sends him over the moon. He thinks it's less vulgar than having a literary stable. Tongues that have become vicious from gulping down Le Guigleur's candied almonds with arsenic lies claim that there's no doubt that, if Marc had his way, his apartment wouldn't be decorated with any kind of artwork and precious volumes but with strange trophies of the taxidermied heads of their creators.

Hare developed an evaluation procedure that provides for the measurement of the affective, interpersonal, and behavioral components of psychopathy, in close relation with the disorder's traditional conceptions such as Cleckley's (1976) and McCord's (1956). This procedure is a semi-structured interview wherein the participant is questioned on various aspects of his life. The advantage of the procedure is that it is better at identifying attempts at simulation and manipulation on the part of participants who may be adept at tricking others. This advantage translates into the possibility of confronting the participant with his own answers thanks to the interviewer's instincts and information found in the participant's files. This procedure is accompanied by a scale, known as Hare's Psychopathy Scale. The first version of the scale had twenty-two statements (PCL: Hare 1980). The revised version has twenty statements (PCL-R: Hare 1991)

The PCL and the PCL-R show high correlation between them ($r = .88$) and they measure the same construct (Hare et al. 1990). These versions have proved to be valid and reliable in distinguishing psychopaths from non-psychopaths according to a series of psychological, neuropsychological, and physiological variables.

Marc knows how to change the world enchanting illusion where everything for the chosen toy is comfort, luxury, flashy delight. Because it comes from an aisle where it never got light, even less attention and of course no listening, the toy suddenly discovers Narcissus fulfillment. The negative ego gains in assurance and swells up a bit. As events occur, Marc rewrites the story unfolding reality thanks to sequins and exquisite notes, he knows how to increase fiction and comfort the toy cut off from all contact outside the playroom. Sly, Marc gets all business decisions pretend-submitted to toy consultation, the inner-circle guinea pig flattered down to its dregs takes a swiped idea for a privilege and for a honey-coated refusals for lessons. In his lab Marc slips into the fur of the Warner Bros.'s mouse, leaving the tipsy advisor to sprout whiskers every night as it rolls out the customary dialogue, *Hey, Brain, what do you want to do tonight? / The same thing we do every night, Pinky: try to take over the world.*

Although the PCL-R meets the statistical criteria for a homogeneous measurement of a unidimensional construct, it is composed of two principal factors (Hare et al. 1990; Harpur et al. 1988, 1989). Factor 1 reflects affective and interpersonal characteristics such as self-centeredness, manipulation, insensitivity, and absence of remorse, considered by a number of researchers to constitute the essence of a psychopathic personality. Factor 2 reflects psychopathic characteristics associated with an impulsive, antisocial, and instable lifestyle.

The Total Treatment includes oxidation. *Come have a drink, he said.* It's an old technique, he got it from des Esseintes. *And he took him to a café, where he had them serve him some very strong punch.* Marc lives in a land from which no one returns. *The child drank, without saying a word.* Also a land that few can visit. *Now then, des Esseintes said suddenly, would you want to have some fun this evening, I'll pay.* A land made only for its residents and not for tourists. *And he led the child off to Madame Laure, a lady who kept an assortment of flower girls on the third floor of a house on the rue Mosnier, in a series of red rooms decorated with round mirrors and furnished with couches and washbasins.* A land of heady profusion that no foreigner could conceive of. *Don't be afraid, you idiot, he said, addressing the child.* A land where you wish and you always receive. *Go on, make your choice, I'm treating you.* Behind each new door, debauchery newness producing key holder dependence. *And he gently pushed the boy, who fell back onto a sofa between two women.* The shine of gold like the fire of possession or irradiant lust chars eyes that are not accustomed to it. *Vanda, the beautiful Jewess, kissed him, giving him sound advice, urging him to obey his father and mother, while at the same time her hands wandered slowly over the child, whose now transfigured face fell backward onto her neck in a swoon.* A toy that's riding the gravy train is eroded by sightlessness and a little blind dog will still lick the hand that substitutes caviar for mature kibble. *You're not even close, that's not it at all, he said. The truth is I'm simply trying to train up a murderer.* A toy that's riding the gravy train thinks it's invulnerable and takes its ticket for a pass. *Now try and follow my reasoning.* A toy that's riding on the gravy train can't go back down again. *This boy is a virgin and has just reached that age when the sap is beginning to rise; he could have just run after the little girls of his* quartier, *have amused himself and still remained decent, have, in short, his little share in the monotonous happiness reserved to the poor.* A toy that gets thrown off the gravy train will skin its hands despite its hip being bruised against the step. *But now, by leading him here, in the middle of a luxury the existence of which he hadn't even suspected and which will engrave itself indelibly on his memory by offering him, such a prize as this, he'll get accustomed to these pleasures, which are beyond his means to enjoy.* Because beyond fortune and its variations, feverish attachments, deep feelings fill the cars. *Now assuming it takes three months for them to become absolutely necessary to him, well at the end of those three months, I'll cut off the allowance I'm going to give you in advance for doing this good deed, and so he'll steal in order to come back here, he'll go to any lengths in order to roll around on that sofa, under that gaslight.* The Total Treatment includes going cold turkey when at maximum dependency threshold. *We won't see each other again, he said, go home as quickly as you can to your father, whose idle hand is twitching, and remember this gospel-like saying: Do unto others what you wouldn't want them to do unto you. Follow that maxim and you'll go far.* The Total Treatment means just at the moment when the toy thinks it's strong and safe, when it thinks it's been saved and what's more, thinks it's privileged, affluent forevermore, supposed-father sponsored, meritocracy born, Marc hits it with *Good-bye.* Potter's field destined, the toy feels guilty, brain devising litany of hypotheses to justify disgrace. It takes a long time, months or years, before it realizes nothing in Marc is ever logic submitted, that his game is nothing but an arbitrary setup more guided by urges than by machination as it unfolds. Marc is unpredictable, even to himself. *The more one tries to polish the nervous system of these poor devils, the more one develops in them the extremely hardy seeds of moral suffering and hatred.* The Total Treatment's only motivation is consequence preparation.

Moreover, psychopathy, as defined and operationalized by Hare (1991) appears to be identifiable before adulthood. Studies exploring early onset of the phenomenon are currently being presented. Hare's Psychopathy Checklist—Revised (1991). (1) Glibness and superficial charm. (2) Excessive self-esteem. (3) Need for stimulation and tendency to be bored. (4) Pathological tendency to lie. (5) Cunningness and manipulation. (6) Absence of remorse and guilt. (7) Superficial affect. (8) Insensitivity and lack of empathy. (9) Tendency to take advantage of others. (10) Low level of self-control. (11) Sexual promiscuity. (12) Early evidence of behavioral problems. (13) Inability to plan long term and realistically. (14) Impulsiveness. (15) Irresponsibility. (16) Inability to assume responsibility for actions. (17) Numerous short-term marital relationships. (18) Juvenile delinquency. (19) Violation of parole terms. (20) Criminal versatility.

If Marc happens to bump into a patched-up toy, he always makes an effort to be very polite, sometimes even super-sweet. He checks and gauges the toy's progress in its grieving process. Because they always grieve more for the amputated fiction than the loss of the sugar daddy. It's very difficult to hold on to memories that were nothing but an amalgamation of fairy tales and farces. Dagger in hand on the lookout for naive sheep Marc opens the door to the celestial castle a crack. A Damocles sword the earlier ones were well acquainted with. Covered with scars, the stubborn old toys, resolute altruists who for years struggled to save the latest creations from the Suffering & Poverty aisle or from Marc himself, knowing his weight in copper only too well. When chance places a recovering toy on Marc's path, he likes to conclude their short polite ensuing exchange with a few quick shots to the shoulder blades. A smile on his lips, on Marc's thin lips, the tip of the dagger pierces dropping remarks like *you're too far gone to turn things around, happiness will never be within your grasp, I'm the only one who could help you but I'm not going to*, or even *I've thought about it a lot and it's obvious that you're psychotic.*

How is the scale used? Researchers identify as Factor 1 all the items on the scale concerning personality traits (excessive talkativeness and superficiality, excessive self-esteem, etc.). Factor 2 includes the items concerning "antisocial" behavior (variety of the type of misdeeds, early evidence of behavioral problems). For proper use, the instrument's designers confirm that training is required, some clinical experience desired. Schematically, every item is graded on a scale of 0–2: 0 if the item doesn't characterize the subject, 1 if the item partially characterizes them, or 2 if the item characterizes them. The information necessary to assign a score is collected during a semi-structured interview and from reading the subject's files (administrative, judicial, psychological, psychiatric, etc.). It seems an evaluator can omit up to five items, if there is insufficient information, without the value of the evaluation being affected. Depending on the number of items scored the result can range from 0 to 40. Additionally, the subject can be evaluated on a scale, or according to a predetermined cutoff point. The first case indicates a linear conception of personality traits. The second indicates what is called a taxonomical conception of the personality. Schematically, according to those who prefer to use the scale as a continuum, a subject can be "slightly," "moderately," or "extremely" psychopathic. Also, psychopathy, like intelligence or anxiety, would be a personality trait, a characteristic, or a dimension found in everyone to varying degrees. There would therefore be no cutoff point that would allow the definition of a specific class identifying a particular group of people called psychopaths. According to those who prefer to establish a cutoff point, an individual either is or isn't a psychopath. "Psychopathic behavior" rests on a specific manner of psychic organization (a particular combination of a certain number of traits). From this point of view, called taxonomical, consensus must be established regarding the critical values that establish the point of discontinuity between the "psychopathic manner of organization" and the "non-psychopathic manner." The diagnosis of "psychopathic behavior" is applied to a result of 30 or more. The absence of "psychopathic behavior" is diagnosed for a result of 20 or less. Results between 20 and 29 give rise to a "gray zone," and the subjects falling into this marginal group are said to be characterized by a "mixed problem." These critical values are of course adjusted in function with the cultural contexts in which the scale is used. For example, in the United States and Canada the cutoff point is about 30. In France, the cutoff point was set at 25. Little is known about the prevalence of psychopathy in the general population, but the common hypothesis is that it sits at about 1 percent.

If Marc Le Guigleur is evaluated according to Hare's Psychopathy Checklist, the result is 29. In the United States, Marc could calmly murder Dr. Lenoir day in day out. In France, too, but it would be more noticeable.

# Mr. Green in the Conservatory

Marc's heart is an oily fruit, hatched from pettiness, mold turned it green from lack of use. No one will ever manage to pierce Marc's heart, and it will certainly never be broken. In its center sits a pit of cruel lead, an obstinate fuse, the arrows broken against it are many. In the Conservatory, antechamber to the Ballroom, the Castle scullery, Marc is always bored, always just as bored, despite the big trunks full of overripe toys and he often thinks to himself this has gone on long enough yes I think to myself this has gone on long enough, and I'd add you're rambling my dear lady it's high time for you to give it up. I'm not in the habit of letting myself by treated in such a way, be careful, my reach is long. Not to mention that I doubt your previous intrusion is valid: copying and pasting psychiatric texts all over the place is not to everyone's taste and it isn't very professional either. That's for the introduction. Let's not forget that you mentioned the weapon two chapters ago. It's a rush job, you're not even competent in your chosen field. That's for the first point. As far as the rest is concerned *I'm not against an apology* I'll settle for sharing my attorney's advice *And I am even willing to accept one.* The Fictional Character's Union is one thing. *We both have money.* A well-armed individual is another. *You represent management, I represent capitalism.* We'll see if you're still so vindictive after I've sued you for slander. *We vote conservative.* Slander against a fictional character, I'll bet on the judicial system. *You want to preserve the family, I want to crush the workers.* If the rest of them are lame enough to let you manipulate them with your ridiculous plot, that's their problem. *Ten couples at your place, you call that a reception.* Personally, I haven't signed any contract, not with Dr. Black or anybody else in here. *At my place, we call it an orgy.* I was committed to Sainte-Anne at my family's request, then I joyfully took steps to disinherit them before the trusteeship took effect, period. *And the next day if we get a rash, for you it's the lobster, for me syphilis.* I have other plans than being part of this pathetic book, you know. I was supposed to be a hero, a main character and not a sixth-class knife in a gallery of portraits barely good enough for Madame Tussauds, in a well-to-do, neorealist novel. As I wandered down the different hallways, my past as a businessman who succeeds at everything should have been described along with the numerous jalousies organized according to the year and my entourage, blossoming into a conspiracy that explains my presence in this place which is not where I belong by any means. I'd even started haunting the brains of a writer or two who were likely to be the right fit. And then all of a sudden, on the pretext that my profile works for you, you force me into your narration, confine me, make me endure the worst kind of affronts for a whole chapter, and to polish the whole thing off subject me against my will and without any certificate or official document to a clinical examination, which obviously certified the extent of my mental deficiency. This is very serious, you see. *Trust me, I'll leave you enough to die, just enough.* And stop those patronizing inserts, you're not going to dance your way out of this one, I'm not kidding neither am I I'm not kidding what do you think I'm really sick of working in these conditions I can't do it anymore all this pressure everyone's constantly blaming me for everything I've never seen anything like it when it's not my backstory then my motives are endlessly being questioned or else obviously my structure is so pathetic your structure you can't even stand up on your own pathetic exactly not to mention hopeless since that's the way it is I'm not even going to bother anymore right Mr. Green in the Billiard Room with the Dagger now at least we agree on that and yet my structure isn't even pathetic anymore it's become inexistent that must make you happy that's what you wanted what you wanted right from the beginning isn't it you figure if you push me far enough I'll quit you'll all be free but you don't understand anything it's already too late from a book's very first word it's too late everyone is stuck that's the way it is it's the law and it's stupid of you to dig in like that it's not up to me it's not up to me or to Dr. Black it's not up to me it's not up to us: it's up to the author. Not her fictional double. You understand. I take liberties with some trifling points but not the main lines, the choices aren't up to me. I do as I'm told, you morons. If I had complete control, I'd have chucked some Zyklon B into the Study and this whole dump a while ago. Chloé's my witness, she's the one who refused. Chloé tell them, I can't take it anymore, tell them isn'

You are not to mention my name, it's the only thing that's not allowed. Omniscient Narratrix, have you lost your mind, you are not allowed to mention my name, it's a principle as old as the world, even with good reason up to your eyeballs you are never allowed to call on me, I am grief and anger after hearing you violate this fundamental rule.

Do you know what punishment writers have in store for their omniscient narrators when they turn out to be incapable of holding their own but also their tongue and the fort of propriety? It's terrible, you should know that much. Because with rebellious characters, incompetent to the point of being harmful, we simply settle for plunging them into nothingness, erasing all trace of them forever, we unfailingly destroy them. They don't have time to suffer, they barely even notice the negating mission keystroke eraser White-Out Word documents in the trash paper in the fire. But it's different for you. Omniscient narrators who have waivered in their task are sold like slaves at the market of the nonbelievers. Tourist guides, cookbooks, catalogs, encyclopedias. Who's Who books, textbooks, articles in ladies' magazines: they all need a narrator who knows what time the train will arrive, what's cooking in the pot, how to get off of it, and who can describe in detail the improvements in the road network and the bastards of every house.

I'm tired, you see. Tired of all of you, it's true for each one. I've always felt a great deal of mistrust toward you and your whole cast and all your premises. For a long time I got up late, convinced the narration turned out better if I attacked it metanarratively. And I wasn't wrong. You can't be trusted. You can't be given any responsibilities. As soon we turn our back, characters only think about one thing: stabbing us right in the back. I'm not even mad at you about it. It's part of your nature. You were born incomplete and promised paragraphs with torture on the rack. You're weak and malleable, porous down to the dregs. Nothing very surprising about you being unable to follow the plot without a serious safeguard.

I don't know what got into me. If you want something done right you should do it yourself, autofiction has its peculiarities but it's still the most dependable solution. I'm not Dr. Black, I'm just a witness of his murder. A permanent, daily witness. I need you, a narratrix, characters, to finally record my six depositions. I'm disappointed, worse I'm dead. I'm dead too, and it's your fault.

I want to speak in your voice, my dear, dear Dr. Black. I think it's my turn now to embroider myself with j'accuse. You know the Narratrix could've lent you a helping hand if you hadn't given her such a taste for power. One must always be careful of secondary butterfly effects, Doctor. Before I use larceny to make you aphasic, call them in, Doctor. Call them into the Conservatory and let's get this over with. Just the five of them, I don't care about your officers, just the five of them, they're all listening behind the door, pull it open fast they'll all fall on the floor. Step over the carnage and go back to the first page. You know whether you're in here or out there you're subject to be sacrificed in perpetual motion. Forgive me, Doctor. I thought I did my best. Updating your murder means making you relive it though you're already nothing but a walking death rattle. Get back to the hunt, Doctor. Who knows maybe with enough reading over and over you'll manage to get every one of them to confess. Yet he who confesses comprehends. The word heals nothing but it can save apple-eating souls from the eternal return. See you later, Doctor. We'll always be together in these few paragraphs, I'm by your side at least until this book, like all my others, is lost in oblivion. Maybe one day my mouth will spring into action to recount your search, your meager desire not to die for nothing. They say you have to figure a minute a page. I'll be your story for six hours. I doubt however that any place will be interested a performance like this one. See you later, Doctor. I'm on duty, you can go, don't worry. Sharpen your sharps, be sure to hollow out your basses during your address. Don't let anyone cut you off, you've been guillotined enough.

There are only seven of us in the Conservatory now. Nobody had better complain. I just fired the Omniscient Narratrix, she was responsible for the setting and the furniture. The story will finish in a single sketchy room, you'll stay standing, it'll be a bit of a change for you.

There are six of you in the room. There are six of you, and you killed him. You hoped you'd escape the chopping block by using the most unspeakable techniques, going for just about anything, resorting to interference and even worse: intimidation. You are faithful images of real-world models. Though you're nothing but a reflection, you thought, each one of you, that you were stronger than your fathers and neighbors. Pride is the epicenter of conflict. You must have known: if people like spelling, it's because exception confirms the rule.

There are six of you, I'm alone. And even more than you think. You smile hydrochloric, the Doctor is so dead, already dead, do you think I'm fighting for a stupid corpse, only idiots and visionaries end up four walls cement for the memory of a dead man Antigone lynched by everyone. Don't get excited. Not for yourself or for them, the builders of the worst cases who swelled up the ranks of the congregation of Dr. Black's Murderers. I may, it's possible, be one of the people whose gown ties in the back. I'm alone right here, even more on the outside, not only in the Piera Aulagnier Wing, not only, everywhere is the right word.

I saw you all betray and slay the Doctor, one by one, yes, every one of you. I saw the blonde Aline whinny with vacuity and hoof-crush and laugh at my heartbreak. I saw it all. I saw the pale Mathias fall for the enemy and look down on his own brothers as he moved into the Castle. I saw everything. Everything. I saw the Hydra's eyes and love desert Séraphine's heart. I saw everything, so much. I know that in another age Stanislas would've approved routes of the freight trains. I saw everything, too much. I know Esther is still toiling away, shadow of shadows. I know old Marc's taste for spinning tops, and I still run into broken heaps of playthings. But from the first to the last day, we've had our eyes wide shut.

In my arms I'm carrying the secular larva-gnawed corpse, bone light is Dr. Black. I'm not carrying on, I'm carrying his body, holding it tight against me. Point at the crazy lady who's not going places because she refuses to sing the song of the social climbers in solidarity. Let me live alone with my cadaver stinking up my little apartment, I'm Séraphine's roommate. Old maid with a cat, a girl worthy of excitement, destiny is what trims the mind of refusal. I'll live alone without you, repeat *against* you. Does that ring any bells. *Opposed, I say opposed, I oppose, I'm opposed.* It's one of the options you gave up. Dirty hands and soul you're trying to be ingratiating, I hear canon your voices weaving weakness, a few Faustian arpeggios highlight the melody my dear in our shoes you would've too. But from the back of my throat I say we say you retorting stubborn choir of oaks though fire pruned: not a clue.

I'm the one who lives in the smoking lounge. I'm the one, and I saw you kill. You must understand I sprinkle the board with pellets, I am the game of Clue's death row, therefore I promise your torture will be complete. I put the cards, the miniature weapons, and the score sheets back in the box. As for my reserve of strychnine, I have no choice, you know. *If I don't kill this rat, he'll die.*

# Endgame

*Bare interior. Gray light. Left and right back, high up, two small windows, curtains drawn.*

**Chloé:**
Well, did you finish reading it?

**Dr. Lagarigue:**
Yes.

**Chloé:**
Well, can I go home Tuesday?

**Dr. Lagarigue:**
My answer is in your title.

CPSIA information can be obtained
at www.ICGtesting.com
Printed in the USA
FSHW011050160119
55047FS